Shadows in Sussex

The British Book Tour Mysteries | Book 5

Emma Dakin

CAMEL PRESS

Seattle, WA

CAMEL PRESS

A Camel Press book published by Epicenter Press

Epicenter Press
6524 NE 181st St. Suite 2
Kenmore, WA 98028.
For more information go to:
www.Camelpress.com
www.Coffeetownpress.com
www.Epicenterpress.com

Author website: www.emmadakinauthor.com

This is a work of fiction. Names, characters, places,
brands, media, and incidents are the product of the
author's imagination or are used fictitiously.

Cover art by Teresa Hanson
Design by Rudy Ramos

Shadows in Sussex
Copyright © 2023 by Marion Crook

ISBN: 9781684922024 (trade paper)
ISBN: 97816849202031 (ebook)

LOC:2022946245

Printed in the United States of America

DEDICATION

To my children

Janice, Glen and the memory of David

ACKNOWLEDGEMENTS

My Beta readers Jill, Janice and my cousin, Richard McKinnon and his wife Linda who read every word and, from their lives as native residents of Kent and environs, pointed out any local facts that needed correction. My thanks to David, the driver of the taxi, who took me to Rye Harbour and the Martello tower, explained the area to me and introduced me to his brother. Thanks to the many strangers who pointed me (repeatedly) in the right direction so I could navigate the streets, who discussed their views of murder in their town and who were willing to enter into my plot with enthusiasm.

The plot is based on the life of a man I knew and the trauma he suffered. This story is, in some ways, his memorial.

AUTHOR'S NOTE

Claire brings her guests to that countryside of Sussex and Kent with its miles of flat delta and inland low hills. In the first year of World War II the enemy bombers came from Occupied France only twenty miles away. Memorial plaques and commemorative statues are reminders of those fearful times when intense bombing caused such suffering. The collective memory goes further back, and I was told tales of the smugglers who operated here in the seventeenth and eighteenth centuries, evading the Revenue officers by escaping through the tunnels from one inn to another. The tunnels, the locals swore, are still there.

I wrote the book during the pandemic when travel was prohibited. When the skies opened, I flew to England to trace Claire's route. I hadn't been to this area for many years, so I was excited to explore and take detailed notes along the way and to find out how my story reflected the landscape. I was chagrined to find I had made mistakes. For instance, I'd set a scene in the Martello, an old defensive tower, which I had assumed was at the edge of Rye. It was near Rye, but three miles toward the sea at Rye Harbour. Surprises like that forced me to re-write the book when I returned home.

I stayed in the Mermaid Inn in Rye where I sent Claire and her guests. The beams are old and crooked and the floors are truly wonky. I stayed in the Falstaff in Canterbury. I tried to experience as much of Claire's trip as I could. The Rother Manor is imaginary but I scouted out the site, so if we could move a few houses, it would fit into the town. The tourist sites the guests explore are real and waiting for you.

I had trouble walking when I was in Sussex and Kent and used a cane. I thumped up and down the streets, poking into corners, hauling myself up stone stairs in castles and towers and generally managing to get where I wanted to go. It was surprising how useful that cane was: propping open doors, poking at vegetation and shore life, garnering assistants in hopping on and off trains, and getting a constantly solicitous attention from the travelling British public. Wonderful countryside. Wonderful people.

I hope you enjoy Claire's travels and adventures as much as I did.

CHAPTER ONE

"Waltzing Matilda" shot into the air above me and rolled down the stairs of my two-storey home carried on the rich baritone of my man Mark. A Welshman singing an Australian song in my English house. The thought entertained me. There was no shower here, so Mark made do with a bath. Obviously, he was enjoying it—a shame I had to leave. Everything was packed in my van. I just needed to run up the stairs to say goodbye.

I pushed open the bathroom door and was met by a full-throated "Up jumped the swagman…"

"Mark!"

He grinned at me—glinting brown eyes, soap suds covering his shoulders and water splashing over the tile floors.

I leaned over the soapy, delectable package and gave him a quick kiss. "Bye."

"Have a good, uneventful tour, Claire." He raised his eyebrows.

I'd managed to meet some dangerous situations in the past, but those days were behind me.

"Of course. It's just Sussex—staid, respectable Sussex."

"Staid and respectable," he intoned like a prophet. "May it be so."

He reached for me but I stepped back and laughed. "I need to stay dry."

I dashed down the stairs and shut the outside door to the sound of "Up came the troopers one, two three…".

1

I smiled at the thought of Mark, his gorgeous voice, his interesting life, his... Ah, well. I would see him in a fortnight. I pulled away from my house, sipped my coffee and considered our life together. Mark and I had relaxed into domesticity over the last few months. It suited us at this time in our lives. He was established in his career as a detective inspector based in Hampshire and I enjoyed my business, The British Mystery Book Tours, with its month-long respite between tours. During that month, I planned the next trip, made accommodation arrangements and updated my website—all of which I did from home. I could take days off to enjoy Mark in that month without jeopardizing my work, and I did. I'd been worried that too much togetherness would create problems between us but, other than minor disagreements about toothpaste and how long to cook an egg, we hadn't argued. Things were going well, entirely too well. It made me slightly nervous.

I turned the wheel to join a round-about and the sunlight glinted off the new diamonds on my finger. I knew the ring was there but it still surprised me when it caught the light. An engagement was a big step for me. My chaotic childhood with my alcoholic father and my poisonous relationship with my old partner Adam set me up to expect disaster. I should be past that and be an evolved, emotionally mature adult, as I had managed my own life for years now. But it seemed I had a collection of entrenched fears and anxieties, plastered over with civilized manners. I supressed the niggling thought that I didn't deserve happiness. Mark wanted to get married. I didn't see any need for it. My sister Deirdre's opinion was, "Be grateful to fate that you've met a decent bloke. Take a chance and stop expecting trouble." I wasn't convinced.

She was partly right about why I didn't want to get married. It would challenge the gods of fate who would trip me up if I expected too much. I know that's irrational, but I half-believed it.

It was early July and my new tour started tomorrow. Gulliver, my Cavalier King Charles Spaniel, was staying at Deirdre's house while I conducted the tour. I'd miss him but I couldn't manage him on this tour. I motored from Hampshire to East Sussex without incident and little traffic. I was looking forward to the new group of tourists. I never knew what challenges the collection of personalities would give me. Usually, the guests were eager, polite and cooperative. Occasionally, not. The odd tourist brought the troubles and complications of their life to my tour and caused havoc, but usually they wanted to forget their every-day lives and partake of a magical fortnight away from their reality. I was happy to provide it.

Approaching the small town of Rye, I marked the route to Canterbury and the road to Hastings where I'd take my guests later in the week, I didn't know this area well but had done two quick reconnaissance trips earlier. Jacqueline Winspear set her books near here in the war years. Her descriptions had given me a sense of familiarity with the green land around me, but the miles of delta before the sea surprised me. Rother Manor, our guest hotel, was large, but not, I was sure, large enough to have ever been a manor house. The name was probably applied to the house recently to attract tourists. The common meaning of 'manor' was a large house on a huge estate, but sometimes it just meant a large house. Mark told me that his colleagues sometimes called their police district their manor. I ruminated on the application of the word. I tended to do that. I'd not brought guests here before, but it looked ideal, sufficiently old to satisfy the North American appetite for a romantic setting but not so old it was decrepit. Laura Wright, the manager, had seemed organized and experienced.

I loved trying out new guest hotels and the whole experience of taking a tour to the sites of mystery novels. The tourists shared my itch for mysteries and were usually interested in what I offered. I'd had a career as a teacher of English to executives in many parts of the world. I enjoyed it as I was fascinated by linguistics and the way people use language. Now at forty-eight, I had achieved stability with a reliable partner, my own house and tour business and a legacy from my much-missed step-father. I should be able to feel comfortable, not always expecting a disaster. I admonished myself. *This time the tour will go smoothly. This is a beautiful house; you will enjoy it here.*

Rother Manor House was a three-storey rambling Victorian and was as close to a gracious house as was possible at the edge of Rye. The grounds were beautiful. Laura's son, Reece Martin, looked after them she'd told me. He was in his late twenties and committed to creating beauty. The owners of the guest house were glad to hire him, Laura had told me, as staff was hard to find. It was unusual to see so much land around a house of this age in a town but it made a picturesque setting for my visitors. Across the street and well below it lay the cricket grounds, still green in the July heat. Beyond the grounds, the salt marsh stretched to the sea. The tourists would love this view.

I pulled my eyes away from the vista and turned into the car park, a graveled area to the left of the entrance. After unloading my small suitcase, knapsack and briefcase from the van, I climbed a few steps to the front door. It was unlocked. I entered into a long hallway and saw a side table with an open guest book and a prominent bell. I called for Laura but there was no answer. I hit the bell. No one came. I hadn't told her the exact time I'd be here. She was likely nearby. I wandered into the lounge which was off the hallway. A small table held two cups and saucers, sugar and a milk jug and a plate of cake. My guests weren't arriving until tomorrow. She could have others guests tonight, but I *hoped* that cake was for me. I dropped my luggage on a chair in the lounge and walked down the hallway to the rear of the house. There was no one in the kitchen. I pushed through the back door and stepped into the garden. The minute I opened the door I heard the keening of a woman in distress, a soft, desperate cry that rose in the air and hung there. There was anguish in every tone. The hairs on my forearms rose and I stood frozen for a moment.

The wail receded, then rose again. It came from the area at the back of the property. I walked towards a shed. I moved cautiously to the open door and peered in.

Laura was sitting on the floor beside a young man who lay still. His skin on his arms was pale, deadly pale. His head was turned so I just saw his dark hair. He was muscular, wearing a black T-shirt, denim jeans, black trainers. At first, I thought he'd fallen or had a seizure of some sort. Then I saw the Prenoxade kit open and the syringe on the floor nearby. Prenoxade, naloxone, the life-saving remedy for drug poisoning. Tour guides carried it; police carried it; teachers had it handy and, apparently, so did mothers.

"Laura," I said.

She stopped wailing, turned her head and looked directly at me.

"He's dead. My baby. He's dead. He said he wasn't using any more. My poor boy." Her shoulders heaved as she struggled to steady her breathing. She stopped keening.

I stood at the door not sure what to do or say. The scene was so wrong; no mother should be mourning like this. Laura turned back to her son, slipped one hand around his shoulders and held his unresponsive hand with her other as if she could keep him safe within her arms. I thought of the Pieta and of Goya's portrayal of mothers finding their sons on the battlefields of Spain—all mothers lamenting the death of their sons, holding them one last time. The terrible weight of grief was heavy in the air. I covered my mouth with my hand as if to keep back any words that might shatter that grief. I wanted to shout out that this wasn't happening, that he was just sleeping, or passed out, that he wasn't dead. I waited a moment, collecting my own emotions until I could speak quietly then asked, "Did you call 999?"

"Yes. Yes, I did." She sat there patting her son's hand as if he could feel her. "I did call them," she said, quiet now. She put his hand to her cheek holding it in hers and covering both with her tears.

We heard the sirens at that moment. Laura glanced at me. "Would you meet them at the front door and send them here?"

"Of course." I moved quickly to the front garden where the ambulance was just pulling into the car park. I gestured toward the side path that led to the the back of the property, then followed the ambulance attendants to the body of Reece Martin.

I hovered near the door of the shed while the paramedics assessed Reece. There wasn't much doubt about his death. He must have been dead for a few hours as now I could see his face had that blank look that the absence of life leaves. But I was no expert on death. I'd seen only a few bodies in my time. I stayed out of the way and waited.

The shed was much more than a storage place for garden equipment. It had a bed, a dresser, a table and two chairs, a small kitchenette and, tucked in a corner, a tiny bathroom. Reece had probably lived here.

The paramedics put a stethoscope on Reece's chest and shone a light in his eyes. They held a low, murmuring conversation with Laura. They pointed to the empty Prenoxade syringe and said something. Laura nodded. She finally released Reece's hand and placed it gently on his chest. Then she stood and came to the door.

She was a little shorter than me and thin as if she lived on worry. Her eyes were a pale blue. Her face white with shock.

"I will go with Reece," She sounded sad and resigned. "I'll go to the hospital with them."

She took a deep breath and focused on me. "You are in room four. You can let yourself in. Everything you need is underneath the counter in the lounge. The keys are there. Make yourself some tea. I'm sorry I can't help you right now."

"Don't give me a thought. I'll make myself at home. My group isn't due till tomorrow so we have lots of time. You have my mobile number?"

She nodded but I wasn't sure she heard me. "I'll want my mobile and my purse. I have to go now."

"Call me when you're ready to come home and I'll fetch you," I said to her back.

She ran toward to the kitchen door, then through the house, no doubt picking up her mobile and purse on the way. She caught up with the paramedics in the car park. I moved more slowly along the side path and watched as they loaded the body of Reece Martin. I saw Laura climb in after him.

The ambulance pulled onto the street. No siren. No need to rush.

I hurried through the hall to the lounge. The key for my room was where Laura said it would be, on the shelf under the counter. I gathered my luggage, trundled up the stairs and found my room —small, but it had a desk. I opened the window, a new one that looked Victorian but wasn't, and let the spring breeze freshen the room. I'd need to be sure the other rooms were ready for my guests. I'd use the keys lying handy in the lounge to check them. But first, I needed a walk. Without the excuse of taking my dog for exercise, I had to remind myself that fresh air and exercise were essential, especially when my nerves were jangling around my shoulders, shaking my hands, making it obvious that I needed to breathe deeply and slow down.

I'd seen an extensive garden beyond the shed where I'd discovered Laura and her son. A gate to the area had been open when I arrived and was still open. I checked the keys in the lounge and found one labelled *Garden Gate* and took it with me. It would probably be wise to lock the gate behind me. The large garden connected to many houses. I presumed the people who lived in the surrounding properties had private access to this common ground with their own locked gates. Only residents could use this park. Well, I was temporarily a resident. I trotted out on the well-kept gravel paths, admiring the larkspur and the roses, splashed like a hasty painting of reds, pinks and whites. A white clematis spread over a brick wall on one boundary near the street. A blackbird perched on vine, a black ebony contrast to the stark white of the flowers. I spotted a robin hopping on the ground, cocking his head, listening for the movement of underground food.

Poor Laura. Poor Reece. No one expected a young man to die, but Laura or Reece had a naloxone kit handy. Reece had been an addict. Addicts were dying of poisoned drugs all over the country. It was a terrible affliction. I took two deep breaths and felt my shoulders relax in the late morning sun. The song of a blackbird in the quiet of this secluded park sifted into my bones as the sadness and grief I had witnessed drifted away. Laura had told me that Reece worked on this garden. He'd created beauty. It helped me, but it hadn't been enough for him. I didn't know what would help Laura.

I carefully locked the gate and returned to the house. There was a new car in the driveway, a small compact. I'd booked the whole house as of tomorrow. Conceivably, Laura had other guests for tonight. But it wasn't a guest.

"Angela. Hiya." a brisk voice announced from the top of the stairs. She was a little shorter than me and younger, probably mid-thirties. Her red hair was caught in an elastic on top of her head but much escaped to form a frizzy halo around her face. Bright green eyes surveyed me. In one hand she held a bottle of glass cleaner, in the other, a paper towel. The cleaner. Laura must employ a cleaner.

"Claire Barclay of The British Mystery Book Tours," I introduced myself and added the inevitable Sussex greeting. "Hiya."

She stepped back and ushered me in. "Laura told me you were coming. Do you think your lot will get drunk and throw glasses at the mirrors?"

"I hope not. Has that happened?"

"Once. An infamous crew from the Continent. Some kind of spiritual group who thought they were going to discover their inner selves. My theory is they did discover their inner selves and were severely disappointed."

As she was talking, she led me into the lounge. The table for two was still set and the cake still looked inviting.

Angela continued talking. "I can't think where Laura's gone. I know she wanted to be back in time to have tea with you and to help me set up the rooms."

"Let's sit down," I said. "I have something to tell you."

Angela shot me a sharp glance and moved over to the table. She placed her glass cleaner and towel on the floor and settled into the chair. I sat opposite her and explained what I had found when I arrived.

"So," I said. "Laura is at the hospital. She'll either find her own way home or call me to fetch her."

Angela let out a huge sigh. "I really liked that boy. He'd been trying so hard. It's tough being an addict. Not much help for him. He was such a nice guy. Laura is going to be shattered. He's all the family she has... had." She corrected herself. "Blimey. I'm so sorry."

"Is there any other family," I asked. "Anyone who could help?"

"The poor bugger has a father but the arsehole never wanted anything to do with Reece. Some guys are like that. I've seen it before. A good enough father when the kid is little, then turns away when their adoring kid becomes a teen. The kid wants to be himself and the father wants a clone."

"Should I call the father?"

Her eyebrows shot up to disappear under her falling hair. "No, don't. Laura wouldn't like it. She'll call if she wants to."

That was good advice. I didn't know enough to avoid making mistakes.

"What you can do," Angela said, "is help me set up the rooms."

"Right you are," I said glad to do something useful. While I was helping Angela, I could check out the rooms to assure myself my guests would have everything they needed. Keeping busy would also keep me from thinking about Reece.

"First," Angela said with renewed energy, "we'll have tea." She picked up her cleaning equipment and whisked away to the kitchen, returning in a few minutes with the promised pot of tea.

"Help yourself to the cake," she said. "Laura made it." She spoke rapidly as if she had to get all her thoughts out immediately. "She's good at cakes. She's good at cooking. She's good at making people feel welcome. She runs this place really well." She took a bite of cake, swallowed and continued. "She's a good mother, too. Reece was doing fine in the garden shed. He looked after the common area. Everyone in the garden association was happy with his work and it takes some doing to satisfy that lot. He did heavy lifting for Laura when she needed it, kept out of the way of the guests and was polite when he did meet them. Such a nice guy. I'm so sorry." A tear escaped and rolled down her cheek. She brushed it away impatiently.

We had a mini wake there at the tea table for Reece. Angela talked to me about what Reece had been like when he was younger—a bit of an athlete in school, popular with friends, devoted to his mother, estranged from his father who had a new family, a young one.

"Reece couldn't keep a job for long," Angela said. "The drugs grabbed him every once in a while. It was like he had to go back to it. Laura was always waiting for the next time. But between those binges he was a gem. She's going to miss him badly."

We took the tea things into the kitchen. The cake had been delicious—Victoria sponge.

Angela collected the cleaning trolly from a first-floor closet and opened all the rooms using her own set of keys. We dusted, hoovered, cleaned bathrooms and generally tidied. When we had the rooms sorted to Angela's exacting standards, we went through them putting on the clean sheets and straightening the counterpanes. When all was satisfactory, Angela loaded the trolly and trundled it back to the first-floor closet. She threw the laundry down the stairs to the ground floor, followed it down and gathered it into a basket, taking it to basement. I heard a machine grumble as she came back up the stairs. She closed the basement door and shut out the sound.

"I'm off then," she said. "Thanks for your help. It was necessary. I only have so many hours here, and I couldn't have done it in time without you."

"Do you have a family you're going home to?" I asked.

"No, I don't have to make a dinner for anyone but myself, but I work as an artist and I start in an hour." She pulled her mobile from her pocket and checked the time. "I have a commission I need to finish."

I was impressed by all this energy.

She stopped momentarily at the door. "Tell Laura I'm sorry, really sorry. I'll be back tomorrow." She left and I heard her car start.

She was finished, but I wasn't. I went to my van and pulled out the baskets I'd arranged for each room. They contained a map of the town, some interesting facts about Rye and the surrounding area, a list of mysteries set in or at least tangentially associated with the town as well as a list of recommended restaurants. Of course, I added chocolate to every basket and a small bottle of water. I checked the bits and bobs Angela had set out and saw that each room had tea, coffee and hot chocolate available and a hot pot and cups. I added biscuits and some shortbread.

The physical work had helped me settle, but enough had happened in the day that I was in need of a calm, uneventful walk with good food at the end of it. I hiked down High Street, to West Street and to The Mermaid Inn for dinner. Laura would return eventually. The day wasn't over.

CHAPTER TWO

I ordered from the Mermaid's extensive menu and gratefully accepted a glass of dark cabernet sauvignon. I was sitting in a small alcove where it was relatively private, so I called Mark.

"Shit!" was his reaction. "You haven't even been gone a day!" He sounded as if it was my fault Reece had died. I had to remember that in Mark's world death can be violent and suspicious.

"It's not murder, Mark. The boy was an addict so it's likely he was poisoned. Laura gave him Naloxone."

"It happens." His voice was soft now.

"Far too much."

"It sounds like his mother had been supporting him and that he'd been trying hard to deal with a drug problem. So many drugs are chancy."

"Contaminated, you mean?" I said.

"I mean that, yes. Fentanyl's in everything. It just takes a tiny bit to kill someone. And then there's carfentanyl where an even smaller amount can kill. Just a fleck. We need more safe drug testing sites. More safe drugs period. More help for addicts." Mark hated the way society accepted deaths from drug poisoning. His sister, his only sister, a teacher and a well-loved woman, had died from the same cause.

We were quiet for a moment thinking about the magnitude of the problem. Contaminated drugs were everywhere, cavalierly mowing down thousands, from habitual users to first-time experimenters. Poor Reece.

Laura came home about eleven. I heard her unlock the front door and met her in the lounge. She hadn't called me, so she either called someone else or took a cab.

"Would you like tea?" I asked "I can make it."

She flung her purse on the kitchen table and sat with a thump. "Please," she said. "It's been a long night."

"I'm so sorry, Laura," I said as I filled the kettle. "So very sorry."

She stared at me for a moment her large blue eyes wide then spoke slowly. "It's not that I didn't expect it at some time, you know, just not now. He was doing so well. He hadn't been using. No, he hadn't been using. He was working and even talking to friends. His old girlfriend, Beth, had him hooked up with a psychiatrist. He'd made up his mind to talk to her, the psychiatrist. Beth had managed to get it all paid for. I don't know how she did it. She's amazing. In a quiet way she gets things done."

"Who's Beth," I asked. I poured the hot water into the teapot and set it in the table. The mugs were already there. I sat down opposite Laura and waited. If Laura needed a listening ear tonight, I'd listen.

"Beth and Reece used to be a couple but Beth couldn't deal with Reece's drug problem. It was hard because, when he used, he also stole. Drugs are expensive and he never made enough money to pay for them. Our wallets would go missing. I couldn't have him around my guests when he was using. I had to send him away then, so I didn't blame Beth when she did the same. She stayed in touch with him because she cared. I thought she was good for him. When he wanted to try hard to get off the drugs it made sense for him to talk to Beth. And she helped him. I thought things were going well." She repeated that as if she couldn't believe she had misjudged her son.

She blinked and looked straight at me. "He liked his garden shed. He had his computer, his books and music. He had a small hot plate and fridge. He said it was ideal because it was surrounded by garden. But I guess his fears and his cravings were all too much for him again."

"He sounds as if he had a tortuous time," I said.

"So true." She poured the tea into both mugs and took a sip. She was quiet for many moments. I didn't talk, just waited.

She sniffed, took a sip of tea and continued. "He needed some kind of drug to keep him calm and stable. Why couldn't they prescribe something legal that would work on him.? They have insulin for diabetics. Why can't they have something for drug addicts? He was a wonderful boy—compassionate, loving. I'm going to miss him badly. He had a brilliant sense of humour. I'm going to miss that." Tears rolled down her face. She closed her eyes. I expect she was going to cry for a long time.

I stayed with her for about an hour while she talked about her son. Finally, she brought up her plans for the next few days.

"Do you have to notify people?" I asked.

"I suppose I'd better let his father know."

"His father?"

"Yes he lives in Maidstone with his new wife and family. I don't think he's seen Reece in the last five years. That's sad too," she said. "Reece used to be his shining boy. His pride." She was quiet for a moment. "I had Reece before I met Malcolm. My fiancé died just before our wedding." She took a deep breath. "It was hard, but my parents helped. I met Malcolm when Reece was three. They bonded right away. Malcolm said he'd wanted a son and, when Reece was five, he adopted him and gave him his surname. Malcolm was the only father Reece knew. We were a happy family. They did a lot together when Reece was young, went to the cinema. Malcolm taught him chess." She looked a little dreamy and half smiled. Then she looked up at me and sat straighter. "By the time Reece was ten, his dad had found someone else and left me. To tell you the truth, it was a relief for me because I was tired of Malcolm's self-absorption, narcissism, and his constant criticism." She stared at her tea and let out a long breath. She looked up at me. "Other than his devotion to Reece, I couldn't see any reason to stay in the marriage. When he started to distance himself from Reece, I couldn't believe it. He had been so close. It was as if Reece belonged to me and he didn't want anything to do with me or mine." She shrugged and took a sip of tea. "It was hard on Reece. I guess he didn't understand why his father would leave him. Kids see divorce as something that's about them. That's common, the counselor told me. Malcolm just left Reece behind like he was a pet he didn't want any more. I didn't understand it either." Her brow wrinkled. After all these years, she was still puzzled by it. "I can understand not wanting to have the same wife. I *can't* understand leaving your son behind. Malcom didn't live far away, just in Maidstone. He could have had him for weekends, taken him to the cinema. He didn't do anything with him."

She looked away. I had little experience with fathers other than my own who was an alcoholic and not reliable, my step-father who was loving and supportive even with less-than-perfect sons and my brother-in-law. I tried to imagine Michael, Deirdre's husband, leaving Josh and Kala. I shook my head. I *couldn't* imagine it.

"Malcolm did pay for Reece to attend a good school but he never went to any of Reece's rugby games or his swimming meets or even his graduation. It was odd, but then Malcolm is odd," she said. "Still, I better tell him. Who knows he might even send a wreath?"

I left her to her grief and went back to my room. It was a heartbreak for her and I did appreciate how hard the next few days and the next weeks were going to be, but I needed to work out how I could keep my guests from being touched by this tragedy. They were coming to Britain to experience a wonderful holiday full of fun, laughter, exploration and learning. They weren't coming to be part of Laura's sorrow. I had to keep my compassion for Laura separate from my plans for my guests. Before I started concentrating on the tour, I wanted fresh air to clear my head and my heart of all the emotion I'd absorbed. I expect fresh air is my panacea for all troubles.

I let myself into the communal garden again and walked around slowly appreciating the well-tended beds, especially the rose beds. Reece's work, perhaps. Even though it was dark, there was enough light from the street and from the lamp posts within the garden to allow me to appreciate it. The scent from the roses was heavy in the air.

My sister is usually the first person I call when something unusual happens, but I'd been preoccupied. I called her while I was in the garden. It was late, but she was usually up until midnight.

"How is the tour?" She answered the phone without the customary 'Hello. How are you?'.

"The manager's son died."

He voice went from brisk and cheerful to concerned. "Tell me about it. I'm ready for bed but I have some time."

I told her about Reece.

"It sounds like an accidental poisoning by a street drug. That's all too prevalent and sad. Mark will investigate thoroughly if he's involved." Deirdre's law practice made her an expert on many subjects.

Mark would investigate if he was asked, but his Major Crimes Investigation Team would not likely be called to a drug poisoning. Those were far too common.

"How is Gulliver?" I could use Gulliver's warm body and affection right now.

"He's fine. He hasn't been here long enough to miss you. Don't fuss." She was quiet for a moment. I shouldn't take more of her time, but she continued. "Tell me about Mark's parents."

That was a change of subject. I hadn't met Mark's parents until recently as they lived in northern Wales. I'd meant to tell Deirdre about our dinner but she'd been chief barrister on a murder trial and unavailable. I thought about the family meeting.

"We went to Jack's pub."

"The Rose and Crown?"

The pub was close to my house in Ashton-on-Tinch in Hampshire and Deirdre had been there many times.

"Yes. I was sure we'd all enjoy an informal pub meal rather than try to make conversation at an up-scale restaurant or even at home."

"That was wise. Especially since you can't cook anything impressive. What are their names?"

"Annwyn and Elis Evans."

"Very Welsh."

"They *are* Welsh. What did you expect?"

"I don't know. David and Cati."

Those names were more common. "Annwyn brought me a book on birds of south-western England. She must have asked Mark what I would like then asked her brother Lionel what book was the best. He's a birder in Cornwall."

"Thoughtful. That's a good start. You'll be able to identify birds with him."

Mark told me afterwards that he had been afraid his mother would give me some of her jewellery. "Trust me, *cairid*, you wouldn't want it. It's ugly."

"They both seem pleased that I was Mark's choice—or they have excellent manners. It's hard to tell."

"Don't sell yourself short. They're probably delighted."

"I hope so."

"Did they ask when the wedding's going to finally take place?"

"They have better manners than you do so, no, they didn't."

"I bet that question hung in the air, though."

"Perhaps." It certainly lurked in the back of my mind.

"Mark wants you to name a day." Deirdre wouldn't let the question alone.

"He does."

"You're too cautious."

"My mistake with Adam makes me careful."

"Not careful. Afraid. Which is ridiculous. You never married the loser. You just stayed far too long. And Mark is nothing like him."

That was true enough. Mark was straightforward and had no side to him,. He said what he meant and didn't make snide or sarcastic remarks. While he liked a drink, he didn't get drunk and I wasn't afraid of him. Notably different from Adam.

"Besides you love him."

"That too. I'm just not in a hurry."

She stopped pressuring me then, and we said our good byes. I returned to my room and contemplated the up-coming tour. It was going to take some planning, and some energy.

I didn't realize how much energy until I met the new tourists the next morning at Heathrow Airport. I'd parked the van in the spot I'd reserved and for which I paid a yearly fee. It made picking up guests much easier than trying to find a vacant spot in the public car park. The first to arrive were from Washington State, Howard and Poppy Mickleson. They had flown first class and were the first off the plane.

"Would you like to wait in the VIP lounge," I said, "while I collect the other guests?" Their tickets allowed them to use it. They looked at each other.

"No," Howard said. "Richard and Heather are our friends and they unload from economy, so we'll wait with you."

"They won't be long," Poppy said.

We chatted for a few moments. Howard was a short man about my height of five-foot- nine and shaped like a pear—heavy on the bottom. Poppy was at least six inches shorter than Howard and a thin woman. They were both relaxed and sociable.

"I'm the mystery buff," Poppy said. "I read everything set in England that I can get my hands on."

"I like thrillers," Howard said, "especially the English ones like Dick Francis and Ian Rankin."

"I believe Ian Rankin is Scottish," I said.

Howard grinned at me "So he is, and the Scots like to make that distinction."

"They do," I agreed. The English did as well.

My next two guests arrived. Richard and Heather Shelley. They emerged from the Arrivals door with Richard in front, his thin body jerking a little as if he was excited or nervous. I didn't know which. They were a handsome couple in their sixties. He was almost six feet with white hair worn long, an elongated face with a sharp nose. She was about five-foot-seven and looked fit. She had clear skin, a round face, short, gray hair, deep brown eyes and a ready smile.

"Over here," I called. I'd looked up everyone's picture on Facebook so that I could recognize them. I did have a sign saying *The British Mystery Book Tour* but people didn't always see it. Heather turned her head and caught my eye. Howard and Poppy waited.

"Over here, Richard," Heather said to her husband and they walked my way.

"Hi, Howard." Heather smiled at him. She hugged Poppy briefly.

"Howard," Richard said and nodded at his friend.

"You must be Claire Barclay." Heather put out her hand.

"Yes," I said. "Nice to meet you."

Her husband turned to me. "I'm Richard." He shook hands.

I smiled. "Welcome to Britain, Richard."

"We flew economy," Richard said, "and it was most uncomfortable. I could really use a coffee and I'd like it right now."

Oh, my. Was he used to servants? Not if he flew economy.

"First," Heather said firmly, "we need to get our luggage. Then we can have coffee, I'm sure."

"Indeed," I said.

"I can't do without my coffee and not that stuff they serve on the airlines."

Richard might not be as bad as some. Coffee was fairly easy to find. Perhaps if I kept him full of coffee, good coffee, he might be amiable. It was better than keeping him full of alcohol which some guests seem to demand.

I escorted all four guests to the luggage carousel and loaded their luggage onto my porter's cart, then showed them the restaurant where a good cup of coffee was easily obtained. I left them there while I went back to meet the next flight.

Amber Stone, Julie Johnson, and Trinity Joseph came together on a flight from Toronto, Canada. They were three Indigenous women who attended art school there and had decided that they wanted an expensive and catered trip to broaden their horizons. Julie had emailed me to explain that they were trying to understand the British Literature perspective in order to counteract it with Indigenous stories. They were serious about upsetting the canon taught in the school system and decided they needed to know more about Britain. They didn't really want a stuffy historical tour and thought the Mystery Book Tour would suit them better as they were all mystery fans. That seemed a complicated motivation to me but I would do my best to satisfy them.

Julie was the oldest in her late twenties; the other two were just out of their teens. They came down the corridor like three chattering sparrows, full of energy and looking with interest all around them.

"Hello," I said to Julie. "It is good to meet you."

"You too," she said. "These are my friends, Trinity and Amber. We're really looking forward to this. It should be so much fun."

"I'm really looking forward to you," I said. "You are going to enliven his tour, I'm sure."

"Be careful what you wish for," Trinity said.

I laughed and really looked at her. She was the youngest of the three and the smallest. She was thin and wiry with long, straight black hair. Her brown eyes sparkled and she almost danced. "This is going to be amazing. We are going to be treated like Disney princesses. I'm going to love it."

"I'll do my best," I said. I would cater to her as much as possible and try to give her the experience she was expecting.

"We researched you." she continued, "At least, Julie did. She likes research, and you came up top of the small tour list."

I was taken aback. I didn't know there was a list.

"'Individual attention and willing to adapt to special interests,'" Julie quoted from my website. "We have some requests."

Oh. Oh. No tour guide wants to hear that her carefully planned itinerary will be changed.

"We can certainly talk about those requests," I said diplomatically.

I escorted them to the luggage carousel. They didn't have much luggage. I saw only one small bag each.

Amber, the third member of the trio was about five-foot-six, also slim with long, black hair but with a lighter skin tone and more delicate features. "We may need to buy luggage to pack what we buy," she said. "We're starting off light anyway."

"Good plan." I herded them to the restaurant to wait with the Washington State foursome. Howard stood as we approached and Richard stood as well to welcome them.

"Lovely to have you with us," Heather said graciously. Poppy echoed her.

"And nice to have you with us." Julie said, effectively robbing Heather's comment of its unintentional patronizing tone.

Heather blinked, then smiled. "It's going to be a pleasure," she said warmly.

Julie smiled. Those two understood each other. I've seen it before. Instant connection.

"We're looking forward to it." Amber shrugged off her knapsack.

I had one more guest to meet. Susan Cooper was coming in on a flight from Portland, Maine. She was from Barre, Vermont, and was a retired English teacher. I hoped she would add a lot to our tour. I waited as the hundreds of passengers streamed down the corridor. She was one of the last. She used a cane. She had told me in an email that she could manage quite well but would avoid long walks. I had a wheelchair in the back of my van if she needed it. She was the reason I couldn't bring Gulliver with me. I couldn't manage a wheelchair and Gulliver.

When Susan and I joined the others at the restaurant, Richard was pontificating about the value of Shakespeare to the British canon. He was a drama teacher from Friday Harbor, Washington State, and I was afraid he was going to be quite dramatic on this tour. He was presently the director of a series of plays at the San Juan Island Theater which he had informed me on an email was a prestigious company.

I'd seen Poppy's name at the bottom of the brochure he'd sent me as being in charge of marketing so perhaps that explained the couple's friendship.

"Shakespeare was a genius, of course," Richard said. "There's never been before him and there never will be after him anyone who could use language with such efficiency, proficiency and accuracy."

"No kidding?" Amber said, causing Richard to hesitate for a moment.

"I'm not kidding," Richard said. "It's true."

"Truth is such a slippery concept," Julie said quietly. "What's true to you might not be true to me."

I remembered that Julie and her friends were all students at The Ontario College of Art and Design University in Toronto, Canada, and were likely used to debating ideas.

"This is unequivocally true," Richard stated flatly.

"Richard, would you like more coffee?" Heather asked. "They have a really nice cappuccino here. Would you like me to get you one?"

Richard was distracted. "Maybe I should have something to eat, too," he said.

"Oh, good idea," Heather said. "Why don't you come with me and we'll choose something? Would anyone else like something to eat?" She looked around.

"I could use a coffee," Howard said and stood.

"I'll join you." Poppy accompanied them.

Richard hesitated between waiting for Heather to serve him and joining his friends, but left us to approach the serving counter.

When he was out of earshot Trinity commented, "Snappy as a Rez dog."

"Yep. Could be as vicious." Amber said.

Julie murmured, "He's going to be a bit of work."

It's not a good idea for me to encourage criticism in my group, so I simply smiled.

"This is Susan Cooper," I said. The young women introduced themselves. Susan was a tiny woman, barely five feet tall, small-boned and fragile. But she had bright blue eyes and looked alert and interested. "You all look to be native people of Canada. Is that true?"

"It couldn't be more true," Amber said and laughed. The others picked up her allusion to Richard's ownership of truth and smiled.

"I'm Anishinaabe," Amber said, "from central Canada."

"I'm Gitxsan from the northwest of Canada," Julie said.

"And I'm Anishinaabe and French from central Canada." Trinity said.

Susan looked delighted to be surrounded by theses vibrant young women. "I come from Barre, Vermont, and I must tell you that my society there is mostly white. I am looking forward to getting an education from you."

A look passed swiftly from one to the other, then Julie said, "We call our elder ladies 'auntie'. Would that suit you?"

Susan sat back, sat perfectly still for a moment then beamed at her. "I would love that."

"Well then, Auntie," Amber said as she stood. "Would you like me to get you a coffee?"

There was a silent moment when Susan absorbed her new status. "That would be splendid. Decafé, please." She was wise enough not to offer to pay for it.

These young women were generous and compassionate. I was lucky they had chosen my tour. Richard, on the other hand might be a problem. Still, Heather seemed to be Richard's minder so she might be quite useful in keeping Richard in line. Howard and Poppy implied they were well used to him, so they may also be helpful. Years of experience with tourists told me that I was going to get very tired of Richard.

CHAPTER THREE

The drive from Heathrow to Rye was uneventful. Richard dozed and the others looked out the windows of the van, taking in the miles of houses on either side which finally gave way to a green, agricultural vista.

I took the London Orbital Motorway, as it is the fastest exit from the Heathrow area. Aside from Wisley Common where we had a small stretch of green land, albeit with the A3 bisecting it, the motorway ran past suburbs, miles and miles of dwellings without a charming one in the lot. Tourists from North America don't want to see acres of houses. They want to see green and verdant pastures—their notion of England, even in July. I couldn't adjust the landscape, but I could get them through the urban spread as quickly as possible.

"What's this road?" Heather asked.

"The London Orbital Road."

"The London Orbital Road," she repeated. "What we would call a Ring Road?"

"Indeed. We usually just call it the M25."

"The London Orbital Road is a mouthful."

I stayed on M25 when it veered south, bypassing Sevenoaks. The road turned into A21. Roads and streets in England often change their names for no apparent reason. It can be confusing, even to the English. Finally, we came onto the vast expanse of farms, woodlands and the South Downs stretching out on either

side of us to the horizon. Hedgerows bisected the fields as they
had for hundred of years. The farmland looked as it must have one
hundred years ago although they probably didn't have the bright
yellow rape seed in the fields back then. I glanced at my rear-view
mirror and saw both Richard and Heather sleeping. The young trio
from Toronto were snapping pictures. Susan was also watching the
view. We were in East Sussex now, where there were farms which
had been feeding Londoners for centuries. At Hastings, I took a
secondary road to avoid the downtown area and turned along the
coast on the Old London Road. I followed the coast along Pett Level
Beach. Heather and Richard woke when the others exclaimed at
the sight of the sea.

"France is so close," Julie said.

"Less than twenty miles," I said.

"That must have been scary during the war." She stared
out the window probably imagining the bombers relentlessly
droning overhead. East Sussex and Kent suffered badly in the war,
particularly in the summer of 1940 when ports such as Hastings
had no anti-aircraft guns and were at the mercy of the bombers.
Hitler planned the invasion of Britain for that September and sent
his air force to clear the way for the German army. That summer
the Battle of Britain was fought in the air over this area. The
British resistance was so fierce that Hitler changed his mind about
the invasion. Instead, he sent his air force to drop bombs on the
cities, particularly Canterbury, and shell harbor towns like Dover,
Folkstone, Hastings and Ramsgate from the guns along the French
Coast.

Julie had written to me about her interest in Second World
War novels. She said the cohesion of the populace and the sense
of purpose was unusual and admirable. She wondered if her
own Indigenous community had a parallel spirit, opposing the
oppression they experienced. She and her friends wanted to write
mysteries set in wartime Britain in which Indigenous women

featured as strong characters. That sounded intriguing to me. There were a lot of Canadians stationed here during the war. It's likely some of them were Indigenous people.

I drove away from the sea and into Rye. Since everyone in the van was now awake and seemed alert, I took them around the small town and showed them points of interest. Many notable writers had lived at the Lamb House, including Henry James. The Benson brothers lived there at one time, one of whom wrote the Miss Mapp books. They are tedious to read these days, but they were popular in their time. Godden and Diddakoi lived there and Rudyard Kipling visited, but none of the former residents were mystery writers so were not of great interest to my guests.

"Did Jacqueline Winspear live in any of these houses," Trinity asked. "Julie goes on and on about how great a writer she is."

"A master story-teller," I agreed, "but I don't think she stayed here."

"Many of the cozy mysteries are set in the Kent countryside which is close to Rye," Susan said.

"Elizabeth Peters sets Amelia Peabody's home in Kent," I said, "although she was rarely there. "

"Rhys Bowen puts Georgiana Rannoch in Kent in several books," Julie said.

"Yes, in *Heirs and Graces*. I love that character," Heather offered. "She's lively, intelligent and not your usual high-society lady as she is constantly trying to make ends meet."

"Even though she's thirty-fifth in line for the throne," I said.

Heather laughed. "So she says."

We gossiped about imaginary characters as if they were mutual acquaintances.

"Characters are often popping down to Eastbourne on the train." Susan must read the novels set in the 1920s and 30s.

"Now-a-days they'd be entering the Chunnel at Folkstone," Heather contributed.

If I'd stayed on the M25 and not turned off, that is where we would have gone—under the sea to France. I pulled into the front entrance to Rother Manor.

"This isn't my idea of a manor house," Richard said as I parked the van. He sounded like a petulant teenager. I turned and looked down the center aisle to Richard at the back. He was peering out the window and, as I watched, he turned back to me. "It's *not* a manor house!"

The air conditioning whined to a stop and the temperature in the van started to rise. There were huge beech trees around the perimeter of the car park. I could smell the spicy scent of lavender on the hot afternoon air. No one wanted to stay inside the van. Julie and her friends rose and blocked the aisle, so Richard subsided. No doubt I'd hear more from him later.

I got out, leaving the door open and walked to the rear of the van. I pulled all the luggage from the back and set it on the ground. My guests disembarked and gathered around me. Before Richard could start on his disappointment with the accommodations, I began to speak.

"This is Rother Manor Guest House. We will be occupying most of the house. The accommodations are luxurious and the food is Michelin quality, but the manager, Laura, has recently suffered a bereavement. Her son died," I said without going into detail. "She will be here but not as much as she usually is. Please come to me for anything you might need and I will take care of it."

"This is NOT," Richard repeated in a loud voice, "a manor house."

We turned as one to view the house. It was Victorian, with a rendered finish painted gray and curved windows on either side of the front entrance. It looked charming, immaculate and welcoming. What it wasn't was a huge pile of stone with forty bedrooms, a ballroom and a wing for the servants along with a thousand acres of grounds.

"What were you expecting, Richard." I tried to be patient.

"Elegance, luxury. We're paying enough."

"I promise you luxury and elegance," I said

"But not size," Richard said. "I expected a huge mansion. A manor house is a mansion."

"This one," I said, "has eight guest rooms and is of luxurious standard. It is in the middle of Rye so you can't expect a huge manor house and farm. A manor house, I agree, can be a large house on a manor, that is with farms and agriculture around to support it. This is not one of those. This is a guest house so one does not expect it to be big."

"Well, I did," Richard said.

"Richard," Heather called, "could you help me with my suitcase?"

Richard glared at me then turned to help his wife.

I hoped he would accept the accommodation because I wasn't going to find anything else. I turned to assist Susan with her luggage but found that Julie had placed Susan's small bag on top of her own and was carrying it to the guest house.

"Julie," I said, "do you need a hand?

"No, I'm good," she said.

Howard and Poppy had picked up their luggage and were walking up the stairs.

I did get all kinds of people on my tours with diverse personalities like Richard who was concerned primarily with himself and Julie who automatically looked after the elderly. I like some better than others, but I find most of them interesting. Some just take more patience than others. At least, that's what I tell myself.

Angela was in the foyer to greet the guests and hand out the keys. I took Susan's bag from Julie and thanked her.

"When you have settled in," Angela said, "come down to the lounge and have tea." She gestured toward the room behind her.

Trinity peeked in. "Wow," she said "Cake and everything."

Angela smiled. "Fairy cakes, biscuits, Victoria sponge, Eccles cake and some fruit."

"We will be down for sure." Amber said.

"It looks lovely," Poppy said.

I waited with Susan until the others had climbed the stairs then carried her suitcase while she followed. She managed the stairs without difficulty, but slowly.

I settled Susan in her room and showed her the tour package I'd left for her. She said she had slept on the plane so she felt quite fresh and would be down for coffee in a few minutes. I suppose I could stop treating her like fragile porcelain because, in spite of her age and some limitations, she was active and capable of getting on and off the van and up and down stairs.

"I'm just down the hall in 106," I said, "in case you need me."

"I'll be fine. Thank you," she said.

I dropped my knapsack in my room and walked over to take in the view from my window. I was at the back of the house so overlooked the guest house garden and the communal gardens beyond. I had been looking at the garden for few minutes before I realized there was yellow police tape around the garden shed. Why would there be police tape? As I was thinking this through I saw a man come out of the shed and head toward the back door of the guest house, then another appear and follow the first.

Police tape. Were they police? *Who else would they be, Claire?*

I didn't want them anywhere near my guests. I rushed down the stairs and headed toward the kitchen. I met Angela who was looking down the hall. I expect she'd heard me coming.

"What's going on!" I demanded.

"You'd better come in," she said as she stepped back into the kitchen and made room for me. "We've got trouble."

Laura was standing at the kitchen door. The two police officers were outside, facing her.

"Mrs. Wright, we ran a test on your son's blood. We're doing a study for the government Health Department on fentanyl poisoning and we routinely take samples for the survey."

"Yes," Laura said. "I gave permission for that. I'd do anything to get the government moving on doing something for addicts. I expect that you did find fentanyl." She sounded resigned as if she knew her son had never been far from his drug habit.

"No, madam," the first officer said. "We did not find fentanyl. We found a different drug. An unusual drug. So we are now treating his death as suspicious."

I thought about that. 'Suspicious' was police jargon for 'likely a nasty mess'.

"A suspicious death," Laura echoed. She frowned.

"An accident," I said, "or mur…" my voiced trailed to nothing.

"Murder?" Laura was incredulous.

"A suspicious death," the officer corrected her. He wouldn't go so far as to propose murder— but it was either an accident or murder.

"It must be an accident. Accidental toxicity. I always knew that might happen."

"We don't believe that likely," the officer said. "Although it is a possibility."

"You'd better come in."

None of my guests would be implicated in Reece's death. They were in the air over the Atlantic when he died, but I didn't want them involved in the investigation.

Laura stood back. Angela and I moved toward the kitchen table and sat.

The two officers followed Laura. The taller one, Detective Sergeant Travis Flynn he'd announced, was about thirty, handsome with defined cheek bones, black in the way some of Jamaican heritage are coffee-colored black, and broad-shouldered. He was dressed in light brown trousers, a pale blue shirt and a long black leather jacket. He'd fit into a group of uniformed police. His acolyte, Detective Constable Jas Sandhu was much shorter, more my height, with lighter skin color than Detective Sergeant Flynn and with much more flamboyant clothes. His shirt was canary-yellow and he topped it with a green jacket and a red and yellow scarf handkerchief tucked in the jacket pocket.

"Coffee," Angela offered, standing, then moving toward the stove.

"Lovely," Jas Sandhu accepted for both. "But make it tea, luv, if you would."

Laura gestured to the chairs and we all sat. She passed her hand over her face let out a long breath, "What's this all about then?"

Travis Flynn spoke slowly and clearly. He had an educated accent. He was a Detective Sergeant. Probably had a university degree. I stopped speculating on the nature of his diction and listened.

"The drug that was in your son's body was not one that he could have found easily. We're worried that there's either a new drug available to contaminate supplies, or he somehow found this drug and used it with intent, or someone gave it to him knowing what it was."

Laura looked at him and I could see her trying to work out what was bothering the police.

"You think," I said, trying to help her process along, "that Reece would not have used this drug deliberately unless he intended to kill himself."

I saw Laura wince, but I wanted to get this out of the way. "A deliberate death is unlikely. If he wanted to kill himself he could have done it in many ways that didn't involve finding an esoteric drug."

Travis Flynn looked at me. "That was our thinking," he said.

"So he could have taken a drug that was being sold as something it was not, poisoning unsuspecting users."

"That's possible. Until we know where he got the drug we are going to be very interested."

He looked down at his tablet and scrolled down. "It would have made him sleepy not high." He returned his gaze to Laura. "It's not a drug that has appeared in any other sample in the survey. We don't want it circulating and need to find the source."

Laura considered his information, then said, "Whoever gave it to him might not have been trying to harm him. I mean they might not have known it was lethal."

"That's true, but we don't want that purveyor of death selling this to anyone else."

I didn't believe searching for the supplier of the drug was an explanation for the crime tape around the shed.

"Or somebody deliberately killed Reece," I said.

There was a long moment of silence.

"Someone murdered him?" Laura said and looked at Travis Flynn with an incredulous stare.

"I'm sorry," Flynn said, "but that is what we're considering."

Of course they were. After securing the site of Reece's death, the two detectives were starting their investigation by interviewing Laura.

He continued. "We will search for whoever supplied him with the drug but we must consider that someone might have given it to him deliberately."

"Oh," she said quietly trying to absorb the horror of it. "Oh, dear God. What was he mixed up in?"

Reece's death, as difficult as it was for Laura, was just made worse by the thought he'd been involved with criminals and that someone, perhaps a member of a gang, had murdered him.

CHAPTER FOUR

Angela had distributed the tea and we sat for a moment or two in quiet. Jas Sandhu had been taking notes but put his notebook down to drink his tea.

"Excellent tea this," he said to Angela. "What is it?"

"Ceylon," she said almost absently then shot a quick glance at Sandhu, probably realizing she was giving Indian tea to someone from India or at least of Indian heritage.

"I thought so. It's my mother's favorite." He smiled. His eyes were lit with humor, but also with compassion. He gave the appearance of a flighty, fashion-conscious, rather shallow personality, but I was beginning to think he was more complicated than I'd first assumed.

Angela smiled in response.

Laura ignored this exchange and leaned toward DS Flynn. "Detective, what can I do to help? Not that I think I know anything that *could* help."

His calm face, quiet movements and air of serious contemplation must make others feel that he was someone they could trust. Behind that demeanor was intelligent watchfulness. "Take some time to consider who might have wished him harm. I'll return to interview you more fully." DS Flynn was direct without being particularly warm or supportive. Laura might appreciate this no-nonsense approach from someone who kept her informed. I would be more likely to confide in Detective Constable Sandhu.

She nodded.

"In the meantime, I'll call in the Scene of the Crime Officers to take fingerprints, samples of food and give a more thorough search to the garden shed where your son lived. That means a lot of people coming through this garden."

Laura touched his arm. "Could you be as discreet as possible? I have a house full of guests and I don't want them upset by the coming and going of the police."

"Right." Flynn agreed.

I was concerned that my guests if they knew of the police investigation would be curious and interfere with it. I'd do my best to keep them way from it.

"We understand." DC Sandhu leaned forward. "We'll try to be quiet. We also don't want your guests interfering with our investigation. They weren't here when your son died, were they?"

"No, no." She looked at me. "No, they weren't."

"I was the first of my group to arrive and I came after Reece had passed away," I said. "My guests came after me." It was comforting to know that the police also wanted to keep my group out of their way.

Flynn reassured her. "We won't want to interview the guests. We'll try to be unobtrusive."

"Thank you," Laura said.

DC Sandhu finished his tea. "We'll come and go like ghosts," he said. "You won't know we're here."

Angela snorted, then gave advice. "You tiptoe through here; you manage quiet; you'll get tea."

Sandhu grinned. "That's a deal," he said and they departed.

We sat where they left us considering what we'd heard from them when there was a knock on the kitchen door. Angela opened it.

A thin, blonde woman who looked to be in her late twenties hesitated in the doorway.

"Oh, Beth," Laura said. "Come in."

"I'm so sorry, Laura."

Laura opened her arms and Beth dove into them. They were both crying. I stood to leave but Angela gestured at me to sit.

She brought a chair and guided her into it. Beth and Laura held hands.

"This is Beth," Angela said. "Reece's friend."

"Claire," I said.

Beth took the paper towel Angela proffered and blew her nose. "Sorry," she said.

"It's normal," I said and I decided that it was normal and Laura and Beth could cry as much as they wanted to. I sipped my tea.

Laura began telling Beth about the police investigation when there was another knock on the kitchen door. Before Angela could answered it, it opened and a woman stood there. A short, plump woman of about fifty or so, round glasses, graying hair, thin and smiling.

"Hiya. I'm Jessica Weatherby from the *Rye News*. I just popped by with an obituary form." She waved it in the air then stepped into the kitchen and placed it on the table. "You can hand it in at the office or fill it out on line. Credit cards are an easy way to pay on line."

Laura stared at her.

Angela rose to her feet but before she could say anything Beth jumped up. "Miss Weatherby! How could you?"

"Why it's Beth from the library. What are you doing here?" She didn't wait for any answer. "I see there is police tape around your shed, Mrs. Wright. Has there been a crime?"

Beth advanced on her, fury propelling her to confront the intruder. "You are not welcome at this time. Leave at once."

Miss Weatherby backed up. "Certainly. ...certainly." She backed out the door. Beth slammed it, locked it and burst into tears.

Angela comforted her this time. I picked up the obituary form and placed it on the counter. "You may want to look at that later," I said.

"I suppose." Laura found her voice.

"Who is she?"

Angela broke out the brandy and topped up our tea. Beth chugged down a few gulps and shivered.

"She's a teacher, if you can believe it. A teacher at the infant school. She bosses those poor kids like she's their commandant."

"She said she was from the newspaper," Laura said.

"She does that part time. Reports in local events like the guides' picnic, the art show, that sort of thing. Once in a while, she gets a report in the *Sussex World* out of Hastings. She gets paid for that. She's always looking for a story." Beth took another drink, more slowly this time. "I should be more understanding, I guess. But she surprised me and it was just too much."

Angela patted her hand. "You got rid of her, so you did just fine."

Beth smiled. "I did, didn't I?"

I left them and rushed to my room to change for dinner. It was good to meet Beth and good for Laura to have someone sharing her grief. That Miss Weatherby took the biscuit. Some people ignored social boundaries.

I shook out my dark blue and turquoise print cotton dress. It was simple but fitted well. I obsessively love shoes and it's always difficult to restrict the number I take on a tour. I chose my low-heeled sandals which added some sophistication to my outfit. I picked out a silver chain and a bracelet with a deep blue turquoise stone in the center. I seldom wear earrings now as my glasses have multicolored turquoise and blue frames which is enough color around my face. I needed to hurry to meet my guests. I walked quickly to the stairs, mentally going over what Flynn had said. If Reece's death was murder, Mark might be involved. I'd call him later.

I'd put Reece and his mother out of my mind while I concentrated on my guests. They had to be cared for and pampered like the special people they were and I wanted all to go brilliantly for them. I was taking them to the Mermaid Inn for a relaxing and elaborate meal. Their first dinner in Britain should be one of elegance and gourmet quality food. I'd eaten there last night; I knew The Mermaid Inn could do this.

My guests were distinctively different in their dress choices. Julie who was about five-foot-eight and solid, wore a silky, sleeveless, red top over a long, floaty, cotton skirt. She had silver bracelets and dangling silver earrings which had some design engraved on them. Trinity, much shorter and much smaller, wore a light, woven skirt with elaborate beadwork sewn on most of it in multicolored hues of orange, yellow, and brown. She topped it with a long-sleeved white silky shirt, and over that a hip-length vest in a butternut color with elaborate beadwork sewn over the lapels: stylish and unique. I wanted to spend more time studying the designs.

Amber wore black light-weight cotton capris and a black tunic top with silver jewellery encircling her neck and her arms. She wore silver rings with engraved designs on four fingers. The trio looked like exotic birds with their dark skin, brown eyes and long, dark hair. Tonight, all three had let their hair hang loose down to their waists. People would turn to stare at them on the street as they drifted towards the Mermaid Inn— a phenomenon I'm sure they were used to.

Richard wore jeans and a white, short-sleeved shirt open at the neck. He was presentable—he wouldn't be turned away at the door because he wasn't sporting a tie—but he was not up to the dress standard of this restaurant.

Poppy was a poem in a lavender silk blazer over a dark blue sheath. Her shoes were Fluvogs. I envied her those shoes, gray-blue with a low heel that somehow appeared to be a blue twisted rope. Classy. Howard wore a dark summer suit with a pale gray shirt and a Paisley tie. He looked distinguished and comfortable. He probably wore suits often.

I'd offered to drive everyone as The Mermaid Inn had a car park close to the door. Susan and the two couples agreed to the ride, but the three young women decided to walk as it was a fine summer evening. Roses were in full blossom and bobbing over walled gardens. Hanging baskets with their cheerful red geraniums adorned many of the medieval buildings. I hoped the route would show them the charm of this English town.

The two couples, Susan and I had some flavor of the town as, after I'd parked, we walked out through the arch to Mermaid Street. Susan could walk that far on the flagstone walk beside the cobblestones but it was narrow and uneven so we just went a few yards and turned back.

"Look at the color of those roses," she said, staring at the peach-colored ramblers on the wall nearby.

Heather took a deep breath. "You can smell them. It's heavenly."

"Medieval," Richard said, looking up at the black and white timbered buildings.

When we approached the front entrance of the Mermaid Inn, Richard stopped dead and stared at the sign affixed to the wall: *Mermaid Inn re-built 1420.*

"Look at that, Richard," Heather said. "It was *rebuilt* before Shakespeare was born. Do you suppose he ever came here?"

"I doubt it," Richard said.

"He could have. It's been standing here since those days." Heather was not going to give up on her romantic notion of a Shakespearean visit.

"Remarkable," Susan said to me, stopping on the pavement and staring at the inn.

"Yes," I agreed. It was remarkable. I was pleased it was making an impression. That was a good start to the tour.

"Gorgeous," Susan said, enamoured of the building. "Look at those timbers."

The outside of the inn was typically Tudor in design with

vertical dark timbers alternating with white rendering. Diamond leaded panes in the windows established it firmly in a bygone era.

"This is more like it," Richard said.

"Classy," Heather agreed.

"All this fifteenth century grandeur makes me feel positively young," Susan said.

She looked like one of the present King's cousins, with her perfectly-waved white hair, her long-sleeved ivory silk blouse, and a single strand of what looked like real pearls around her neck. She didn't look young, but she did look alert and aware.

The hostess showed us to our table which I'd reserved in the main dining room. This was not a replica of an old building; it *was* an old building. Weathered timbers held up of the roof.

Heather stared at them.

"They've been there for centuries," I said.

"And will be probably be standing here for a few more." She looked around at the posts and beams.

I wasn't sure I had her faith in the future. Climate change, plagues and political idiocy might interfere, but I kept those thoughts to myself.

We'd just sat at our places when the three young women arrived like a flock of vibrant parrots, not that Julie was talking, but Trinity and Amber were chattering.

"Wow," Amber said as she sat down beside me. "This is beautiful."

It was handsome. Red walls, red carpet on the floor, and red cushions on the seats added warmth to the dark room. Pictures with gilded frames adorned the walls. Carriage lamps hung from the ceilings between the dark wood beams. Sparkling white linen on the table brightened the room and, while it gave a feeling of luxury, it also gave a feeling of comfort. The posts in the center looked ancient. The waiters must learn to dance around them.

"It hits you between the eyes with 'This is England,'" Trinity said.

"It really is authentic England," I said. "At least authentic in medieval times."

"We aren't going to write about characters who lived that far in the past," Julie said, "but it's fascinating."

Even Richard was positive. "I like this. Shakespeare would have been comfortable here."

I supposed that meant Richard as a drama director was comfortable here. I wondered if he saw himself as a modern-day Shakespeare? They both produced plays.

The waiter appeared with the menus. I'd ordered two bottles of Chapel Down Flint Dry 2019, a local white. Richard ordered bourbon. The waiter caught my eye and I shook my head in a slight movement. Extra liquor orders did not go on my bill. Richard would get a tab at the end of the meal. Howard, after consulting with Poppy, ordered two gin and tonics.

The menu intrigued them all.

"Juniper-smoked duck breast," Julie said, "with poached gooseberries, beetroot, gin and gooseberry puree."

"Could you make that?" Trinity asked Julie.

"I could get the duck and the juniper out on my lands, but probably not the gooseberries."

"Could you substitute salmon berries?" Amber suggested.

Julie raised her eyebrows. "Maybe."

"I want beef," Richard said. "It says 'Cote de Boeuf with bone marrow and Jersey Royals' so that's beef, but I want more than bone marrow."

"The bone marrow is for flavor," Heather said. "'Jersey Royals'" must be the beef. Probably tenderloin."

"Why don't they say so?"

Heather didn't respond, just went back to studying her menu.

Amber, who was sitting beside me leaned toward me and murmured. "He'd complain the sky was too blue and the ocean too salty, that one."

I smiled but didn't comment. It's never a good idea to join in criticizing the customers. Jersey Royals were potatoes but I'd let the waiter explain the menu to Richard.

It was Julie who enlightened Richard about the menu. "'Cote de Boeuf' is bone-in rib-eye steak. You'd probably like it."

"Oh," Richard said "Thanks. I'll have that."

"Good choice," Howard said. "Love to have it myself, but Poppy here has me on a Mediterranean type diet. It's surprisingly good."

We smiled, but I doubted any of us believed Poppy was in charge of him or that he adhered to a Mediterranean diet.

Everyone ordered and conversation circled around the food and the fifteenth-century ambiance—both notable.

It was after the desserts—I'd chosen rose, wood sorrel and rhubarb sorbet— that the conversation turned to what the guests wanted from this tour.

"I am the director of the San Juan Theater. We are deviating from Shakespeare next season and performing Christie's *The Mousetrap* which is set in a manor house. I want to see a manor house. I only came on this tour because Heather said we were staying at a manor house." He turned to his wife, "Rother Manor is NOT a manor house."

"You're quite right, Richard. It's not." She didn't look at all apologetic.

"I can arrange for you to tour a manor house," I said, hoping to prevent further complaints.

"Howard and I would like to join that excursion," Poppy said. "I work in the office of Richard's company, so I have an interest."

I wondered if Poppy with Howard's backing kept that company solvent. They seemed quietly competent and confident. And wealthy.

"Does anyone else have a special request?"

"Julie really wants to see a Second World War Museum," Amber said. "We all need to see one if we are going to write this mystery together."

"Set in the war years," Trinity elaborated.

"In Kent," Julie added.

'I'll arrange something for you," I assured them. There were many mysteries set in the Second World War era. Presently there was a trend in mystery readership for that genre, so they might find a market for their book.

As we left the inn, the late evening sun lit the walls of the houses lining Mermaid Street. Sunset would be an hour yet. Across from the inn, brick houses nestled against white rendered walls, and brick and half-timbered buildings. Centuries of style crowded harmoniously to the edge of the narrow street. Shadows hid the doorways. The two couples and the Toronto trio elected to walk back to the guest house. The streets of cobblestones and flagstone pavement would be difficult for Susan to navigate in the fading light so I drove her home.

When we arrived at our guest hotel we found Laura had left out the makings for tea, coffee and cocoa in the lounge. I offered this largess to the group when they arrived but they declined and went to their rooms. It had been a long day for them. I took a cup of tea up to my room, and settled at the small round table, Georgian, I think, and prepared to call Mark.

He answered immediately. "Hello, Claire *bach*."

"I love you, too," I responded to his endearment. He used some delectable words.

"Good. How is your tour going? Will they be much trouble?"

"Probably," I said, thinking of Richard.

"Not harboring a murderer this time?" Mark asked.

I've only had that happened once and I never wanted to experience it again. "I don't think so." I repeated that with emphasis. "No, it doesn't look likely. But it does look as though Laura's son Reece didn't die a natural death."

"I thought he died from drug toxicity."

"He did, but it wasn't a drug they expected to find."

"And?"

"They think it's unlikely he got it by accident. They have police tape up around the garden shed."

He knew that indicated a suspicious death. "Do you think Major Crimes will be called?"

"Probably," I said. "The detective who came was just a sergeant. Either he doesn't have an inspector above him here, or the inspector's away or sick or something, because the sergeant came to interview Laura, and he was the one who said that Reece's death was suspicious."

"So the police suspect he was murdered," Mark said. "I see. I might get the case. I'll let you know if a request comes through."

"All right."

There was silence for a moment.

"If I do get the case, I can't stay with you."

"I suppose not," I agreed. "Too close to the action."

"I hope there will be no more action, but too close to the suspects. I would have to interview Laura, and anyone else who might have seen something. It would compromise my investigation to be staying in the same house."

I understood that. He might not even get the case because I was staying here. His superintendent, the querulous Marjorie Addison, didn't approve of my being anywhere near Mark's cases.

"Is Laura a suspect?"

"Everyone's a suspect, Claire, you know that. It's rare a mother who kills her son, so don't worry."

I hadn't considered Laura as a murderer. That was ludicrous. "She's devastated, Mark. You'll need to look elsewhere for your killer." I know there were deviant personalities wandering around disguised as normal people, but not Laura.

There was a moment of silence. Then he said, "I'd like to keep you well away from any local killer. I don't suppose you can change accommodations?"

"Impossible," I said. I wouldn't be able to find accommodation for all of us. It was high season. *I* couldn't be the only one to move because I had to be available to my guests. "Laura is absolutely no threat. Anyway, no one is likely to be interested in me, certainly not Reece's killer, if he was killed."

"I've heard that before," Mark said.

He had a point. I did seem to attract attention from the wrong people.

"So I might see you tomorrow," I said brightly, deflecting the conversation from my propensity to attract nefarious characters.

"I'll let you know as soon as the request comes in," Mark said. "I should know in the morning."

I disconnected. It would be lovely to see Mark. However, I knew that if he was assigned this inquiry and was sleeping somewhere else, I wouldn't see much of him.

I was up early to help Angela set the tables and put out the breakfast. Laura was cooking in the kitchen but didn't want to face a roomful of strangers just yet.

"She'll have to get it together soon," Angela said. "The owners appreciate her and will give her some time to recover, but not forever."

Grief doesn't have a predictable timeline. Perhaps Laura couldn't know when she'd be ready to face her guests again. Angela's expectations were unreasonable.

"It was bad enough that she lost Reece to a drug poisoning, one that she thought was accidental. Deliberate murder? That's a very hard concept to accept." I couldn't help but let a little censure seep into my tone.

"Oh, I get that," Angela said. "It's hard. It's even wicked. Bloody wicked. Imagine someone wanting to do away with Reece? He wasn't at all offensive. Always polite. Even when he was using."

"It's a shock," I said.

"Yeah, well it is at that," Angela said.

I went to the kitchen to fetch some salt and peppers. Laura was taking muffins from the oven.

"Those smell delicious." I admired the browned muffins, uniformly perfect.

"Thank you." She smiled at me "Before you ask, I'm better this morning. I will have to manage this somehow. I need this job, so I'll have to do it. I will be better tomorrow." She carefully picked the hot muffins from the pan and piled them into a basket on the counter. Then she turned to look at me. She bit her lip and tears welled in her eyes.

I opened my arms and she moved into them, laying her head against my cheek as if taking comfort.

"I'll never see Reece happy. I'll never be a grandmother."

I patted her back and simply held her.

"All those dreams of him finding solace and eventually contentment are gone. He was such a wonderful son."

I held her for a few moments longer.

Then she sniffed, pushed away and reached for the basket. "Here take these muffins, if you would." She passed them to me.

The muffins steamed. "Beautiful," I said. "I'm going to sneak one before the others get here."

"Go ahead." She touched my arm. "I was thinking last night that there might be something on the surveillance tapes."

"You have surveillance tapes?"

"Well, yes. Everyone does. I should tell the police, shouldn't I?"

"You have the sergeant's number."

"I do. I'll call."

I took the muffins into the breakfast room, put them on the sideboard, helped myself to one and took it to my table. I brought out my mobile and texted Mark. "Did you get a request to take on this case?"

"Just got it. See you soon."

I texted back. "There are surveillance tapes."

"Good to know. Thanks."

I scoffed the muffin and remembered I hadn't picked up the salt and peppers. I fetched them then followed Angela's directions, getting the food onto the side table. As I bustled after the fast-moving Angela, I ruminated on this last piece of information. I wondered what area of the surrounding garden those surveillance cameras covered and whether they would give Mark a solid lead.

CHAPTER FIVE

By the time the guests trickled in, Angela and I had the breakfast room ready. There were four small round pedestal tables of dark polished wood and four larger square tables. We had put a dark brown mat at each place setting of teal blue crockery. Blue was the restful, predominant color in the room. The wallpaper was white with pale-blue feathery plants. The sideboard was painted deep slate blue. Angela and Laura had placed a few white and maroon-colored small cosmos in tiny vases in the center of each table. It all looked charming—and very Victorian.

The hot dishes steamed on the sideboard: boiled, scrambled and poached eggs, bread for toast, muffins, bacon, sausage, fried tomatoes and even black pudding. The muffin I'd just eaten was fast fading into memory. I could do justice to this largess. Angela was ready with the coffee carafe.

The three young women from Toronto and Susan sat at one of the tables and Richard, Heather, Howard, and Poppy at the other. I chose at a small round table beside the window.

Richard complained to Angela as she was topping up the coffee in his cup.

"This house is not a manor house."

Oh no. Richard was going to be tedious. I didn't want to have to deal with him without fortifying myself with coffee.

"Is that right?" Angela paused, the hot carafe in her hand and a belligerent look in her eye. "So what's your problem with it?"

Richard sputtered a little but persevered. "It's not big enough."

"Are you one of those guys who thinks bigger is better?"

Richard blinked while he absorbed the sexual inuendo. Everyone was quiet. No one laughed. Angela turned her back. I was happy that she hadn't poured the hot coffee on him.

All was peaceful after that as we tucked into our meal.

When we were finished and relaxed drinking coffee, I reached down to the basket I'd brought with me and distributed the daily goodie bag to each person. Each small bag contained a map of Rye, a Lion bar and a small package of biscuits.

I wanted them to have an interesting day, but I didn't want to over-tire them. "This morning I will take you on a tour of Rye. I'll show you points of interest such as the Art Gallery, St. Mary's Church and the Heritage Center. This afternoon will be a time for rest, shopping, reading or exploring on your own. We'll meet back here at six for dinner. I will be arranging an excursion tomorrow to a manor house for our Washington State contingent." I smiled at Howard and Poppy. "And I will arrange a trip to Folkestone and the war museum for the three ladies who asked for it. Susan what would you like to do?"

She thought for a moment, then said, "I'd like to see the manor house. I've never toured one and I doubt I could keep up with the young ones in Folkestone who will want to dart into galleries and other museums when they get a chance."

"That would work out well," I said. "Can you all meet me in the foyer in forty minutes for today's exploration of Rye?"

They agreed, took their gift bags and moved toward the stairs.

Angela swung into the room with a tray upon which she began to pile dishes.

"Want me to poison that Richard?" she asked.

I shuddered. "Don't joke about it."

"Oh!" She looked stricken. "I forgot about Reece for a moment. I don't know how I could. Oh bloody hell. I'm really going to miss him."

We did forget dreadful events or we blotted them from our minds periodically. It was as though we could only mange reality a few minutes at a time. I remembered the days after my mother died. I'd not think of her for hours at a time then something someone said, or some scent I smelled would remind me of her. Angela had forgotten. It's what we do.

"It's all right." I looked at the crockery she was carrying and hesitated.

"You go on," Angela said. "You've done enough this morning. Laura and I can cope. It's better if she has lots to do."

I also had tasks to accomplish. I cancelled the excursion to Hastings by boat that I'd planned. I had to pay a penalty but such are the exigencies of tour guiding. I called Godinton, one of my favorite manor houses, and was able to book a tour with a guide for tomorrow. I went on line and purchased train tickets to Folkestone for the three budding mystery writers. I managed to do all that and be in the foyer before the group arrived. It was wise of me not to bring Gulliver, even though I missed him. This tour was going to keep me busy.

While I was opening the van, I noticed a woman on a bike, stationary on the other side of the road. I saw the bike first. It was a new electric one, a sensible choice for Rye with its hills. Then I noticed Miss Weatherby, the woman who had burst into the kitchen yesterday. Was she hanging around trying to see if there was any police action here she could report on? She saw me watching her and sped away. She could be a nuisance.

Once my guests had loaded into the van, I drove only a short distance to the Lamb house. I asked them to wait for me there while I parked and hurried back. My group were wandering over the cobblestones when I returned in danger of being hit by any oncoming vehicle. Susan, sensibly, was at the extreme edge of the road. I expect the others assumed this was a pedestrian pathway to the Lamb House, but it was a usable vehicle street, the English version of a street, which was narrow. They were lucky not to have had to flee oncoming cars. I should have warned them. I didn't want to make phone calls to bereaved relatives to explain how I had dropped their father, mother or sister into traffic. Everyone had their National Trust passes and followed me. I was relieved when I had them safely inside.

"As you could see by the symmetrical design of the exterior and the high ceilings inside, this is a Georgian house, built in 1722. The owner, James Lamb was the mayor of Rye, elected thirteen times. He entertained many notables in the house, including George I, and apparently Mayor Lamb occupied it for some time. Henry James, the American writer, bought it in 1899 and many well-known authors and even a book illustrator lived here."

I stopped talking and let the house declare itself.

"One family lived here?" Trinity asked, incredulous at the notion of so much space for so few.

"Fireplaces everywhere," Julie said. "Who brought the wood and stoked the fires?"

"In 1722, I expect it was servants," I said.

Trinity imagined it. "They must have had one man whose total job it was to look after the fireplaces. Maybe John, the wood guy. All day he'd chop wood, bring it to all these fireplaces, feed the fireplaces and keep the place from burning down." I could see her imaginary John. Perhaps she *would* write a book.

"Well," Amber said, "it would be work and maybe he liked the job."

"And he'd get fed," Trinity added.

"Today these fireplaces, at least some of them, are gas," I said.

"Well sure," Amber said. "No one wants to haul wood today. It's not environmentally sound, in any case."

"Neither is gas," Julie said.

They were enjoying their wander through the house. Richard particularly liked the oak study with its impressive portrait of George I. Howard liked the billiard room.

Julie was fascinated by a framed excerpt of Henry James'
writing that described his fear of the threat from war. It read: 'In
looking over from the old rampart of a little high-perched Sussex
town at the bright blue streak of the Channel, within a mile or two
of us at its nearest point [...] just on the other side of that finest
of horizon-lines history was raging at a pitch new under the sun;
thinly masked by that shameless smile the Belgian horror grew.'

"It's that sense of fear we want in our novel," she said.

"Henry was talking about the First World War," I said. "It was
even worse during the Second."

She nodded and moved on to read other examples of his work.

Amber and Trinity were examining a portrait of Henry James
by Sir Philip Edward Burne-Jones.

"Cool brushwork," Trinity said.

"Too careful," Amber said.

Heather approached me. "Are there any mysteries set here?"

"Joan Aiken wrote *The Haunting of Lamb House*. She was born
in Rye on Mermaid Street. Her father was Conrad Aiken."

"An American writer," Howard said.

"He was. And her mother was Jesse MacDonald, a Canadian."

Susan beamed. "That's delightful." I expect she was seeing the
parallel with this group of Americans and Canadians.

They seemed happy with their visit. I led them out of the house
and down West Street. I noticed Trinity was guiding Susan along
the flagstones that ran beside the cobblestone roadway. Susan had
a walking stick but cobblestone and flagstones can be difficult
underfoot, especially this narrow, uneven one. We toured the twelfth
century St. Mary's Church with its sixteenth century working bell
clock. Howard was intrigued by the mechanisms of the bell clock.

While the others were still wandering through the church, I
returned to the van and fetched the wheelchair. Susan could ride
down East Street to High Street and to The Fig Restaurant where
I'd planned to have lunch.

The walk invigorated them and they were in good spirits over the meal. I wasn't sure how the food would appeal to them. I had the shredded chicken, roasted kale, goat cheese, figs, blood orange, black rice, mint, pistachio, and pomegranate. Delicious. Others had pulled pork tacos. Amber had a frittata. There were many vegetarian and vegan choices and, while no one had indicated they must have that choice, both Julie and Trinity picked from that menu. I watch their preferences in case someone was quietly dissatisfied with the food.

Richard praised the acoustics he tried out in St Mary's Church. Howard marvelled at the wheels and cogs and engineering ingenuity of the bell clock.

"I suppose you met at your theater." I said to Richard, indicating Howard and Poppy.

"Actually," Howard interrupted, "we all met years ago when Heather and Richard wandered down the wharf to our boat. We keep it at Roche Harbor which isn't far from Friday Harbor, both on the San Juan Island. We invited them on the boat for a drink. It was then that Richard got Poppy interested in working with the theater." It sounded as though they'd been friends for some time.

We sat with our lunch coffees while the guests decided what to do. They had the afternoon free as I know guests often liked to take a jet-lag nap.

"There are several galleries here on High Street," I told the three artists. "The exhibitions are wide-ranging."

"Are there any textiles?" Trinity asked.

"There are. At least, there were the last time I visited the gallery. The exhibitions do change, so I can't guarantee it."

"Oils?" Amber asked.

"I expect so," I said. "But probably not carvings."

"You never know," Julie said. "If they don't have any, they might be interested in mine."

"Do you have some with you?"

"No, but I can get their email address and hook them up to my website."

"We should all do that," Trinity said.

"Julie's our most accomplished entrepreneur," Amber said. "I have trouble getting my artist brain to move over and let my business brain work, but Julie does it instantly."

"Practice," Julie said.

Trinity turned to Susan. "Would you like to join us, Auntie, while we tour the galleries?"

"It sounds just right," Susan said. "I'm very interested in different forms of art, although I'm not educated in it."

"We'll probably bore you to tears," Julie said.

"Not much danger of that. I like to hear you talk in any case."

"Will you need the wheelchair?" I asked.

"Are all the galleries on High Street?" Susan asked.

"Yes, they are."

"Then I think I can manage," she said. "I do fine when I walk a bit and sit a bit. Perhaps I can give you a call or text if I feel the need of a wheelchair?"

"Right you are. Do that and I'll come over with it. The Rye Heritage Centre is at the bottom of Wish Street so you might want to call if you decide to go there," I said. "It's marked on the map I gave you. And, of course, there are several book stores. You can have the books sent to the guest house if you buy too many to carry."

"Richard and I are going to take the steam train excursion on the East Sussex Railway. What time would you like us to be back" Heather asked. "I know it's out of town but we can take a cab."

"Dinner is at half seven." The station was only six miles from Rye, so a cab would not be costly.

Heather turned to Poppy. "Would you two like to join us?"

"I think I'd like to shop and nap," Poppy said. "Thanks anyway."

"No point in sleeping your vacation away," Richard said as he stood and left the restaurant.

Heather gathered her handbag and stood. She leaned down to Poppy and said, "Five will get you ten he'll sleep on the train."

Poppy laughed.

I was settling the bill— this lunch was on my account—when Mark and his Sergeant Andrew Forsyth arrived at the café. Mark spotted me, smiled and engulfed me in a big hug. It really did feel wonderful to be surrounded by his familiar, tough body. He smelt like pine and sawdust for some reason. We disengaged and I turned to Andy.

He gave me a brief hug.

"Where are you staying?" I asked

"The Rye Lodge," Andy answered. "Very posh."

"We get a rate," Mark said.

The Hampshire Constabulary would pay for it. I imagined the department got reimbursed by a national program somehow. The Major Investigations Team had a complicated administrative system.

"How are the boys?" I asked after his sons. Andy and his partner Bruce had adopted two boys who were now five and three.

"Keeping Bruce very busy," Andy said. Bruce worked from home and so had the primary caretaking role.

I accompanied them to their table where they quickly chose from the menu, ordered and accepted a cup of coffee from the waiter. I declined any more coffee.

"How's the tour?" Mark asked me.

"I have one guest who wants to argue about everything. I'm not sure yet if that will create cohesion in the rest of the group as they band together to make comments about him or it will result in everyone trying to avoid each other,"

"Sounds like you have your hands full."

"I might." At least Richard didn't seem homicidal, suicidal or manic. So far, I could cope with him. I turned back to Andy. "Tell me about the boys."

He brightened. He's a pale man: pale hair, white complexion, blue eyes, shorter than me by about an inch. Many a criminal underestimated his strength. He worked out and kept fit. Mark said he was a good man in a corner.

"They're doing splendidly," he said. "You know that Charlie can read already."

"He's only three," I said. "That's a remarkable boy."

Mark gave me a quick glance. I interpreted it to mean, don't get him going on his family. On the subject of his sons, Andy could extoll for many minutes.

I changed the subject. "You're here to investigate Reece Martin's murder?" I asked.

"We believe it's murder," Mark said. "What's your take?"

"I don't know very much. Laura is devastated, as you can imagine. By all accounts, Reece was a nice young man who was an addict. His mother understands relapse happens and wasn't surprised that he overdosed. Grief-stricken but not surprised."

"She knows the police here don't think he did this to himself. That's why we're here."

"Yes, she knows now."

I recalled our meeting with DS Flynn and his revelation. That reminded me of Miss Weatherby. I told Mark and Andy about her. "Can she hang around and watch the place? It's a bit macabre. Laura hasn't noticed her yet but she may do so soon and it will be upsetting."

Mark thought for a moment. "She can stand on the public road and watch as long as she doesn't come onto the property or try to approach Laura."

"It seems ghoulish."

"Small town press don't usually chase police news. They're more interested in civic events and are respectful and careful because they depend on the local people for their existence."

"Beth thinks Miss Weatherby wants to sell a sensational story to the *Sussex World*. They are more cosmopolitan than the *Rye News*."

"You could let Flynn know, although there isn't much he can do about it."

"I may do that. "

"What do you think of Detective Sergeant Flynn? I've never worked with him."

"He's well aware he needs a supervisor. He said his inspector is off with an injury."

"Knifed," Andy said. "He'll be all right."

I shuddered. I hoped that inspectors, especially my inspector, rarely ran into knives or guns.

"Competent?" Mark asked.

"Yes, I think so. I expect he will have evidence correctly tabulated and entered into a computer program. He's the one who suspected homicide, so he's a bright officer, probably a little stiff but cooperative."

"And the DC?" Andrew asked.

I smiled. "An interesting character."

Mark and Andrew looked at each other. "What does that mean?" Mark asked.

"Unique. Imaginative, I think." I recalled Cst Sandhu's flamboyant clothes.

"That can be a problem. Cocky?"

"No. Confident."

"Thanks."

I left when their meals were served and returned to the guest house. Sergeant Flynn was in Laura's kitchen when I arrived.

"Claire, sit down," Laura said. "Detective Sergeant Flynn has more news. It's difficult to hear." Her eyes implored me to share whatever had upset her.

"What is it?" I slipped onto a chair.

Laura turned to Sergeant Flynn. "Please tell her what you told me."

"We think," Sergeant Flynn said, "that someone gave him this drug—because it wasn't a street drug; it was Nembutal. That used to be commonly given to help people sleep but is seldom prescribed anymore. There might be a stash of it somewhere and we're looking for it. We doubt that Reece would have taken it because the effect is to put you to sleep which is not the effect an addict wants."

Laura looked overwhelmed by this. "It must be a drug dealer who's got hold of some old drugs and is selling them as if they were something new and exciting. Or it might be a drug dealer who did it on purpose. Perhaps Reece owed money. He told me they had no conscience. He was always afraid that they would come after me if he didn't pay his bills. But I think all those bills were paid and I was sure he wasn't using—and I do not believe he did this intentionally."

Flynn was quiet for a moment as if reflecting on what Laura had said. "You might be right, Mrs. Wright. He might not have been using at all and someone gave him this."

"That's despicable," Laura said.

"Just so," Flynn agreed.

We were all silent for a moment.

"I suppose," Laura said, "it's going to get in the papers. The fact that it might be murder, I mean." She must have been thinking of Miss Weatherby.

"Possibly," Flynn said.

"I better let his father know Reece is dead. I haven't done that yet. I keep putting it off."

"Any particular reason?" Flynn asked.

Laura shrugged. "Just putting off a distasteful job. His father hasn't had much to do with Reece over the years. He wanted to reinvent himself with a new family. He paid for courses for Reece when I demanded he do so, but the money was always pried out of him."

The divorce had happened many years ago. She was still bitter, but more for the sake of her son than herself.

She took a deep breath and continued. "I failed Reece because I didn't give him a caring father." She looked up at Flynn. "his biological father died before he was born. Malcolm was my choice to be Reece's father. He adopted Reece at five. I gave him a father who was good to him the first few years but was no use to him after that." She swallowed. "I feel so guilty about that."

We were quiet. She probably felt guilty about many things.

"I do have to let him know." Her voice sounded firmer. "He is legally Reece's father."

"We can do that for you," Flynn said.

Laura looked tempted by the offer, then shook her head. "No, I'll do it. Reece would expect me to."

I left her with DS Flynn. He would have practical information about when the body could be released and how to contact the funeral parlour. The funeral director could help her with the obituary. It was going to be a difficult week for Laura.

CHAPTER SIX

All my tourists gathered at the Rother Manor guest house well before seven in the evening. Again, we turned out in our finery. Julie wore black trousers and long tunic with a large, engraved silver pendant hanging low. Amber wore a black tank top with silver designs painted on it. It was unique. Her short skirt was black but without any embellishments. I wonder if she'd made them both. Heather's sun dress was of a soft, gray material that moved with a swish when she walked. Susan had her inevitable pearls with a pale pink blouse and knee-length gray skirt. I wore a multicolored cotton sun dress with a turquoise gauze overshirt. I chose my Echo sandals as those cobblestones can turn an ankle.

The men were wearing the usual drab, respectable dark trousers, white shirt and dark lightweight sports coats with ties—at least Howard wore a tie. Richard had a loosely-tied pale lavender scarf wound around his neck and hanging down his chest. Trinity was the most colorful of us in a green, blue, and turquoise long top over black capris. She wore chunky green leather sandals. I'd like a closer look at those.

Webbe's at the Fish Café was just up Cinques Ports Street. The name of the street changed as they tend to in Rye as it was called Tower Street at the east end. Susan could manage that distance. She used a walking stick but didn't seem to lean on it. The three young woman floated down the street, drifting from the flagstone pavement to the cobblestones without any hitch in their gait— in spite of the shoes they wore.

The Fish Café has a solid brick wall with an impressive arched entrance projecting staid respectability as if it housed a bank or a prestigious center of commerce. Inside the décor was more modern and simpler than The Mermaid Inn. The food was excellent.

"This place just serves fish," Richard said. Obviously, he had not read the itinerary. Everyone had agreed to a fish dinner.

"There will be meat," I said. There is often someone who won't eat fish.

The wait staff had put two round tables together with wooden ladder chairs around them. It looked inviting and everyone settled in with a rustle of finery and clicks of knapsacks and handbags settling around them.

The waiter was a young man with a dark complexion and bright brown eyes who passed out the menus and suggested we consider a drink before we ordered. We sorted that out. I had ordered two bottles of crisp white for the pre-dinner drink, but anyone could order what they liked as long as they paid for it. Howard and Richard had scotch.

"Rye Bay scallops, ceviche, avocado and orange," Amber said. "That sounds delicious."

"I'm going to start with seaweed salad," Julie said. "I miss that. We get that at home on the west coast. I never see it in Toronto."

We made our choices. The conversation was muted as we enjoyed the wine and the delicate flavors of the starters.

Most of my guests chose the delicious seafood on offer for their main course but, predictably, Howard and Richard ordered the grilled sirloin—without the spinach.

Richard had another scotch with his meal. I hoped he was the kind of drinker who simply went to sleep when he had too much alcohol, not the kind who got loud and obnoxious. He was speaking emphatically, but not yet loudly.

"I want to produce the best *Mousetrap* ever performed," he told Susan.

"Now, that's ambitious," Susan said. "It's been running in London for fifty years, so you have competition."

"I know. I know." Richard laughed. "But I have a good cast."

"And," Julie murmured beside me, "a colossal ego."

"Hey. Hey," Trinity said. "Roosters must crow. It's in their DNA. You don't know what mess the poor man inherited."

"Genes aren't destiny," Amber said

"They can be," Trinity argued. "For some things."

"What do you think, Auntie?" Julie turned to Susan.

She took a small sip of wine and considered the question. "I was a high school teacher so I come down heavily on nurture as opposed to nature. I think destiny can be averted by directed care, love and teaching. So no, I wouldn't agree that it is all in the genes."

I had been looking at Susan and listening to the conversation, so I was not paying attention to my surroundings. I only became aware when every one at the table stopped talking. I turned around and there was Mark.

He smiled at me and nodded to my guests.

"My name is Mark Evans," he said. "I'm a detective inspector with the Hampshire constabulary and I'm the fiancé of your tour guide, Claire." He didn't mention Reece, so he was here socially.

Susan was the first to respond. "My name is Susan and I'm delighted to meet you. I'm a great mystery novel fan and I have met many detective inspectors in the pages of books. It's a pleasure to meet a real English inspector. Please join us."

"Bring a chair," Heather said. "I would love to talk to you about the way English detective inspectors actually deal with a mystery."

Mark smiled at me again and I could feel my heart expand. I knew he came to the café because I was having trouble with Richard and he wanted to help. I was sure I could handle Richard without any help as Heather was used to dealing with him and the three young women seem quite able to deflect and control him. But my heart warmed at the notion that Mark would come and see if he could be of use to me.

I was so distracted it took me a moment to realize that Andy Forsyth was with him.

"Please join us," I said, then turned to the guests. "This is Detective Sergeant Andrew Forsythe. He's Mark's teammate."

"Hello, everyone," Andy said. "We have eaten, but we love to join you for tea."

Andy was dressed impeccably in pressed jeans and a blue, open-necked sports shirt. He wore a gold earring and the wedding band I'd watched his husband Bruce put on his finger. That had been quite the society wedding. Bruce comes from a wealthy and supportive family and they had hosted an elaborate reception.

Susan brought me back to the present.

"That would be wonderful." Susan invited him by a gesture to sit beside her. "What's it like to be a sergeant in the Hampshire police force?"

He laughed. "It's pretty busy."

"I was wondering if the police still give those warnings that I read about in novels."

"Not quite the way you read them in the novels," Andy said. "I read thrillers myself so I pay attention to police procedure. We do make a statement when we make an arrest, but not the one you commonly see in fiction."

Mark was at the other end of the table and seemed to be having quite a lively conversation with Heather, Richard, Howard and Poppy.

I ordered some small fairy cakes and some chocolate and nuts to be passed around with coffee and tea. The guests stayed for some time chatting with each other and with Mark and Andy. The group was enjoying themselves but eventually prepared to leave. The older guests were returning to Rother Manor House. The three young ones told me they were going to visit a pub.

"Waterworks Pub is a nice one," Andy advised. "It's just down the street on this block."

"Sounds perfect," Julie said. "We're not big drinkers. We just like the liveliness of the English pubs. At least we think we will."

"You have my mobile number," I said. "Just call if you need help or for anything at all."

"We'll be fine," Julie said. "Thank you for a delicious dinner." Off they went, leaving Mark, Andy and me at the table.

"How do you like working with DS Flynn?" I asked.

"He's a marvel," Andy answered me. "Meticulous, conscientious. Digs for information."

Mark leaned forward. "He's so competent that if the Super gets wind of him, Andy will be recalled."

That was a possibility. Superintendent Addison wasn't one to waste personnel.

"What about DC Sandhu?"

They both grinned. I expect Jas Sandhu had that effect on most people.

"I can work with him," Mark said. "He seems a good team player with Flynn."

I could see that: one was methodical and one imaginative.

"Flynn put Jas onto tracing Reece's movements on his last day. Once Travis has the info, he'll put it on a chart for us."

"We're looking into a gang motivation. That's my job," Andy said. "I have an appointment with someone in the know later tonight."

"Be careful," I said.

"Shouldn't be a problem."

I don't know why I urged Andy to be careful. He was always careful. It must be some kind of superstition that makes those of us who have no control over the situation offer a kind of blessing on the one in danger. My mum used to caution me to stay dry if it looked like rain. Of course, I'd try to stay dry. But cautioning me was her way of trying to protect me. It can be annoying.

"Do you still think Reece was murdered?" I asked into the silence created by our mutual concern about a gang contact.

"Looks like it. He would be unlikely to get hold of Nembutal. None of that drug is circulating in this area."

"We aren't positive, though," Andy said. "All we can say is that he died of Nembutal poisoning and it is unlikely he gave it to himself."

"He could have taken it by accident, thinking it was something else."

"He could have, but we are going to treat this case as homicide until we can prove it isn't, or until we run out of leads."

Andy left us at the door of the café to walk back to the Rye Lodge Hotel while Mark escorted me to the Rother Manor House.

I invited him to my room where I plugged in the tea kettle and set out two cups and some biscuits—not that we needed any more to eat. While the room was small, it had a table and two chairs near the window.

For some reason we talked about birds. Mark had recently visited his Uncle Lionel and gone on a birding venture with him along the coastal walk of Cornwall. Mark was only mildly interested in birds, but enjoyed his uncle's enthusiasm. Like Lionel, I was keen on birds, so I listened to Mark's descriptions, enjoying the sound of his voice.

We spent quite a few minutes saying goodbye, but he finally left me for the night. I heard the front door close but couldn't watch him leave from my back garden window.

It was going to be a busy day tomorrow as I had to drive Richard and the older guests to Godinton House and deposit the three young women at the train station in Ashford. I checked that I had fresh supplies for their daily packs: chocolates, biscuits, hand sanitizers and tissues. I wished Mark could have stayed but

I understood his need to be with Andy and available to the local constabulary. We were both working. We were used to being apart for weeks. Still, he wasn't far away but I wished he was with me. I conjured up a picture of Gulliver. I expect he was cuddled up with Deirdre's two dogs and was happy enough. I missed him as well.

CHAPTER SEVEN

In the morning I offered to help Laura and Angela set up for breakfast.

"Not today, thanks" Laura said. "I can cope."

She and Angela were an efficient team, so I just took a cup of coffee and sat at the kitchen table out of their way. Laura put a plate of scones and a small dish of jam in front of me then joined me with her mug of tea.

"How is it going?" I asked. She looked knackered.

"I'm getting used to it," she said. "It's difficult. I still haven't called Malcolm. I will do that this morning." She frowned as if contacting her ex-husband was going to take prodigious effort.

Angela slipped into a chair and leaned both elbows on the table, cradling her tea in her hands, sipping cautiously as it was hot.

"You should send him one of those black-edged cards announcing Reece's death," she said. "The kind you send to distant relatives who will eventually send a card but have no real involvement."

Laura half-laughed. "That's tempting. No. I'd better have a conversation with him. He did support Reece through high school. Claremont was expensive with all the sports Reece was involved in and all the equipment he needed. Malcolm paid for quite a bit of that. And Reece was happy there. It was only after he finished upper sixth that Malcom pretended he didn't have a grown-up son."

"Spoiled his image," Angela said. "Made him look old"

"Maybe." Laura shook her head as if to say: I don't want to think about it.

"That was ten years ago." Angela persisted. "What kind of father is he?"

Laura looked straight at Angela. "Almost nonexistent. But I will let him know."

"Don't you have a vindictive bone in your body?" Angela demanded.

"It's too much trouble." Laura stood and put her empty mug in the dishwasher.

I went out to the breakfast room to meet my guests. Conversation was sparse. Angela bustled in with carafes of coffee, leaving one on each table. That was a good idea. Usually, Americans and Canadians were morning coffee people. I had acquired that habit as well when I lived in Seattle. Angela and Laura took orders for a hot breakfast and soon we were all eating eggs, bacon, ham, croissants, scones and fruit. No black pudding for me. When all had finished and we're on their second cup of coffee, I brought up the itinerary for the day.

"Richard," I said. "I've found a manor house for you. It's Godinton House and not far from here. It began in the fourteenth century and was reconstructed in 1620 with additions and renovations over the last six hundred years. It's a medieval manor house and quite beautiful."

"Big?" Richard asked

"Huge," I said. "Who else would like to accompany us on our tour of this manor house?" I assumed compliance from Richard.

"I would," Heather said

That was a relief as I didn't want to deal with Richard by myself. Susan piped up, "I would like that very much."

"Sounds good to me," Howard said. "What about you Poppy?"

"A medieval manor house sounds wonderful."

"They call it a house," Richard said, "when it's really a manor.

They call this," he looked around, "a manor house when it's really just a house."

"Well, that's England," I said. He was going to have to take us as he found us.

"Did you magically produce a war museum for us?" Julie asked.

"Yes." I handed out brochures to the three young women. I didn't tell them I had spent an hour cancelling a boat trip I'd reserved for today and substituting the trip to the war museum and to the manor house. Sometimes being a tour guide was all about juggling events.

"There is an excellent War Museum in Folkestone, a short train from Ashford. I'll drive you to the Ashford Railway Station on our way to Godinton. I have your return tickets and I'll pick you up at the end of the day."

"I'd love to go on the train," Amber said. "How long is the ride?"

"Twelve minutes," I said.

"Cool," Trinity was happy. "Twelve minutes. I love British trains."

"You've never been on one," Julie objected.

"I love their precision," Trinity insisted. "Twelve minutes, exactly."

I would have to ask them at some point why they were so interested in setting their novel in the time of World War II and in England. It seemed an odd choice. These young women probably had a good reason—although anybody could write a book about anything set in any time without needing to justify their decision. That was the beauty of books; they were individual and surprising.

Everyone piled into the van and picked up their bags of goodies from their seat where I had placed them. Today's treat bag included chocolate from The Chocolatier in Maidstone, Kent.

It didn't take long to get to the Ashford International Railway Station. I handed the trio their tickets which I'd printed out on my small printer.

"Just be sure to get off in Folkestone," I said. "Or you'll end up in France."

"The train goes through the Chunnel?" Amber asked.

"It does."

"Under the channel in a tunnel so, of course, the chunnel." Trinity was delighted with the term.

Amber said, "Maybe we should stay on the train. It might be an interesting experience."

"Not today, Amber," Julie said.

"Okay. Okay."

"Where would we end up if we didn't get off at Folkestone?" Trinity sounded intrigued as if she was living in a 'choose your own adventure' novel.

"In France at the train station of Coquelles." I supplied that information.

"Wow," Trinity said. "France."

"Not today, Trinity," Julie said again.

Because Ashford train station is an immigration stop for the travelers coming from France, it's enormous. I parked and took the time to escort the three women into the station and point them to the correct platform. I showed them where I would meet them at the end of the day and at what time. I made sure they had my mobile number so they could alert me when they were near the station on the return trip.

Back in the van, we left Ashford and headed toward Godinton. It's not far from the train station. It just took a little time to get onto the road then past the suburb of Godinton and out into the country where the manor house was located. The green farm land on each side of the road contributed to a feeling of distance from the busy and bustling Ashford.

"Does the National Trust own this building?" Howard asked.

"A trust owns it, but it's a private trust set up by the last owner Major Wyndham-Green. It was in private hands for centuries, first by the Tok family in the fourteenth century. They owned it for 455 years then it passed to the Wyndham family. Just recently, in 1996, it was given to and is run by The Godinton House Preservation Trust."

"That recent, huh? It was a family mansion for centuries."

"They will have brochures for you when you join the tour in the house." The public had to have a tour guide in order to enter the house. I was lucky to find one who worked for the trust and who was willing to take on my group—for a hefty fee, but I had contingencies like this built into my budget.

"If I remember correctly, the building was started in the twelfth century and there is one window that indicates that early time. It was developed more in the fourteenth century then added to in the seventeenth century. It has a remarkable Jacobean staircase with carvings all over it."

"Sounds fascinating," Heather said, "and it's so beautiful. Look at the lake there." She pointed to the side.

"They have gorgeous gardens." I said. "I particularly like the Italian Gardens."

"I can't wait for that," Susan said. "I enjoy seeing how someone can make a piece of ground beautiful. I can appreciate it without having to pull any weeds."

We were lucky with our weather as well, so we'd likely get a good view of the gardens. I would use the wheelchair for Susan on this outing. There was a lot of walking ahead of us.

"You said this was medieval," Richard said. "*The Mousetrap* isn't set in those times."

Richard was taking a lot of patience. I took a slow breath before speaking.

"The manor house started in the medieval times and it has incorporated the old Medieval Hall into its new design. But it has been lived in and renovated, so it would fit into *The Mousetrap* era. After all, the last owner only died in 1996."

"Oh," Richard said.

"Really, Richard," Heather said. "It's fabulous."

"It is impressive," Richard agreed.

I wished he'd stop complaining, but I shouldn't expect miracles.

We met our tour guide just inside the entrance. She appeared to be in her sixties, wearing a tweed skirt, a blouse with pearls and Oxford shoes. It must be some kind of uniform. I had a vision of a factory turning out these tour guides, identically outfitted in what I consider a 1950s style. Obviously, there are a great many women who consider a tweed skirt, twin set and pearls acceptable fashion. And I suppose it is. I just wonder why there isn't a little more individuality. In spite of my prejudice against their fashion sense, they were usually knowledgeable.

"Come this way, please," she said and began the tour.

The manager had assured me on the phone that there were ramps and the tour was accessible by wheelchair. Susan smiled at me when I offered to push her through the manor house.

"My dear, thank you so much. This will make a big difference."

"My pleasure," I said and meant it.

It was when we were at the foot of the grand staircase with its elaborate odd creatures carved on the top of the newel posts that my mobile buzzed. I looked down: Mark.

I read the text. "Checking out gang activity. Have one lead. Can't find anything on the drug."

I stepped back from Susan's wheelchair. She was engrossed in the guide's explanation of the carved staircase and wouldn't miss me for a few moments. I moved a little further away down the hall.

"Why don't you talk to a chemist?" There were chemists at every pharmacy in every village and they were knowledgeable. I thought one of them could be helpful. Mark had probably considered it.

"I plan to do that. Dinner tonight?"

"Yes, great. My group is on their own for dinner."

"Want to meet at The Hoof?"

"Sure."

"See you then."

I smiled at my mobile which was silly as he couldn't see me, but I felt like smiling. I disconnected and rejoined the group

The manor house was fascinating and all six of us enjoyed it, even Richard. There was no restaurant in Godinton House, so I took my group out to the Swan and Dog Pub in Great Chart for lunch. The tour guide had agreed to this. I suppose she wanted a break as well.

"The Swan and Dog has steak and hamburgers," I said to Richard. To the rest of the group I said, "It has seafood and typical pub food, as well as Mexican. We can sit outside if you like."

It was a warm day but not too hot, so outside seating might be a good idea. They were happy with the plan and I was able to find enough tables for us.

"The beer is locally brewed and excellent." I'd spent an hour researching Godinton House and The Swan and Dog Pub on the Internet last night.

Everyone had beer, including Susan, although she had only a small glass.

"I used to be able to drink more." she told me, "when you get older, your body shrinks and doesn't handle alcohol the way it used to. That's one of the things that annoys me about getting older. I can still taste beer, true enough, but if I drink enough to get a buzz I'll go to sleep. Very annoying."

It seemed to me she was handling advancing age with energy and courage. She was on the tour after all, not home watching the telly.

We returned to Godinton House for the second half of the tour and managed to spend some time in the gardens.

"Look at those roses," Susan enthused. "My heavens! They must have one gardener who does nothing but look after roses."

They were spectacular. Every shade of crimson to light pink

and copper orange to pale yellow. She was no doubt right about the amount of work involved in looking after them.

Julie texted me as we were loading into the van about half-four to say they were on the train and would be in Ashford shortly. We drove to the station and met them.

"Did you have a good time?" I asked.

"Fabulous," Trinity said. "We saw tons of stuff in the museum."

Amber leaned forward from the seat behind me. "Those gas masks are creepy, like something out of a sci-fi movie. Did people really wear those things?"

"They did," I said, having heard stories about those days.

"Julie took tons of notes," Amber said, "so we really have some good research material for our mystery novel."

"You still want to set it in Kent?"

"Kent's a pretty interesting place," Amber said, "and I imagine it was very busy place during World War II."

Enemy aircraft had dropped bombs on this area. "Yes, I agree. It must have been a busy place." There would have been enough intrigue, fear, death and destruction in those days to fuel many books.

We arrived back in Rye before six. I handed everyone a list of restaurants in Rye and listened to their plans for the evening. As usual, the three young women and Susan were headed in one direction to a restaurant and the two couples were headed in another. I checked again that everyone had my mobile number and wished them a good evening. Then I went to my room.

Six o'clock meant Deirdre would likely be home.

"How's the tour going?" she asked me

"I haven't pushed anyone in front of a bus yet," I said.

"Not even that one man who's annoying?"

"He was better today. He was genuinely interested in Godinton House."

"That's a captivating place. I can even keep the two kids occupied there looking at everything they have on display."

"How's my dog?" I asked.

"Charming, as usual," she said. "The kids are spoiling him rotten. My dogs are even spoiling him. He's playing with my two who seem to calm down their roughhousing and treat him gently."

My Cavalier King Charles is much smaller than her Labradors. "That's good. I miss him."

"Well, I can't say he's missing you. He is having a good time."

"I suppose I should be grateful for that."

"Yes, you should," she said.

"How's work?" I changed the subject.

"I spent it chasing details, but I like to check them all off, so it was a good day."

"No trial today?"

"Not today," she said. "How's your homicide coming along?"

I don't suppose many sisters have this kind of conversation, but we have over the years talked about murder. For one thing, it was her business as she either prosecuted or defended murderers and, for another, I'm so connected to Mark, I also have been involved with murders.

"Nobody's actually sure it is homicide," I told her, "but they're highly suspicious of it."

"I trust your copper's instincts," she said.

"Mark is astute," I agreed, "but he says he's not sure."

"What's he looking into?"

"The drug. He needs to pin down where that drug came from."

"I expect he'll do that. I have to go. Dinner will arrive any moment and I have to supervise the servings."

"Did you order takeout?"

"I did indeed," she said.

"The kids will love it."

"They will."

We disconnected.

I looked over my clothes wanting to select something attractive before I met Mark. One thing about driving my own van is that I can take as many clothes as I'm willing to carry. I chose a pair of gray, lightweight jeans, purple tank top that looked good on me and a lavender overshirt that was almost gauze. It was warm tonight but not hot, and we would be inside. I wished I had a pair of those engraved silver earrings that Julie wore, but I made do with a pair of plain silver dangling ones. Plain works better with my glasses anyway. I can't resist shoes and had brought six pairs to chose from. I recognized bringing so many shoes is irrational, but I feel comforted by shoes. I picked out a pair of deep purple Bottega sandals that were easy to walk in and set out for the pub.

CHAPTER EIGHT

I met Laura in the foyer just before I left for my dinner date. "Is everything all right with your guests?" she asked. "Mr. Shelly requested more towels and said the water wasn't hot enough. I can't do anything about the temperature. The Health Department regulates that." She frowned.

Richard again! "It's all right, Laura. Richard would complain the king wasn't regal enough or the sea wasn't deep enough. I'm sorry you have to put up with him." I've had other guests like Richard—thankfully not many—who harangue those who are paid to listen to them like servers and hotel staff. "I love the charm of this place and so do my guests."

She smiled. "I'm glad. I work hard to make it appear calm and comfortable."

"As well as elegant," I said.

"As well as elegant," she agreed. "I know are you are all out for dinner at this time so could you let your group know I have left the makings for cocoa and tea when people come back in the evening?"

"That's kind of you. In the lounge?"

"Yes. Everything's set out there as well as some biscuits. The bar is locked. Sorry about that."

"Understandable. I'll text everyone so they know they can help themselves to what's available."

"Ta." She started to turn away then glanced back. "Where are you off to?" she said, as if she just remembered she was a host and needed to show interest.

I appreciated the effort she was making. "I'm meeting my love at The Hoof," I said, naming a pub that served excellent hamburgers.

"That nice detective?"

"The very one," I said.

"Have a good time." She hurried away. I imagined she had myriad details to look after.

I walked up Hilder's Cliff Road which turned into High Street which eventually turned into Mint Street where the pub was located. It was an easy walk and took me about twenty minutes. The Hoof was housed in an unpretentious brick building with newly-painted slate gray window frames and door. Inside, it looked homely with wooden tables and unmatched wooden chairs painted blue. Mark was waiting at a table for two near the window.

He stood when I arrived—his manners are always lovely—reached out and gave me a big hug. I kissed his cheek and sat down across from him.

"How are you?" I asked.

"Frustrated," he replied. "Addison is recalling Andrew. I'll have Flynn who is a good man and Sandhu who looks like a loose canon but might be useful."

"She thinks you have one sergeant too many?"

"She does. And she's given me ten days to wrap it up."

"That's ridiculous."

"That's Addison. I need a beer. We can talk after I've fed the inner man."

"Good idea." I had my mind on a hamburger but when Mark ordered a sirloin steak it sounded so good I ordered the flat iron steak along with the grilled tomato and peppercorn sauce. I had a glass of pale ale and Mark had a pint of Cheshire Plain Dark. We gave intense concentration to our food and drink and only relaxed, ready for conversation, when the server brought us tea.

Mark plunged into his activities of the day. "I followed up all the leads I could find on gang activity in this area, but nothing leads me to Reece's death. I know who's targeting who in the gang world." He shook his head. "This particular murder seems to be outside of their quarrels."

"At least you eliminated that as a possibility." I sipped my tea and thought how lucky I was to spend time with Mark. I not only loved him; he was interesting.

"I know, but it doesn't get me much further," Mark said. "I could be wrong. Reece could have owed someone in the gang money for drugs, but poisoning isn't the usual method of disciplining those who don't pay."

I probably didn't want to know but curiosity overcame reluctance. "What's the usual method?"

"Something more violent, although the end results the same. Usually knifing or shooting—a dramatic example to deter others from avoiding payment. Poisoning with an exotic drug just seems too sophisticated for our local gangs."

Anyone who watched the news understood that gangs members saw themselves as celebrities, rich and sophisticated, people who lived an exotic life style. Poisoning would not be dramatic enough for them.

"I read in my news feed about the thousands of refugees landing in Kent in small boats."

"Right,' Mark said. "Those poor bastards. They're fleeing war and poverty to come to Britain and a better life, and they hit the displacement policy."

"The policy of sending them to Africa?"

"That one. I don't think the government can legally do that, and, as far as I know, they haven't loaded refugees on planes and dumped them in the middle of Africa like they're threatening to do, but they aren't welcoming them with open arms."

"Do you think Reece might have been mixed up with trying to rescue some refugees?"

Mark looked away for a moment, obviously thinking about it. He shook his head." Naw. That's not on. Those refugees—they're asylum seekers, not legal refuges—get picked up immediately by the Border Guard and after a health check, get taken care of by the Home Office. They aren't wandering around Sussex."

That was another aspect of British life that my guests didn't have to observe. I was committed to fulfilling their expectations of a calm and pleasant land and not one of political idiocy and random murders.

"So now what?"

"I'll do more interviews. I should talk to Laura again."

I looked over his shoulder. "You'll get your chance. She just walked in the door."

Mark swiveled his head and saw her.

Laura hurried over to us. Beth trailed behind her, long blond hair hanging down her back, bright blue eyes darting to us then behind her. She was frowning.

Laura spoke to Mark. "This is Bethany Williams, a friend of Reece's. She wants to talk to you."

The restaurant was not full. There was privacy at our table.

"I'll get you a couple of chairs," he said, "if you care to join us."

"Don't move," Laura said "We'll get the chairs."

"Hi, Beth," I said when she was seated.

"I swear I saw that crazy Miss Weatherby behind us. She's got a new bike, but I think it was her. Would she be following us?"

I shrugged. "She might be looking for a story."

"She's harmless," Laura said. "As long as she stays away from me."

"She was our teacher in infant school. I didn't like her then, and she hasn't improved." Beth was annoyed.

Mark interrupted. "I'm Detective Inspector Mark Evans." He was letting Beth know he was listening to her as an official of the police.

She nodded and brought her attention to Mark.

"You wanted to talk to me?" he asked.

"I want to tell you about Reece. You need to understand him." She put concerns about the journalist aside, leaned forward, put her elbows on the table and grasped her hands together. Her voice was quiet but intense. We listened.

"Reece and I went to infant school at the same time and met again at Claremont Senior School. He was lovely...smart. He played rugby and swam for the competitive school team. We went out a little when we were in the sixth form but drifted apart when I went on to uni and when ..." She hesitated.

"When he started using," Laura supplied.

"Yes." Beth looked at Laura gratefully and continued. "I didn't use drugs myself and I couldn't understand why he did." She took a deep breath and continued. "When I got the job at the library here after I graduated, I ran into him at a pub one night and we got talking. We started dating again." She stopped for a moment and studied her hands. The she looked up at Mark. "You have to understand that Reece was compassionate, thoughtful, sweet and caring. I didn't have much of that in my life and he made me feel important and loved."

We were silent paying tribute to what must have been an emotionally fulfilling time for her.

"My parents didn't approve of him. My dad's a barrister. He thinks he's more important than God, and if you aren't a toff and especially if you don't have money, you aren't worth knowing. Laura didn't have enough money to impress Daddy. Reece's dad's might have qualified. He's a dentist, married to veterinarian so they have money. She has old money, so my father says." Beth looked away for a moment, then continued. "But Reece's dad didn't help him and my father knew it, so he was sure I'd live in poverty if I married Reece. Daddy went on and on about it. Reece and I weren't at the stage of wanting to get married. I knew Reece was using and I couldn't live with that, but I also recognized that he was worth knowing."

It must have been very difficult for her to love someone and be constantly worried that he would self-destruct.

"In the last month of his life, he didn't use—at least very little. He hardly used much before that, but in the last month, he didn't use much at all. Just enough, he told me, to keep from going crazy. He had an appointment with a psychiatrist. I found one who specialized in addiction and in the trauma that caused addiction, Dr. Masterson."

She had us a spellbound now. What was she going to reveal?

"I knew something had happened to Reece when he was a child, but I didn't know what. He was going to go to a psychiatrist to deal with that. He said he'd tell me about it when he had the words. He thought the psychiatrist would help him find the words."

Tears were flowing down Laura's cheeks. I swallowed. I was almost crying myself. These two young people should have had a chance at life. I felt a growing anger at whoever had cut off that chance.

"Do you think Reece's appointment with Dr. Masterson contributed to his death?" Mark asked the question that was in my mind.

Beth looked at him for a moment. "I hadn't thought of that. Do you think so?"

"I have no idea," Mark said. "He just had an appointment, but he hadn't seen the psychiatrist yet?"

"That's right," Beth said. "He was going next week. It takes time to get into the psychiatrist without having to pay a lot. National Health will pay, but you do have to wait. He wasn't suicidal, you see, so he wasn't urgent."

That's how our National Health system works. Everyone is triaged.

"I'm very sorry for your loss," Mark said to Beth then nodded at Laura to include her.

Beth wiped her eyes, took a deep breath and faced Mark squarely. "Why don't the police arrest dealers for murder? The dealers know some of their drugs are poison. That's murder. If someone stood on the corner of the street selling cupcakes with poison in them, the police would nab them for attempted murder. Why don't you do that with drug dealers?"

Mark looked at her for a long moment. "I don't have an answer. You have a strong point."

Beth sniffed.

"Thank you for telling me this." Mark took out his tablet and swiped it open. He called up his notebook. "What is your legal name?"

"Bethany Pamela Williams," she said.

"And your address and phone number?"

She gave them to him.

"And your father's name?"

She stared at Mark. Was her father now a suspect?

"I need to be thorough," Mark said.

She sighed. "In for a penny, in for a pound." She sounded resigned as if she now realized how her information might be used by the police. She may not have thought beyond unburdening herself. She was realizing the consequences of that now. If her father objected to Mark, he was a suspect.

"His name is James Williams." She gave his phone number and address. "He's not going to like this."

"No doubt," Mark said. He was used to people not liking his official interviews.

"And the psychiatrist?" Mark asked.

"He didn't go."

"We don't know that until I asked him or her."

"Oh," Beth said. She checked her mobile and gave him Dr. Masterson's phone number.

It was possible that Reece had seen the psychiatrist and not reported to Beth.

Laura stood and Beth joined her. Mark stood as well and went to find the server to pay for our meal. He likes to pay. I'm the one with the most money but Mark pays for our meals out. It was one of the compromises we made when we dealt with my legacy. Mark has particular things that he firmly decided mattered to him. 'I'm paying for our meals out' was one of them.

I accompanied Laura and Beth outside where they'd chained their bicycles to a post. I waited with them while they punched their codes into their padlocks and stored the cables in the pouches strapped to the back.

When Mark joined us, Laura said, "We are going to have a small memorial service at the house sometime after coroner's office allows us to have Reece's body. We will have a cremation and spread the ashes in the garden. When will we have his body?"

"Probably tomorrow," Mark said

"I will look after it, then."

My heart cracked a little. It was wrong for a mother to be burying her child.

"When are you going to have the ceremony?" Beth asked her, her toes stretched to touch the ground while she sat on her bike,

"It won't take long to arrange. Maybe for a few people. So just after the cremation." Laura swung onto her bike.

"Please, let me know," Beth said.

"Beth," Laura said, "I will. I truly will. I'm going to need you there."

"Will his father be there? Reece always wanted to reconcile with his father. I think Reese would want him there."

"I'll invite him. Whether he comes or not is another question." What kind of a man wouldn't attend his son's funeral?

We watched them pedal away and followed slowly on foot. I had a quick look around for Miss Weatherby but didn't see her.

"What are you going to do now?" I turned to Mark.

He reached for my hand and held it while we walked. It was amazingly comforting.

"Travis Flynn is going to check Reece's school mates. He was planning on taking an adult education course in horticulture.

He might have talked to someone at the college. Flynn will check that out."

"How could he manage a college course and take drugs? I mean financially. Drugs cost money and he didn't make a prince's salary."

"Beth said he hadn't been using much in the last month, but he might have lied to her. A user can seem normal, without any signs of drug use. I had a friend who took all his law courses at uni under the influence of cocaine. He did well too."

"What happened to your friend?"

"He had a lot of money, came from a wealthy family, so could pay for his habit without stealing. He met a woman who demanded he stop using or she wouldn't have anything to do with him. As far as I know, he got help and stopped."

"Hard to do."

"*Hynod* hard."

I knew that one. It meant extremely hard.

We walked along High Street and onto Hilder's Cliff Road. There were groves of what looked like beech trees lining the street and casting long shadows in the dusk. It was quiet at this time of night.

"How could Reece afford the course?" I mused.

"We found a check signed by his father. It was the amount of tuition for his courses. He could have afforded it."

"So Martin was supporting him?"

"To the extent of that check at least."

We were almost at my guest house. "What are you going to do now?" The neighborhood was quiet. Night had settled over the delta and over the town. At the top of the cliff here, it felt isolated, magical as if the world was distant. No point is getting romantic now; Mark was thinking about his case.

"I'll look at what Travis comes up with tomorrow and interview anyone who might have more information. I need to interview the father, Malcolm Martin. And, if I have time, Beth's father."

He stopped at the house before Rother Manor and pulled me into the shadow of the tree nearby. At last, a little romance. We had a prolonged good night there. It was like dating—a little frustrating but still exciting.

"What are *you* doing tomorrow?" Mark said as he escorted me up the front steps of Rother Manor.

"Exploring Rye, trying to keep Richard happy and the trio from Toronto involved and interested."

"You like those young women, don't you?"

I laughed. "They're amazing. Full of achievements and energy."

"Nice antidote to Richard."

"That's right."

"I'll text you. We can catch up again tomorrow."

We would both be busy. I wondered if Beth's father had objected so strongly to Reece that he had killed him or had him killed. It seemed unlikely, but Mark might find out something tomorrow.

CHAPTER NINE

In the morning I entered the breakfast room a little later than usual. Angela was drifting between the tables depositing hot breakfasts. She looked up and nodded at me. I waved. Laura must have retreated to the kitchen again this morning. Heather was alone at her table.

"May I join you?" I asked as I stood by Heather.

She smiled. "Certainly."

I fetched a glass of orange juice, two croissants and a cup of coffee and sat with her. She had been served scrambled eggs with toast, fried tomatoes and sausages.

"I love eating a big breakfast when I'm on holiday," she said. "It tastes more delicious when I don't have to cook it."

I smiled. I also appreciated someone else's cooking. It's usually better than mine. "Where's Richard this morning?"

"He's in the room with coffee and some muffins, making notes on what he observed at the manor house yesterday. He really enjoyed that. Thanks so much for making it happen."

"My pleasure." I took that first delicious sip of coffee.

"I must say you've been very tolerant of Richard. Not everybody is as forbearing as you."

I nodded my thanks at the compliment, and didn't say that I was charging Richard enough to make it worth my while, but she must understand that. "I imagine he can be difficult." I understated the problem.

"Impossible," Heather took a bite of sausage. "This is so good."
She really was enjoying her breakfast.

"He can be impossible," she repeated. "Still, I'm not putting up with it for much longer. This is the last trip we take together."

I didn't blame her for not wanting to travel with Richard. She was personable and would no doubt have a great deal more fun by herself than she would caretaking Richard through another trip.

"We've been married for forty years. My girls have gone and started their own families, and I don't need Richard in my life any longer. He doesn't know it, and I beg you won't tell him, but I've engaged a lawyer and I'm getting a divorce when we return."

I stared at her. Forty years. That was a long time. She was giving up the life they'd made together. Why would she do that? Probably because she didn't want to spend the next twenty with Richard. I didn't blame her. He was exasperating. Clever but socially inept.

She was confiding in me. I could ask some questions. "Why are you leaving now? Is this sudden?"

"No, it's been coming for a long time. The first twenty years were wonderful. Richard was interesting and full of his work with the high school kids. It was when he began directing the local theatre that he changed."

"In what way?" Was I going to hear that marriages inevitably crumbled? Was it better not to commit to a marriage if it was going to disintegrate?

She spread some strawberry jam on her toast and savored a bite. "He was an important man in our small town, the director of successful play, and he began to believe he was more important than anyone else. He became someone I hardly knew."

I sipped coffee and pondered her explanation. "But why leave now?"

"Last summer, my daughter asked me why I stayed. I couldn't think of a good reason."

"That is all it took?"

"It was a shock. I hadn't consciously thought of leaving. The next day a poem came on newsfeed. You know how they roll down."

I nodded. Hundreds of news items. Some I wish I hadn't seen like one this morning that shouted, 'Police officer dies of stab wounds'. I didn't want to know that. You read them in spite of yourself.

"It was by Mario de Andrade about grasping a rich, satisfying life. The last lines were

'We have two lives and the second begins when you realize you only have one.'

It spoke to me—that second life. So I made plans.

I liked Heather. She was open and friendly but her assessment of her marriage gave me a chill. It sounded so cold.

"I suppose you stopped loving him."

"I did. But I'm fond of him, so I'll make the split easy. I've already introduced him to someone I think would make him a good partner. She's less educated, so he can feel superior; she's a good householder, so he will be looked after; and she's a realist. She won't expect a great deal from Richard. She lost her husband to cancer a year ago and wants to be married again. A year after I leave, he'll be happily settled in a new life."

I couldn't decide if she was caring for Richard or manipulating him. I was leaning toward the latter.

She spread some honey on a second piece of toast and continued. "I've been doing the costumes for Richard's theater productions for the last ten years and I'm good at it. I've made contacts in the theater world in Seattle and one of them offered me a job, so I will be moving from Friday Harbor to the city. The salary is not large, but it's enough."

I blinked. My goodness. She definitely had a plan. "You're running away to the circus, metaphorically?"

She laughed. "I suppose so. My mother left me a legacy which, my lawyer tells me, I don't have to share with Richard. I think I'll be very happy alone in Seattle." Her voice exuded satisfaction. I imagined she'd made careful plans to disengage from her marriage and move on to a better life.

"I wish you the very best, Heather. I'm sure you'll be successful."

"I believe I will be."

She finished her meal, sipped her coffee and changed the subject. "I'm enjoying this trip. Those young women are inspirational. I've been talking to Trinity about incorporating some Indigenous textile styles into costumes. And I'm fascinated by her beadwork. She showed me some photos of capes and she has a web page that shows more designs. Many of the designs are traditional but some are modern. She's bringing her traditional knowledge of design into contemporary art. It's intriguing."

The change of subject wasn't because she found talking about leaving Richard emotionally difficult, but simply because she found textiles more interesting. This prospective divorce didn't seem to be one of great emotional upheaval. She looked calm.

"Do you have a place to stay in Seattle?" I'd lived there for a few years when working in my former job for Executive English and Etiquette and I knew the vacancy rate on flats was low.

"I have already bought into a co-op near the lake. I think that will suit me."

She smiled. I blinked. She was a little terrifying. She'd bought a house and found a new job and Richard had no idea she'd made these decisions. Perhaps I underestimated older women. I shouldn't. I had a flash of memory of some of the intrepid older women who had been on my tours. They could probably manage a small army.

"Our secret," she said.

"Indeed." I wouldn't even be tempted to share this information with Richard. He would likely have a tantrum and disrupt the tour.

Deirdre had texted me the evening before to ask if she could bring Josh and Kala to the sea with us. It was a teachers' professional day which meant no school for the students.

"You always have something interesting going on and, since you aren't very far from us, we could pop down for an hour or so," she'd said.

"Fine with me." My group would not be inconvenienced.

"Those teachers have far too many days off," she'd complained. "I have to take the day off myself to mind the kids, although I suppose they'd be all right on their own."

"You take in quite a few conferences and professional days yourself."

"But I learn something on those days!"

What could I say? I was silent. She got the point.

"All right. All right. They deserve their professional education days. Can we come?"

I agreed to meet them at Ypres Castle.

All but Richard, who was still closeted with his notes on Godinton House, met me in the foyer at ten and we headed off on a walking tour of Rye. I had unloaded the wheelchair for Susan.

"I'm definitely looking forward to this," Susan said.

"My turn to push." Amber took the wheelchair from me.

No one on my tours has ever been as altruistic as these three young women. Susan would have enjoyed the tour if I was the only one who looked out for her. She had the kind of temperament that looked for joy. But she was having a much better time because the young women included her.

I bent over Susan. "So what are you looking forward to on this part of the tour?"

"I'm intrigued by that small castle," Susan said.

Trinity helped Amber push the wheelchair to the Ypres Tower as the pavement was uneven. The rough ride didn't seem to bother Susan as she held tightly to the arms of the wheelchair and looked around. At the castle, they pushed her up the ramp and into the entrance. Susan dismounted and I left the wheelchair near the door.

"The floors are uneven here and there are stairs," I cautioned her. "I'll be fine."

"You can hold my arm," Amber said.

"I can do that," Susan agreed. "It's just long walks that I have trouble with."

I saw Deirdre swishing up from the street with Josh and Kala in tow. Her loose summer skirt and gauze overshirt fluttered in the breeze, making her appear to be floating toward us. I waved and she followed us into the castle. Josh at fifteen was at least a head taller than his mother with the thin, gangly look of adolescence, and hands and feet that seemed too big for his frame. Kala at eleven was still a girl, with dark braids, pale freckled face and her mother's dark eyes. I hugged them both and introduced them to the group. Deirdre got into an animated discussion with Howard about the wars that Kent and Sussex had seen; Kala stared around her and Josh studied the brochure which showed a skeleton hanging in a gibbet.

There was no tour guide for this Castle at this time, so I had to provide any information my group might want to know. I gave a short spiel.

"We think the tower was built around the middle of the fourteenth century as a defense against French invasions. It was one of the five ports, the Cinque Ports, and used for defense and later for trade. It was utilized as a prison from the sixteenth century up to almost the twentieth then as a morgue. Of course it was damaged in World War II, as many prominent buildings were. You'll see some artifacts and, Trinity, there's some medieval embroidery you might enjoy. I warn you, there's a skeleton hanging in a cage which is impressive."

Howard brightened and looked interested. Josh grinned. It was probably the attraction that had enticed him to accompany his mother and sister.

"He was a prisoner," I said. "The laws in the medieval days were severe. The man's name was John Breads. He died in 1743."

"Really?" Howard was definitely interested in the skeleton. "Why was he killed?"

"Paul Kléber Monod wrote a book called *The Murder of Mr. Grebell: Madness and Civility in an English Town* which tells us that John Breads, a butcher, stabbed Mr. Grebell, the deputy mayor of Rye, by mistake. He meant to kill the Mayor who had fined him for cheating customers. He was convicted and executed."

"Howard," his wife admonished him. "Enough. That's grisly."

"Well, it beats embroidery." He defended his interest. He had a point.

"Was England fighting with France at the time in one of their many wars?" Howard turned to me.

"Yes. The English king and the French King both wanted the territory. England had control of Scotland and much of France at the time. The mid-thirteen hundreds was the beginning of the Hundred Years War with France, so there was every reason for the town to want a defensive castle."

"The French could invade by sea and it would have been much closer to the castle in those days," Howard said.

"It was a port at that time, yes."

"And it was hit in World War II by bombs?" Julie asked, her notebook at the ready.

"It was," I agreed.

"Why would they bomb this Castle? It wasn't strategically important by then, was it?"

Susan offered an opinion. "The bombers flying over from Germany dropped bombs at times indiscriminately, especially if they were going home and still had bombs they needed to get rid of. My uncle used to talk about that. He was stationed somewhere in England during the war. I don't know where. I wish I had asked him about it."

Many of the veterans didn't want to talk abut the war when they returned home, except to other veterans.

"The poor people here," Amber said. "It would be hard to be bombed; it would be worse to think there was really no reason for it. Just some pilot getting rid of left-over bombs."

"The whole district of Kent and East Sussex must have suffered from that," Julie said.

We took our time exploring the castle. One or two of the group would occasionally ask me a question and, for the most part, I could answer them.

At close to one, I left them at the castle and walked back to collect the van. They were waiting outside when I returned and we loaded for a short trip to the restaurant. It was a little far to walk after spending so many hours in the castle. I told Deirdre where to meet us.

The sign on the door said *Ship Inn Circa 1592.*

"Very impressive," Howard said.

"Quaint," Poppy declared.

Parts of the Ship Inn were antiquated—wooden floors, wooden panelling on the walls, stone fireplaces. Parts were more modern—cement floors and rendered walls. It was all charming and the food was excellent. I'd reserved ahead, so we were escorted to a room in which a long table had been set up and menus set at each place.

This was one of the meals that was included in their tour. I offered everyone beer. It is the drink of choice in a pub and part of the British experience. Deirdre managed to get a table near us. She would pay for her own meal and make that obvious to my guests. She often joined my tours for a few hours or sometimes a day. She usually participated in the conversation, but this time with the two kids with her, she kept apart.

"Oh, my," Susan said. "I'll have to try something new. Do they serve Old Peculiar here?"

That was a brand common in many pubs in Britain. "Very likely," I said.

The server was a dark-haired, dark-eyed young woman and chatted to us as we settled into our places. I couldn't understand a word of her thick, East Sussex accent. I listened with concentration but I still could not understand her. Usually, I understand most of what people say to me—but not this time. It was disturbing as I was fascinated by dialects and prided myself on being able to understand people all over Britain. I listened with concentration, but I was lost. I gave up and smiled at her and asked everyone what they wanted to drink, assuming that's what she wanted to know. She had no problem understanding us and took the drink orders. We were soon tasting many different kinds of beer. The menu was varied and enticing. The orders came quickly and we began to eat. I listened carefully to the waitress as she came and went but I still could not understand her. There was no mistaking her cheerful interest, so I finally accepted that this was one accent I couldn't penetrate. I wondered if it had a Romany origin.

I watched Julie while she extracted the meat from the first mussel shell with her fork then used that shell as pincers to extract meat from the rest. She dipped each mussel in melted butter and savored every bite.

"I miss the West Coast," she said. "I can't get enough seafood, at least, not fresh sea food."

"You can get all you want here. We're so close to the sea." No place in England was far from the sea. There is a plaque int Lichfield, Staffordshire, which says it is eighty-four miles from the sea. That's the furthest distance I've discovered.

The Ship Inn was a smuggler's haven in the past. Smuggling had been a way of life here. The tax laws in Britain had made it tempting to import illegally from France even when the two countries were at war. Artifacts from those times displayed here in the pub reminded the patrons of this. A smuggler's lantern hung on a post, and an illustration of it was featured on the menu. Revenue Cutter and Coast Blockade defined the beer.

There were quotes from Rudyard Kipling's *The Smugglers Song* written on the beams above us" baccy for the clerk, laces for a lady, letters for a spy". A hostess came to our table and gave us more history. I understood *her*. There were tunnels under the inn that connected to the Mermaid Inn. Howard looked interested at that.

"They aren't accessible now." The hostess discouraged any exploration.

All my guests were enjoying the food and the atmosphere. Richard was not present to criticize.

I took everyone back to Rother Manor after lunch for a half-hour refresh stop. Then we piled into the van again and headed toward the ocean, with Richard this time. Deirdre planned to join us at the Discovery Centre and let the kids see the exhibits describing the nature reserve but, after that, was returning home.

I drove out of town and turned off on Harbour Road. We traveled through farmlands, then through an industrial area to the sand dunes and the nature reserve. The sediment from Rother River silted in and forced the sea back from Rye. It's easy to see the vastness of it, as it is delta land and flat. Although the nature reserve was only a short drive from Rye, the difference in topography was dramatic. I pulled in at the car park for the Rye Harbour Discovery Centre. Deirdre's car was parked there. I assumed they had gone ahead and were viewing the exhibits. Everyone piled out of the van and stared out at the channel.

"This is a bleak spot," Susan said. "I realize it has its own beauty, but I find it unsettling."

"Why is that?" Juliet asked.

"I'm not sure. Perhaps because there are so few people around, and in a country that is so populated, that seems unusual. It looks as though it's been forgotten."

"Perhaps," Poppy said, "it's because it doesn't have the history that we're used to seeing in England. Like we see in castles, manor houses and even pubs, buildings that have been there for centuries. Everything here is new, has been built up in the last few centuries and it doesn't have that long history."

"It could be that," Susan said.

"Was there anything here during the war?" Julie asked.

"This whole area was mined," I said.

Amber looked at Susan. "That might be why you find it unsettling."

"Perhaps," Susan agreed.

I checked in with my feelings. Did I feel an ominous presence? What was I feeling? *Not a thing, Claire. You are wondering how many birds you might see out there and if the avocet will show today.*

"The people here must have been incredibly resilient," Heather said.

"Like my ancestors," Julie said. "They had a tough spirit. A couple of centuries of oppression and we're still here. We have a similar awareness of our power that the women here had after the war. They realized they didn't have to stay in a subservient position in society. The war had taught them they could do many jobs that used to be the sole domain of men and they could manage their own lives. We're coming of age just like the women did after the war, and society is afraid of us."

"Where's your power?" Heather asked.

"Money. A room of one's own as Virginia Wolfe would say," Julie said

"Money?" I hadn't expected that answer. Connection to our ancestors. Spiritualism. Affinity to relatives. But Julie was a practical woman.

"If you want me to teach a class on Ainishinaabe symbolism in art, you will have to come up with a goodly sum to tempt me." She smiled.

Trinity said, "I get top dollar for my beadwork because it's good and because I use ancient patterns."

"She's a bright one," Julie said. "Artistic, and has a business head—when she uses it."

Trinity grinned. "I have good mentors." She studied me for a moment. "It isn't just our ability to make money. We have strong sense of connection to our ancestors."

"The British have that too," Julie said. "Don't you think? All the monuments, and traditions."

I remembered how we had to memorize the succession of kings and queens from Alfred the Great to Queen Elizabeth II.

"Yes," I agreed. "But I think without your sense of spiritual connection."

Trinity thought about it, then said, "The difference may be that we think in pictures before we think in words. At least we artists do. What about you?"

"I think first in words. Do you think your mystery novel, the one you're going to write will be more. ...more poetic? Because you think in pictures?"

"We'll see," Julie said. "Probably every writer of fiction thinks in pictures."

I unloaded the wheelchair because we had to walk some distance to the Discovery Centre along board walks. The area was flat with pools of water scattered in the dunes. We could see many birds: terns, egrets, darting tiny brown birds I couldn't identify. The center was a long, low building that looked like a giant bird blind.

"Is that a World War II pillbox?" Julie asked me, looking toward the river at the low metal building.

"It was a pillbox. It's been converted into a bird blind," I said. "There are several of them in the nature reserve.

Inside the center we found descriptions of the birds which interested me and a history of how this area had been preserved. I found a description of the brown bird I'd seen, a wheatear. I'd love to see an avocet. It has blue legs.

My groups wandered around the center for a half hour. Josh and Kala poured over the exhibit showing different bird tracks then I said goodbye to my family and suggested to the others that we head back. I drove to Rye Harbour and the end of the road until we saw where the river spilled into the English Channel, then I turned the van and headed back to Rye.

The women started a lively conversation in the van on the way home. Howard did not participate. Richard had been uncommonly quiet all afternoon.

"Are there any writers of mysteries who write about this area?" Trinity asked

"They are quite a few who write about the Romney Marsh," I said. *The Birdwatcher* by William Shaw is set in Kent. That's more a thriller that a cozy, but fascinating."

"I read *The Secret Keeper* by Kate Morton. Again, it's not a cozy," Heather said, "but it was good."

"The *Chilbury Ladies Choir* by Jennifer Ryan, is set in the Second World War, Julie. You might enjoy it, and it's in Kent," I said.

"Yes, I did read it. It really gives you a good idea what life was like in small villages and what people had to do to survive."

"There's Jacqueline Winspear's *An Incomplete Revenge*. That's in Kent," Trinity said. "That one has something about hop farming in it."

They talked about mysteries all the way back to Rother Manor. Dinner was on their own tonight, but they still had time to walk around Rye. When we were back at Rother Manor and before they left the van and went to their rooms, I handed some printed material to them.

"Here is a list of bookstores in Rye. There are at least six bookstores close by: Rye Books, Rye Old Books, Olio Books, The Tiny Book Store, Waterstones and The Paperback Book Trader and possibly more."

I left them to their arrangements for the rest of the afternoon and plans for dinner. They all entered the guest house before me. I was picking up wrappers and tidying the van when I spotted Mark and Sergeant Flynn walking toward me. No Sergeant Forsyth.

"Hello," I greeted them. "Andrew's gone then?"

"Addison called him back." Mark said. "Once she knew I had Travis here with me, she decided Andrew was superfluous. Two sergeants is one sergeant too many. Andrew's gone back to Hampshire."

"Sounds just like Addison," I said.

Travis and Mark didn't head to the front stairs but to the side. I expected they were going to the garden shed, so I accompanied them. We had just gotten a short way along the path when we saw a young man come out the kitchen door. He started up the path, saw the three of us, stopped, pivoted and started to run. Travis sprinted after him like an osprey after a mouse and, it seemed to me, with same instinct for prey. There was no contest. Travis had the young man against the wall of the house with his hands behind his back in seconds. Mark walked up to him. I stayed back.

"So, son," Mark said. "What's your name?"

The young man's eyes were wide and he looked frozen.

"We'll do this slowly," Mark said. "I'm Detective Inspector Mark Evans and this is Detective Sergeant Travis Flynn. We're here investigating the murder of Reece Martin. Now, I take it you knew Reece?"

The young man nodded his head.

"Very good," Mark said. "You might be helpful. I'm sure you want to be helpful."

He waited. The boy nodded again as if afraid to speak.

"We'll start with your name. What's your name? Sergeant Flynn, you can unhand him. He's not going anywhere."

Travis let go of the boy and stepped to the side, blocking any escape the boy might have considered. I realized I was thinking of him as a boy, but he was probably in his late twenties.

"Drew," he whispered.

Mark waited.

"Drew Jones."

"Well, Mr. Jones, do you have any ID?"

He reached into his back pocket and slowly brought out a small government-issue card and showed it. Travis peered at it, then copied down some information.

"That's all good," Mark said. "What can you tell us about Reece Martin?"

Drew took in a deep breath and let it out in a long sigh. "Reece, he was my mate. I didn't want him to die. I'm sorry he died."

"When did you see him last?"

"Uh." He stuttered a little. "I guess, I guess it was the night he died."

"Is that so?" Mark said. "What time?"

"It was early," he said. "About six."

"And he was alive then?"

"Yeah. Yeah. Of course he was."

Mark waited.

"He was excited kind of. He was going to go to school. I didn't get it, but he thought it was ace."

"You were mates?" Mark asked.

"From infant school, but he went to Claremont. I didn't go there."

"You were mates at infant school and after Claremont Senior School?"

"I didn't go there; I got an apprenticeship."

"Good for you. What as?"

"A painter. A house painter. I'm a house painter. Inside and outside. I do it. Work for Acme. You know Acme?"

Mark nodded. "You knew Reece well enough to visit him at his garden digs here?"

"Yeah, sometimes. He was a good bloke. Never made fun of me, you know?"

"That's good. Did you see anyone while you were visiting Reece?"

"Reece." Drew Jones was being sarcastic, just factual.

"Besides Reece."

"No."

"See anyone as you were leaving?"

I could almost see Drew thinking. He rolled his eye up and to the right and held still for a moment, then said. "No."

"Right, Mr. Jones. That wasn't so hard now, was it? You give your address and phone number to Sergeant Flynn here, and we'll call you if we have any questions."

Drew nodded and waited.

"And when we call you," Mark said, "you come straight away."

"All right."

Mark and I left Sergeant Flynn to take the particulars and headed for the garden shed. Someone was going to have to interview Drew Jones further. If he'd seen Reece alive at six in the evening, he might have been the last person to see him before he died.

CHAPTER TEN

"**W**hat do you know about Drew Jones?" Mark asked Travis. The men walked in front of me. Travis was taller by about five inches. He looked pale and slim beside Mark who has dark Welsh coloring and a stocky build. They had formidable brains, so, between them, they should come up with some answers today.

"Lower-level drug dealer," Travis said. "Picked up on petty theft charges. Not vicious. His mother pays his fines. He's only occasionally in trouble. Works as he said for Acme Painters part-time. A brick short of a load, that one."

We passed by the house and took the path to the shed.

"He saw Reece that day, probably not long before he died. He's a suspect." Travis's baritone voice reached me easily.

"What else do you know about him?"

"He lives with his long-suffering mother. There must be hundreds of mothers trying to deal with adult children who aren't very bright. Mr. Jones doesn't seem to be able to think very far ahead. Like I said, he does some petty crime. He's always caught because he's incredibly stupid."

We slipped under the police tape and enter the garden shed.

"What motive could he have?" Mark continued to question Travis. A local sergeant did have the knowledge Andy Forsyth wouldn't have. Maybe Superintendent Addison knew what she was doing.

Travis thought for a moment and came up with, "If he had been supplying Reece, maybe Reece couldn't pay him, so his drug boss gave an order to off him. I don't think Jones would have come up with it himself."

"Poison was too sophisticated for him?" I said. We were inside Reece's tiny home now.

Mark stared around the shed. "Maybe Mr. Jones was doing something illegal, contrary to the gang's wishes, or working for a rival gang?"

"How old is Drew Jones?" I asked Travis.

"Twenty-eight."

"We're talking about him as if he were seventeen."

Travis snorted. "Even his mum and his girlfriend treat him like he's a penny short."

Mark and Travis stood in the center of the room and looked around, then started to open drawers.

"What are you looking for," I asked Mark.

"Just about anything," he said.

I glanced at the room, taking in the neatly made bed, tiny kitchen with its two-burner elements, bar sink and two cups on the drainboard,

"Has everything been dusted?" Mark asked Travis.

"Yes. We didn't get anything off the cups."

"What about the door jamb?"

Perpetrators often forgot that they grasped the door jamb as they entered or exited.

"Nothing there either." Travis said.

I wasn't going to assist in the search. "I'm going inside," I told Mark. "I expect you'll be coming to interview Laura soon."

"Tell her we'll see her as soon as we finished here."

I was sitting in the kitchen with Laura having a well-brewed cup of tea when Mark and Travis arrived. They hadn't stayed in the shed very long.

"Just pull up chairs," Laura said. She half-smiled. "Make yourself comfortable."

"We'd like permission to search the garden shed," Mark said.

This request was after the fact. He had already been searching the garden shed.

"Certainly. What are you looking for?"

"We'll go through his papers looking for any indication he had a meeting with someone or if he was worried about something. Anything that might give us a lead to who did this."

"All right. It's hard for me to accept that someone wanted him dead. He wouldn't have deliberately hurt anyone. Wouldn't have made any enemies." She glanced around her kitchen as if trying to remind herself there was a normal, rational world. She turned back to look at Mark.

"Can you free his body soon?"

"Yes, tomorrow."

"I need to arrange for cremation." She bit her lower lip and sat straighter in her chair.

Travis reached into his breast pocket and pulled out a small brochure. "This is a list of funeral companies. You can be reimbursed for the cost of cremation if you apply to the address at the bottom of the brochure."

"I've never had to do anything like this."

"The funeral directors can be very helpful."

"Thank you."

We left Laura sitting at the table with her tea.

Travis parted with us on the street. He had a wife and baby at home and felt he needed to be with them tonight.

"He's conscientious, isn't he?" I said to Mark as we watched Travis stride toward his car.

"He is," Mark said. "He tries to let his wife know his schedule every day. He's conscientious at work, as well. He attends to detail. He thinks ahead. He's meticulous. But he doesn't have

Andy's imagination, so I'm going to need to bounce ideas off you."

That suited me.

"What about Sandhu? Is he any help?" I brought to mind the engaging detective constable.

Mark grinned. "He's entertaining, but I don't know how much use he's going to be. For the most part, I let Flynn send him out to gather information."

I mulled over information, then asked. "Did you talk to the psychiatrist?"

"I did. Dr. Masterson. Nice woman. She had Reece booked in for an appointment but hadn't yet seen him."

"Too bad. She might have gotten a name."

We headed for The Hoof again. It wasn't very busy tonight. We found a table and settled in. Mark ordered a Romney Gold. I ordered a Bohemian—both beers from the same Romney Marsh Brewery. Mine had a nutty flavor and I sipped it as we waited for our burgers.

"Did you get your interviews?"

"I saw Beth's father, James Williams." He grimaced.

"You didn't like him."

"No, I didn't. He was cooperative in that he gave me an impeccable alibi. He was at a conference in France and even produced credit card receipts to prove it. He just seemed uncaring and pompous."

"And you had to be polite?"

"That was the worst of it, yes." He smiled at me.

I returned the smile. It was hard to be polite to the annoying people we dealt with. I had Richard; he had James Williams. I wondered if he'd had the same trouble with Reece's father.

"How did your interview with Malcolm Martin go earlier today?"

"Interesting guy," Mark said. "He's a dentist with a practice in Maidstone. He and his wife have a large property on the outskirts of the town. A bit posh."

I'd like to know more about the house. I'm always interested in houses, but first, I wanted to know more about Reece's father. "What does he look like?" I asked.

"About six-foot-two, slim, blond hair still thick. Wears it down past his ears. Brown eyes, very good manners, dressed in an expensive suit. No lack of money there."

I tried to build a picture of him in my mind. "What's his wife like?"

"Again tall and blond, sophisticated. Looks like she comes from wealth, but she works. She has a veterinary practice."

"She's a veterinary surgeon?"

"Yes, in Maidstone. She works part-time, but she owns the practice. They have two youngsters one about four and one about six, both girls. She seems to be a competent person. She just came in for a few minutes."

"So Malcolm?" I asked again, looking for more information.

The server put our orders in front of us. I had a white fish burger and Mark had a towering double patty burger. I watched him get his mouth around it. It thought the physics would defeat him, but he managed it. We were munching on the chips when we finally got back to Malcolm Martin.

"Was he really estranged from Reece?"

Mark shook more vinegar on his remaining chips. "He said he tried with Reece but he was a difficult child, and as he grew up, got more difficult. When he started using drugs, Martin said he couldn't deal with it. He had young children, toddlers then, and he didn't want Reece around them."

"Did he meet him someplace else?" Surely, a man who had adopted a son and acted as his father for years would have kept up some kind of contact?

"He avoided Reece. He said his wife didn't want Reece in the house and he could see her point. He'd supported Reece's education and thought that should be enough."

"What about the check he made out? I suppose that was for education?"

"He felt a little guilty and, even though Reece was an adult, thought he could support more education, so he sent him that check."

"He *sent* him the check?"

"So he said."

"What did you think of him?" I asked. I was sipping tea trying to make the evening last a little longer with Mark.

"To be honest, Claire. I expected to hate the bloke because of what I'd heard from Laura, but I ended up feeling a little sorry for him. I think his new wife is used to being in charge and tells him what he can and can't do. It seemed to me he was trying to build a new life and felt he had to leave the old behind, including his son."

I was happy that Mark's divorce years ago hadn't involved any children. *I* didn't absolve Malcolm from fatherhood. "I don't think you sign up for parenthood for half a lifetime. I think when you're a parent you parent the child for their whole life, no matter what they do."

"That's a bit much," Mark said.

"Perhaps." It might be my history with my fathers that was influencing my strong opinion here: my alcoholic father who did not care what happened to me and my step-father, Paul, who cared a great deal and who maintained a relationship with me and with his older son in spite of that son's irritating arrogance. Paul, tried to be a good parent his whole life.

We had another lingering good night under the trees near Rother Manor.

I peeked into the lounge to see that my guests had taken advantage of the cocoa and juice Laura had left out for them. I tidied the dirty dishes and carried them to the kitchen. The light was on and I pushed the door open.

Laura was sitting at the table with another cup of tea. She couldn't have been there all this time, but it did look as though she hadn't moved.

"Come on in. Thank you for picking those up. I would have got to them before morning."

She had a book, a type of journal, in front of her. I put the dishes in the dishwasher.

"What are you reading?" I slid onto a chair opposite her.

"I was in the garden shed this afternoon before the police came and I found Reece's diary. I probably shouldn't have taken it." Her hand passed over the journal smoothly as if she were caressing it.

"Does it give any information on who might have killed him?"

She looked at me blankly for a moment. "Oh, his murder. No, but it tells me something important, very important." Her shoulders heaved as she took a deep breath.

I waited.

She looked at me and tears welled up. "He'd been abused when he was eight years old. Eight years old!"

My stomach clenched.

"He tabulated a schedule. Twice a month for eight months. Someone systematically and repeatedly abused him."

I sat in silence. That poor boy.

"I worked out the dates. That was the eight months I worked afternoon shift at the Palace Hotel. I had a babysitter for three hours until Malcolm got home from his clinic at six." She stared down at the journal, then looked at me. "How could she! I've heard of female babysitters abusing children, but it just never occurred to me that it was happening to him. My poor Reece. That was probably at the root of his addiction. I never knew. I would have helped him. Why didn't he tell me?"

I sat perfectly still as I absorbed the horror of it. A little boy, the victim of a predator. His parents ignorant of it. What a dreadful burden for a child.

"Oh, my God," I said. "This is horrible."

"It is," she was quiet for a moment. "It explains so much. He wouldn't have known how to deal with it when it happened, and, I suppose when he didn't tell us right away, it became easier never to mention it, so no one helped him."

The anguish in her eyes was hard to witness. I felt my own tears come just imagining it.

"I don't suppose he could deal with his addiction until he dealt with the abuse. And he didn't want to deal with it." Laurie processed her new knowledge aloud.

Dreadful for a child to be subject to that kind of abuse, over a long period of time and doubly dreadful to not be able to tell anyone about it.

We were both quiet. I was thinking of twenty years of secrecy and confusion that Reece had borne. It probably was easier for him to try to put that abuse behind him and go on with his life than face what had happened. Perhaps he hadn't made the connection between his childhood experience and his craving for oblivion in drugs.

Laura wiped her eyes. "Beth said he had made an appointment with a psychiatrist. Maybe he was going to finally face his demons."

I patted her hand. "That would have been wonderful."

"Yes," she half smiled. "It would have been."

She probably spent many years hoping something would make a difference to her son and he'd find a better life, free of addiction, or at least able to cope with medication.

I was quiet for a moment then asked her.

"Do you remember the name of the babysitter? There's no statute of limitations on child abuse. The police can still charge her."

She looked surprised. "Yes, I do. But Reece didn't name her in his diary, so there isn't much point in trying to prosecute her now."

"If Reece was planning to go to a psychiatrist, there was a chance he would name her. Perhaps the babysitter knew that and wanted to prevent it."

Laura looked horrified." She'd murder him?"

"She had no concern for him when he was eight. Why would she care about him now?"

"She was so nice. Seemed so kind. Reece really liked her."

I didn't tell her that murderers can often seem caring and concerned and abusers made a practice of being loving to their victims. I didn't know a lot about it, but Deirdre had prosecuted abusers and she'd told me a little. "You need to give that name to Mark…and the diary."

"Betty Clarke. Her name was Betty Clarke," Laura whispered. "She's married now. I sent her a gift certificate for her wedding. Her married name is…" she hesitated for a moment as if searching her mind. "Sanderson. That's it. Betty Sanderson. She has two kids. They live in Canterbury. I haven't been in contact with her for the last few years. She may have moved." She took a deep breath and straightened. "She's had twenty years of normal living. Reece had twenty years of struggle." She was angry now and pounded her fist on the table. "How could she? How did I miss it?"

"Reece didn't name her?"

"No." Laura sat back. "I may be rushing to conclusions here. How could she know he was going to see a psychiatrist?"

"Give it more thought. See if you can come up with more names of someone who might have abused him: an uncle, a boy scout leader."

"We didn't have any relatives nearby, so it wouldn't be an uncle. But Reece took swimming lesson. He was on the swim team."

"His swim coach. Or there might have been a teacher at the school."

"He was in scouts and there was a teacher at school, one he really liked. He taught math. He made Reece feel special. Could it have been him?"

"Name?"

"Lexington. I don't remember his first name."

"Tell Mark." I would tell him in any case. "Make a list and give it to Mark."

"I'll do that. I'll make a list and give it to him in the morning. Thanks so much, Claire. Thanks so much," she said again. "I need something to do, something to help."

I contemplated her situation as I went up the stairs to my room. The guilt she'd experience now she knew about the abuse would be oppressive. She'd feel guilty that she hadn't discovered the abuse then, and that she hadn't helped Reece deal with it. She needed to take some kind of action to help. She would spend the night trying to remember who interacted with her son twenty years ago. An eight-year-old boy wouldn't have a lot of contacts. Perhaps an older brother of one of his friends, a Sunday school teacher, that school teacher, Lexington, or the coach. It might get quite complicated to find out who might have abused him. Then, it would take some work to find out whether anyone would have anything to gain by murdering Reece.

CHAPTER ELEVEN

Before I went to bed I texted Mark and told him about the journal Laura had lifted from Reece's shed.

"Brilliant!" he texted. "I'll need that."

It was the best lead he had. The predator from the past might not be the murderer, but at least it was something Mark could investigate.

In the morning after breakfast, I gathered everyone for our trip to Tillingham, a winery about three miles from Rye. Again I had a bag of goodies: a fridge magnet of a Kent oast house, a keychain featuring Ypres castle, some tissues, wipes, and, of course, chocolate. The drive to the Tillingham winery was short—north to Peasmarsh then west—with pastures and crops on either side divided by hedgerows.

"All these roads here are called lanes," Heather commented. She'd been reading the sign posts. I had turned off the highway onto School Lane, then Dew Lane, which turned into Tillingham Lane.

"That's true. Starvecrow Lane is my favorite."

Heather laughed. "And the name 'lane' is apt. It conjures up something picturesque with draping trees on either side and, right now, that's what I'm seeing."

The 'lanes' here would be called roads in another part of the country, and they were picturesque. I pulled into the car park before ten. The staff were ready for us as I'd booked ahead.

Trinity squealed as she dismounted from the van and caught sight the farm pens. "They have pigs here!"

"And chickens and sheep and probably goats," I informed her

She squatted on the grass in rapt contemplation, peering through the fence and watching the pigs root up the ground as they snuffled and snorted.

"Do they have names?" she asked me.

"Marvin, Brick, and Tumbler," I introduced the pigs. "This is Trinity."

"They really *do* have names."

She cast an eye around the farmyard, looking for more animals.

"You can wander around after the tour," I said, encouraging her to join us as we entered the winery. She waved to the pigs and followed me. The view from the tasting room was spectacular.

"Is that the English Channel I see?" Richard asked.

"It is. And the river in front of us is Tillingham River."

"Beautiful," Heather said.

"Sir Paul McCartney has a house just west of here across the fields." I pointed.

"Really?" Susan squinted her eyes as if she could see the famous singer and song writer if she tried. "I think he's a genius."

We were interrupted by one of the staff. "Hello. I'm Marcy." An energetic young woman with dark curly hair almost bounced up to us. "I'm your tour guide."

From this point on, I could relax and remain quiet as the guides were excellent.

Susan had opted to walk with just a walking stick. She said walking on level floors was not a problem. She was near the front of the group and seemed interested in the wine making.

Marcy held their attention. "We don't grow grapes and then add a lot of things to it make it ferment and give us the flavor we want," she said. "We till the soil and add nutrients and organics so that the grapes do the work and give us wonderful wine. It's the land, the *terroir*, that creates the wine."

"What difference does that make?" Poppy leaned forward.

"It gives a more complex flavor. And we don't put our wine in oak barrels to age it. We bury the wine in quivas."

"Now that sounds like a Latin word," Susan said.

"I expect it is, because they are the same kind of amphoras that the Romans used when they made wine."

"So it's an ancient process?" Susan was intrigued.

"Yes. Like the Romans, we don't use pesticides on the weeds that grow between the vines. We plant nettles to control pests and allow only natural fermentation."

"Isn't that a little risky?" Howard asked. "I mean you couldn't control what you get every time. You wouldn't get a reliable, consistent product."

"That's right." Martha sounded pleased that someone got the point. "We can't control exactly how the wine is going to turn out. It's very exciting."

"I think it would be a financial nightmare," Howard said.

Poppy smiled at her husband. I expect she admired Howard's shrewd financial acumen.

Marcy smiled. "Not so much. Because once we get the wine, we blend it and make a spectacular taste. You'll see."

My group continued to be interested in Marcy's enthusiastic educational tour of the winery. She finally brought us back to the tasting room where small round tables held several different wines. Everyone had three glasses in front of them and Marcy poured about an ounce into each glass. She discussed the wine and allowed everyone to give an opinion. The three young women from Toronto were outdoing each other with adjectives.

"Complex substance," Julie said of the Pinot Noir.

"Musty," Amber said.

"Perhaps even a tad earthy," Trinity said then giggled

"You're reading from the label." Julie said. "Not fair."

Howard twirled his glass and gazed at the deep red wine. "Remarkable wine. I don't know how you do it. Such an uncontrolled process, and you get this. This one is a blend of ten different grapes. You must have a genius vintner."

"It's delicious," Poppy said. "Can we get this in the States?"

"Not yet," Mercy said, "but soon."

Poppy laughed. "We'll just have to drink all we can while we're here."

Howard bought three bottles of the Pinot Noir. The three Torontonians bought one bottle of the Sparkling White to be shared.

"English champagne," Julie said.

It did taste like champagne.

We took a few moments to let Trinity become acquainted with the goats and sheep before we loaded into the van. I wanted to vary the tour somewhat so did not stay at the winery for lunch but drove my group to The Playden Oasts Inn where the old oast houses with their distinctive cone shaped roofs provided a change of atmosphere.

"Oast houses are where they dried the hops. Right?" Howard asked.

I went into tour guide mode. I sometimes think I have a compartment in my brain, like a computer file that holds all the information I need for a tour. Ask a question and a file opens.

"Yes this used to be a big hop-growing area. They still have hops here, but not as many as they did in the past. In the late 1870s, there were 77,000 acres of hops grown in Kent. Today, there about 3,000. In the thirties and forties, pickers came from London and spent a few weeks in September picking hops. Today, much of the picking is done by machine. It must have been lively in the old days with extended families camping around the hop fields."

We left behind the acres and acres of grape vines that stretched out in rows along Tillingham Lane and traveled through the mixed farming country as we headed south.

"Does anyone know any mysteries set in wineries?" Heather posed the question that kept the group talking on the short trip.

"Ellen Crosby," Susan said, "but she set hers in Virginia."

"Joey Fulger set them in Texas," Heather said.

"Niki Sands set hers in the Napa Valley, California." Susan offered.

"Did anyone set them in England?" Julie asked.

There was silence while we considered it.

"The closest I can come is Alaux and Balen and they set theirs in France." I didn't know any set in British wineries. Some author should do that.

I drove into the car park at the Playden Oast Inn where I stopped for a moment so all could appreciate the distinctive circular towers with their cone roofs and miniature cones on top of the peak.

"They look like something out of *The Hobbit*." Amber said.

They did.

The restaurant was expecting us and the server ushered us into the reserved area. The menu was interesting and varied.

"All locally sourced as much as possible," I said. "The seafood will be fresh which, in my opinion, is the only way to eat it."

"I'll get the seafood," Julie said. "Today's catch is my preference. I particularly miss salmon, but I don't expect to get that here."

"You can get salmon, but I'd go for the scallops, the cod or any white fish." I eat fresh salmon in Scotland.

They busied themselves with ordering. I asked for two bottles of Tillingham White to accompany the meal.

While the server was taking their orders, I slipped out to the cloakroom. Before I returned, I texted Mark. "Did you talk to Laura?"

For a wonder, he answered me right away. "I did. Thanks for the tip."

"What about the babysitter?"

"Later," he texted.

That was frustrating. If I wanted to know what he learned, I'd have to wait until tonight.

The group enjoyed their lunch. Howard even deviated from his steak and potatoes menu to Steak and Ale pie.

"I want to try something English," he said.

Poppy was amused and smiled at him.. "Good for you." She obviously recognized how slight his deviation was.

When everyone had been served and enjoyed most of their meal, I brought up today's itinerary. "The rest of the day is free to shop or do whatever you like until this evening when we're scheduled to go to Imopera."

"What is that? I don't believe it's opera." Richard was suspicious of the event and clearly not eager to try something new.

"No," I said. "It's not truly opera. It's improv theater, so the audience participates. It's really is a lot of fun."

"I'm looking forward to that," Amber said. "I'm up for fun."

It was difficult for Richard to say he wasn't up for fun, so he remained quiet.

I wouldn't be able to talk to Mark until quite late. The Imopera finished about nine-thirty. After that, we would go for supper. It would probably be about eleven before I was back at the guest house. I texted that information to Mark.

"I'll come around then," he texted back.

The Imopera was located at the Rye Creative Centre just across the river off the A259. I had warned the group that, although there was a bar, it was outside. Still, the evening was warm and clear.

"What kind of opera is this?" Richard asked. "I'm familiar with the usual ones: Puccini, Verdi, Wagner. But I've never heard of imopera."

"You're in for a treat," Heather said. "It's improv. As the audience, we create our own opera." She had read the material I'd sent out earlier in the month. Only about half my guests do read it before they arrive.

"Music and all?" Amber asked.

"You'll get help there." I'd experienced this about a year ago. The troupe provided the music; the audience created the lyrics.

"It should be fun," Trinity said. "Do I get the yell out my suggestions?"

"You do. It can get pretty lively."

The actors were professionals and well used to handling audiences, so the evening, while on the edge of raucous, was still controlled. Everyone enjoyed it except, of course, Richard.

We were settled around the pub table after the performance. We didn't go to the Mermaid Restaurant this time but to the more casual atmosphere of The Mermaid Pub. We put some tables together and ordered the locally brewed house beer.

"I thought we created a fabulous opera." Amber said.

"Really stimulating," Julie agreed. "We're a good team."

"I was entranced at the way the story twisted," Susan said. "We got a little carried away with the plot there, making it very melodramatic."

"But operas are melodramatic," I insisted. "Think about *Il Travatore*. It starts with a mother telling us she threw her baby into a fire. Now, *that's* melodramatic."

"True enough. Melodrama is what gives you the license to really go for it," Susan said.

"I found it unrestrained, wild, totally unbelievable, and without the beauty of a decent libretto," Richard's voice held a querulous tone that set my teeth on edge.

Everyone turned and stared at him, even Howard.

He tried to cajole Richard into a party mood. "Come on, Rick. It was great fun."

"The audience was manipulated by those actors," Richard persisted..

"You do the same thing when you direct a play." Heather argued with him. "You want the audience to react with a certain emotion and you direct the actors to present the story in a way that will get that reaction. That's obvious manipulation."

"Well, yes." Richard gave her that point. "But it's all within the canon, the literature canon. Everybody knows the rules."

"I for one." Julie said, "am tired of those rules. I have every intention of changing the canon. It hasn't done my people any good." She leaned forward. Trinity and Amber put their elbows on the table and also leaned forward.

"Yes, yes. I see your point," Richard said, backing off. He was wise enough not to take on the three women staring at him with firm intent.

Mark was sitting in his car in the guest house car park when I arrived. I waved to him. He got out of his car and followed us into the Rother Manor.

Heather touched my arm. "Could we have some brandy in our room?"

Laura wasn't licensed to sell alcohol after hours, but I had some brandy stashed in my supplies. "I'll bring it right away."

I caught Mark's eye and waved toward the lounge, indicating he should wait for me there. The rest of the group headed for their rooms. I attended to Heather's need for brandy. If I was married to Richard I might make that a nightly ritual.

Finally, I joined Mark in the lounge. He had his tablet in front of him and had been checking his notes. In anticipation of a long talk, he had two cups of tea ready. He smiled when he saw me, stood and reached for me. We had the privacy for a warm greeting and made the most of it. Then we settled at the table.

"Any progress?"

"I located Betty Sanderson. She wasn't hard to find, but I wanted to talk to a psychologist before I talked to her so I'd know what questions to ask and how to phrase them. I'm out of my depth with female abusers. They've never come my way before."

That was a good idea and typical of Mark to approach the problem methodically. "*Did* you talk with a psychologist about how to approach her?"

"Yes, on the phone. We have a consultant on retainer in Hampshire. I need to be careful not to lead Mrs. Sanderson or to let her know what I'm looking for. We'll see if I can manage that. I'm scheduled to see her tomorrow." He checked his notes. "I did interview the scoutmaster, the one Laura named. He remembered Reece. I said I was looking for childhood trauma and he knew right away what I information I was after. He'd been in charge of all the scouting for Rye, so he had records on all the workers. He said he was always alert for the possibility of abuse and didn't think it had occurred under his watch. He had one group himself that Reece was in and remembered him as quiet but attentive. He was quite sure none of his leaders were predators."

"What do you think?"

"I'm inclined to think he's honest. There were no allegations against him. I checked. He might be wrong about his assessment of his staff, but I'll take his word for it right now."

So, no abuse from the scout leader—another lead that had petered out.

"What about the gangs? Do you think that Reece was killed by a gang member?" I still thought that was a possibility as gangs were synonymous with violence.

"I sniffed around a little and got Travis to do the same, or, more accurately Travis got Sandhu to do that. There's some activity here, but there doesn't seem to be anything related to Reece. It's possible that a small-time dealer objected to not being paid by Reece and killed him, but the manner of the killing doesn't look like retributive murder and, by everyone's assessment, Reece wasn't using. Although Travis would say addicts are only *sometimes* not using."

"Are you feeling frustrated? Are you running out of leads?" It was as if every lead he had disappeared when he examined it.

"No, it's early days yet. I still have to find the teacher Laura mentioned as being particularly interested in Reece. Lexington. Travis should have an address for me by tomorrow."

I mulled over the information Mark had so far. I wondered how anyone could have gotten at Reece to murder him. I suppose he had been alone out there in the garden shed and whoever poisoned him was likely somebody he knew, so he didn't object to their visit.

"What about the surveillance cameras?"

Mark scrolled down and read a note on his tablet.

"The camera —there is only one—shows three people on three separate occasions walking down the side of the house that evening toward the garden shed. There's no evidence they went into the shed. One is Beth who has already told us she visited Reece. One looks like Drew, his erstwhile friend. He said he'd been there late afternoon. The other is a man over six feet but the surveillance photos are grainy."

"Not Betty Sanderson then?"

"No, but she could have approached the garden from the communal property at the rear."

I hadn't thought of that. Anyone could have come to the garden shed through the back gate. Even if they did find the man on the surveillance cameras, it didn't mean he was the murderer. The murderer might not have walked past the surveillance camera. Someone or several people could have approached from the back. That definitely widened the suspect list. It was frustrating. Laura wouldn't expect a quick arrest, but she would be upset with no progress.

"Meanwhile, Laura can go ahead with the funeral?"

"Yes, the coroner released the body today."

Laura didn't have a lot of support. There was Angela and Beth but no family. I'd try to attend the funeral.

CHAPTER TWELVE

Laura was cooking and serving breakfast. She would have a lot to do today. She'd have to arrange the flowers, the hymns and the organ music. She would probably have to spend time on the phone calling relatives and friends.

"Cremation today. Funeral tomorrow," Angela said. "I'll be cooking and getting things ready for tomorrow's reception. Are you coming?"

"To the funeral? Or the reception?"

"Both."

"Do you think Laura wants me there? "

"She does."

"In that case, I'll come," I promised. I'd have to juggle my schedule, but I'd come.

I took everyone out of Rye for the day and into Crowborough, the home of Sir Arthur Conan Doyle and the site of the Miss Seeton mystery novels. My groups appreciated the inland country and the quaint village atmosphere of Crowborough.

The next day was Saturday. I dispatched the trio along with Heather on e-bikes. There was a cracking good bike trail along the coast and lots to see in the surrounding area. I'd ordered a lunch and they packed it into their paniers. I made sure they had full water bottles and a small bottle of wine.

I put some effort into worrying about what to do with Richard and had secured a lunch date with the manager of the Bowler Crab Theatre Company. They were putting on a one-man Shakespeare production around the subject of Shakespeare's sense of comedy. I felt guilty saddling the theater manager with Richard, but I compensated him with a huge fee.

Susan said she wanted to go back to Lamb house and spend more time looking at the artifacts and the books in the building. I consulted with Angela about who I could hire to accompany Susan. She offered her niece and I hired her. Harold and Poppy wanted to see Dover. I bought them train tickets and sent them on their way. I scattered the group, something I'd never done before on a tour. But I did want to attend the funeral and this seemed the only way I could manage it.

Funerals usually weren't arranged quickly as this one was, so I was surprised to see so many at the church. I knew Laura had not yet put the obituary in the Rye News but there was a small notice of the funeral place and time there. Miss Weatherby, no doubt, was responsible for that. It was a good idea and could be the reason there were so many attending. The funeral was held not in the imposing St. Mary's but in the smaller Methodist church on the Square.

I met Mark just outside the church door. We stepped aside so we could have a conversation and also to allow people to enter. Both Mark and Travis were in light-weight dark suits, white shirts and ties. They screamed officialdom. I don't know if that would comfort Laura or make her nervous.

"No tourists with you today?" Mark asked.

"I've managed to keep them occupied for the time of the funeral and the reception. How is the investigation going?"

"Travis is onto what the gangs are doing around here and nothing seems to come back to Reece."

"Can't find anything," Travis said. "Not even a smidgen of a rumour. Jas had a good nose for rumours and he hasn't heard anything either."

"What about Reece's friend Drew? He looks a little dodgy."

"He might have been supplying Reece at some point," Travis said, "but he might just be an old friend. A doubtful prospect. He isn't bright enough to plan a shopping trip much less a murder."

We heard the squeal of tires as a small compact car stopped behind the hearse. Jas Sandhu emerged, grinning at us. He left the door of his car open as he strode toward us. "Reporting, gov," he said to Travis.

I took in his dark pants and dark sport shirt, his idea of proper funeral attire, interrupted by the bright red trainers that winked at convention.

"What's up?" Travis said.

"Thought you'd like to know I found a witness who was feeding the birds in that communal garden for two hours in the afternoon. Imagine spending two hours with birds. It'd drive me crazy."

I could spend two hours watching birds. They were fascinating to me.

"Did he or she see anyone enter the gate to Rother Manor?" Mark spoke softly in deference to the people still moving past us.

"She. Nice old tabby. She said no one did."

"What time?"

"From 3:30 to 5:30. That leaves us a half-hour window when we don't know if that gate was used."

Travis nodded. "Good. Put that info on the spread sheet timetable."

"Will do." He left.

"Why didn't he just text you that information?" I asked.

"I didn't want to ask. He probably forgot to charge his phone."

Mark raised his eyebrows. Travis shrugged. Jas did get some good information in his own way.

We moved back a little more from the doorway. Travis leaned closer. "We found the teacher we were looking for, Lexington,

Charles. He's still teaching at the school. No priors. One complaint twenty years ago from a parent. Not substantiated."

They looked at each other.

"Worth checking out," Mark said.

I'd been watching the congregation file past us while we were speaking in low tones. There were people of all ages even some young children. Reece had been connected to many.

Mark lifted his head and caught the eye of a tall man just entering the church. He was about six-foot-three, thin, with thick blond hair and brown eyes. He held the door for his companion, a tall blonde woman.

"Malcolm Martin," Mark murmured to me. "And his wife Vanessa Clarke."

I noticed her fabulous, navy-blue Gucci flats with a low heels. Even though they looked plain, I'd price them at about eight hundred pounds. Her navy linen pantsuit look like Balenciaga model, but I wasn't the expert on clothes the way I was on shoes. She looked elegant and beautiful. Martin's wife. I'm not sure if Laura was going to appreciate her coming, but she might appreciate the fact that she had dressed with respect. I was disposed to like anyone who had such good taste in shoes.

We followed them in and took our seats near the back of the church. It was a charming old church more homely than I'd expected from the outside, more ornate as well. There was wood panelling, gold and even candles which I hadn't anticipated in a Methodist church— all contributing to an atmosphere of peace and sanctity. There were flowers on the altar, more candles and an urn. There was also a picture of Reece. In the picture, he was smiling. The tragedy of that smiling face struck me anew. He could have been happy for years.

Laura came in from a side entrance and sat in the front pew. I saw Malcolm go up and touch her shoulder. She looked up, shrugged off his hand and turned away. He turned and moved to a pew behind her. His wife followed him.

Laura was angry with him. What kind of a man ignores his son? A selfish one? Even a narcissistic one? Still, he was here. He wasn't pretending that his son's death had nothing to do with him. He must have redeeming qualities of some kind. Maybe he was trying harder with his new family. I don't know why he would be more successful with a second. *Hold on, Claire, that's too judgmental.* After all, Mark and I were trying out a second relationship with every intention of making it successful. Maybe Malcolm deserves a second chance. Laura said he'd been attentive to Reece when Reece was young—a good father then, she'd said. He'd paid for his secondary school sent and check to education and had contributed a check for Reese's coming tuition for his horticultural course. I should get past my prejudice. He probably sent a wreath. There was a large wreath in front of the altar. Either Laura sent that or perhaps Malcolm. I looked around at the flowers and noted the small bouquet I had ordered.

We sat through the funeral. Mark and Travis were not too obvious in their visual examination of all the members of the congregation. Drew, Reece's friend, was there, as were several young people I had not met. Beth sat beside Laura and I'm sure was a great comfort. There were several older people in Laura's pew who I assumed were grandparents or aunts and uncles.

After the funeral and the disbursement of the congregation, Travis left us to do more searches, this time looking for criminal records on any of their suspects. Mark joined me at the reception at Rother Manor. Laura stood just inside the door and shook hands with people who came to give her their condolences. Beth stood beside her, her hand on Laura's elbow. This ritual of a reception after the funeral was a huge strain on the bereaved. Laura should sit and let people come to her. I moved closer and whispered that suggestion to Beth. She guided Laura over to a chair a little removed from the main part of the lounge. I got Laura cup of tea and put it beside her. I could see it was all she could do to get through this. Her cheeks were pale, her eyes shadowed in purple.

Slowly, people came to greet her. I saw Malcolm and his wife approach. Laura leaned back and looked at him through almost closed eyes. He said a few words and moved off. His wife also said a few words and followed. I could see Laura shoulders rise and straighten. She must be ready to clout him on the side of the head. Indifference can be as cruel as outright aggression. Malcolm's indifference to Reece must have hurt him badly. I don't suppose Laura would ever forgive him for that.

I took my tea cup and moved to where Malcolm and his wife were standing, holding a cup and saucer and a biscuit. While there was some sense of celebration of Reece's life here, Laura had provided only biscuits and small cakes. Guests were not encouraged to linger.

"Claire Barkley," I said smiling at Vanessa. "I know Laura as I have a tour residing here in the guest house." I turned to Malcolm. "I'm afraid I didn't know your son. I'm sorry for your loss." He didn't feel the loss, so my condolences were irrelevant. But I wanted to get this man talking.

"Thank you," he said. "He had a troubled life."

Was he saying Reece was troubled so his death was no loss? "But I think he was doing better. It must feel ironic that such a tragedy occurred."

"He *said* he was doing better, but he'd said that before. I'm sure he would be relieved to stop struggling." Malcolm looked away.

I don't know why he would think that when everyone said Reese had hope. Perhaps he'd often anticipated Reece would stop using and the constant disappointment made him believe it would never happen.

"You hadn't seen him in quite a while?" I asked.

"No, as you probably know," he said curtly, "we were estranged. I have tried but I couldn't deal with his lifestyle."

Of course, it's all about you. Now, *I* wanted to clout him on the side of the head.

"He was a lovely young man," Vanessa said, "when he was not using. But you never knew when that was going to be."

She was sincere in that and seemed to have a bit of compassion.

"I think his murder is shocking," she continued. I hope they find the perpetrator. It's a dreadful thing to have happened. I don't know how Laura will stand it."

Definitely, she had some compassion.

"You never met him?" I asked her.

"Oh yes," she said. "Malcolm and I took him for coffee once, probably a couple of years ago. So I've met him, but I didn't know him, not really."

We were interrupted by Miss Weatherby who came up in a rush, her hand extended. Malcolm automatically shook it. "I'm Jessica Weatherby, Miss Weatherby. I taught Reece in infant school. Such a quiet boy he was. Studious even at that young age. You were so proud of him, I remember."

"A long time ago," Malcolm said.

"Yes. I agree, but children do carry some of their earlier characteristics into adulthood. I expect Reece was still a good athlete."

Malcolm nodded.

"And he probably still kept that journal he wrote in daily."

"I don't know," Malcolm said. "Perhaps."

"This is your wife?" she turned to Vanessa with her bright inquisitive stare.

Malcolm introduced them "And Ms Barclay," Malcolm included me. His manners were good.

"We've met," Miss Weatherby stood back a step, obviously remembering I had seen her hustled out of Laura's kitchen.

"I must see Laura," she said and left abruptly, but she didn't head toward Laura but toward Mark. She spoke to him. He shook his head and walked past her. She left the reception without talking to Laura.

There wasn't much more I could say to Malcom. I was dying to ask him what he was doing on the pertinent day, but that was Mark's job and he wouldn't appreciate me bringing it up. It was a good thing I hadn't asked any awkward questions as Mark joined us.

"Detective Inspector," Malcolm acknowledged him.

"Hello again, Inspector," Vanessa said. "Do you know Claire Barclay? She's a tour guide who stays here."

"Indeed." Mark smiled at me. "She's my fiancé."

Vanessa turned to me. "Oh, my. What's it like to be the girlfriend of a detective inspector? I expect you don't see a lot of him as you must be away a lot and he probably is as well."

"That's true," I said.

"Mr. Martin," Mark said, "I would like to arrange to visit you at your house when convenient."

I could tell by Mark's voice that it had better be convenient.

"Certainly," Malcolm said "Would noon tomorrow do?"

"Yes, tomorrow will do."

Vanessa turned to me. "Why don't you come with him. We can have a gossip while they're talking."

I realized that Vanessa was trying to change an official inquiry into a social occasion. I glanced at Mark who almost imperceptibly nodded. I mentally reviewed my plans for tomorrow.

"I will if I can. I have a full tour right now and so my time is not always my own."

"Well, do try."

I smiled at her. Vanessa was a dear. I still didn't like Malcolm.

CHAPTER THIRTEEN

I left the reception early, as I had to do a round of pickups. I didn't get a chance to ask Mark what Miss Weatherby had wanted from him, but it was probably a statement for the paper which he wouldn't give. Even mentally, I called her *Miss* Weatherby. There was something about her that pegged her into a position of authority which I instinctively tried to resist: hubris? A blatant belief in her own right to know? The conviction that her pursuit of a story was more important than kindness or consideration of social boundaries.

Everyone of my group needed to be collected except Susan who would be delivered back to the guest house by the girl who had looked after her all afternoon. I texted Julie and found that the Toronto trio would be ready in a half-hour to be picked up at the bike rental shed. I texted the manager of the theater.

"Is Richard Shelly ready to go? Do you want me to pick him up?"

The answer was succinct. "Please."

I picked up Richard first and shook hands with the manager who was a tall, thin, gaunt man.

"Thanks," I said as I passed him a substantial tip. I was sure he'd earned it.

He raised his eyebrows and nodded his thanks.

"A good theater company," Richard informed me as we drove to the coast to pick up the three young women. "Not as good as mine, of course, but they had an interesting marketing plan. Mind you, the manager didn't seem very well informed about it and I might have to go elsewhere to find more information."

I let Richard prattle away and pulled into the car park at the bike rental shed. The women were waiting and looked dishevelled, flushed and happy.

"Wonderful," Trinity said. "It felt great to be sweeping along the trails. No cars. No pedestrians. It was sublime."

"Just blew all the cobwebs away," Julie said. "The breeze from the ocean kept us cool. How was your day Richard?" she asked hospitably.

"Yeah," Trinity said. "What was the theater company like?"

"Small but adequate. They need better marketing." He started to continued, no doubt with criticism but Trinity interrupted him with a burst of laughter.

"I'm going to start calling you Eeyore."

Richard look affronted. I hid a smile. Richard did sound like Eeyore from *Winnie the Pooh*, the donkey who was perpetually pessimistic and always complaining.

I gave everyone a chance to rest and change clothes then drove them to Amici's in Ashford for dinner. It was a half-hour drive but worth it.

We left town on the a A259 which, as it passes Brookland and for no obvious reason, turns into A2070. There was the farmland of Kent on both sides of the road with cereal crops in the fields. It was a beautiful view on a warm July evening with some hay already harvested and lying in huge round bales. I watched for slow-moving farm vehicles on the road, those mammoth beasts that crawl in front of a line of cars, imperious and unchallenged.

I turned left just before Ashford onto the A2042 then right ninety degrees. The road was still A2042 but in true English fashion a road that changes direction can retain its name and a road that goes straight can also change its name. If tours come from a city or from a community that has a grid numbered system for their streets and avenues, this confuses them. It confuses me at times. I don't trust a road will either keep its name or its direction.

I maneuvered through the city to the restaurant. Amici's had the seafood Julie craved, the aged British steak Howard and Richard preferred and many options for the others. This was one of the meals that I included in their tour package. I'd ordered three bottles of Chianti and hoped everyone would enjoy themselves. My group appreciated the warm, Mediterranean atmosphere as we passed by the smaller tables to our reserved table at the back.

Everyone settled, and happily began on their starters. I excused myself and went to the cloakroom, stopping in the courtyard to text Mark.

"I won't be able to attend your interview with Malcolm and Vanessa if it's tomorrow. I'm taking the crew to Canterbury where we're staying overnight at the Falstaff."

I didn't get an answer. I expect he was busy.

I sent a quick call to Deirdre." How's my favorite guy?"

"I take it you mean Gulliver, not Michael or Josh."

"Exactly," I said.

"They're all fine," she replied. "How's it going? Did you tell me you had a murder?"

"I don't have a murder, but Mark does." I was going to be very involved with Mark's investigation except to act as a sounding board for his ideas.

"He's there, is he?"

"Yes."

"With Andrew?" Deirdre liked Andrew Forsyth.

"Not Andrew. He has a sergeant on loan from the Sussex Constabulary called Travis Flynn."

"How's that going?"

"Travis is fine, but the investigation is going nowhere. All leads all seem peter out."

"Mark will find the creep," Deirdre said. "He's very good."

"But not miraculous." It was wise to be realistic about Mark's abilities and not idealize him. After all, he only made conclusions on the evidence he found.

"Is he staying with you?"

"No, he's staying in a hotel nearby. There are suspects in my house."

Deirdre's voice held some alarm "Are you in any danger?"

"I don't think so," I reassured her. "I have a grieving mother and her friends around me. Suspects—but unlikely ones."

"Take care," she cautioned.

I rushed back to my group. They hadn't missed me. They were talking amongst themselves. Richard was sitting at the other end of the table and, if he was complaining, I couldn't hear him.

In the morning, everyone had had breakfast and was packed and waiting for me in the foyer. I loaded the van and we were off to Canterbury where we would stay overnight at The Falstaff and return to Rother Manor the following night.

I took the same route to Ashford as I had last night except this time I skirted the city to the south and joined the Canterbury Road, heading east. We traveled through farm lands with pastures and crops on either side. It was a beautiful morning. The sun lit the fields, brightening the patchwork of variegated greens and bright yellow. The traffic was light even as I approached the cathedral city. The route to St. Dunstan's Street was free of traffic.

The Falstaff Hotel is a 600-year-old coaching house. It's just outside the walls of Canterbury but is part of the city. It's been modernized so it doesn't obviously reflect medieval life. There's parking behind The Falstaff, so I was able to get quite close to the back door.

My group followed me into the hotel and stared at the décor. The leaded paned windows, exposed stone walls, the wooden beams and the wooden panelling were reminiscent of its history, but the lobby and breakfast area were open and spacious and the furnishings were modern and bright. The manager was ready for us and escorted my guests to their rooms. Although I got a discount rate for the rooms, they were still pricey, as The Falstaff was committed to giving guests a sense of luxury. I hoped the trio from Toronto, in particular, appreciated all the little touches of elegance. I'd booked the family room for the three women as that was the largest available. Trinity was small, so I hoped she'd be comfortable on the sofa bed. She wouldn't complain, in any case, but I did want her to be happy and feel pampered.

My own room was a 'superior' room which held a queen size bed and an en-suite bath. I've stayed here in the off season when they gave me one of their 'luxury rooms'. In those rooms, the bath is inside the bedroom. I preferred this room. I wished Mark could share it.

We assembled in the lounge. I'd pulled out the wheelchair for Susan and we started off for The Garage Coffee House about seven blocks away.

I gave a short history of Canterbury, although most of them had read Chaucer's *Canterbury Tales* and had some understanding of the city as the center of pilgrimage in the medieval days. I pointed out the Marlowe Theatre, a huge building and one that would appeal to Richard. There were many independent shops along the streets. The women were attracted to the knit shops, galleries, and vintage clothing. The 1930s to 1970s styles especially interested Trinity.

"I'm going to come back here." She stopped to stare at the sumptuous brocade waistcoat displayed in the window. I expect there were many specialty shops that would fascinate her.

The Beaney House of Art and Knowledge, an eighteenth-century building, caught Poppy's eye. "I'm going to have to come back to this."

The aroma of roasting coffee reached out to the street and drew us into The Garage. It was a roasting house as well as a café and a source of varied and delicious coffee.

I handed out maps of Canterbury with circles around places I thought would interest them, individually marked to cater to each person's interests. They had the afternoon on their own, but this morning, I wanted to wander with them to be sure they understood what they could do together and what they could do on their own.

We took two hours to explore some of the nooks and crannies. I led them past the cathedral, but not in it, as they could join one of the excellent guided tours in their free time. I made sure they all had the location of bookstores on their maps. There were eight in the downtown area, because, after all. Canterbury is an historic literary center. I'd marked museums as well, so I hoped the Toronto trio would enjoy those. We wandered through the town to High Street and back to the Falstaff Hotel where I'd booked a special meal.

After they had gone to their rooms, deposited their packages and freshened up they met me on the terrace. I'd ordered the typical afternoon tea package, although it was a trifle early for it. They were pleased with the presentation: Scones with jam and cream on one tier, sandwiches on the next and pastries on the top. The choice was confusing. What to eat first? We started with the sandwiches.

"There were many books of mystery set in Canterbury." I needed to make sure I fulfilled their expectation that they would learn about mystery novels while they were with me. "Most of them, such as Paul Doherty's, are set in medieval times. I expect it's all the information in Chaucer's *Canterbury Tales* that fires modern-day authors to set their mysteries back in those days."

"Maureen Ash wrote *The Canterbury Murders a Templar Knight Mystery*." Heather was the most informed on mysteries.

"She did," I agreed. "There was another interesting book called *The Canterbury Sisters* but it wasn't a mystery."

"I read that one," Amber said. "Who wrote that?"

I thought for a minute. "Kimberly Wright."

"It was interesting but not as interesting as a mystery." Amber was defining her reading interests quite young. Most people read in many genres before realizing they preferred a particular one.

She continued. "I don't want to write a story about understanding love and the purpose of life. It's depressing."

"We're not old enough for that," Trinity said.

"I'm looking forward to those experiences, though," Amber said. "The actual living experiences of love and making choice about my purpose in life will be exciting."

"You hope," Julie said.

"Of course." Amber was sure. I hadn't been so certain when I was her age and had not expected adventure and love, which was just as well as I hadn't found it until I was in my forties. I shuddered to think I might have lived my whole life and missed Mark and my tour life.

Before they headed out to their afternoon of shopping, I asked them to meet me at The Falstaff at four-thirty that afternoon. I'd booked a boat to take us to on the River Stour at four forty-five. It would be beautiful at that time and cool on the river. I planned to stop and give them a glass of wine at a riverside pub then have them back at hotel by seven-thirty. The play at the Marlowe started at eight-thirty. The timetable should work if no one got lost, no one got upset, no one got sick or had an accident.

No one did. We were on the water at four-forty-five, enjoying the slow movement of the current and the patter from the guide on the history of Canterbury. We drifted past lawns, flower-beds, the shady beech and plane trees of Westgate Gardens, noticing the many walkers out enjoying the parks on either side.

Trinity peppered the guide with questions about what it was like here during the Second World War. He wasn't old enough to have lived through it. but he probably heard a great deal from his parents and family.

"My Gran said that the planes seem to fly overhead all day and sometimes late into the night. They dropped bombs, some of them. She had a cat that could tell the difference between our planes and the Doodlebugs—those unmanned flying bombs that the Germans fired from France. The cat would head for the closet when she heard the Doodlebugs. Everybody in the house would follow the cat."

"A lot of bombers flew over here?" Julie encouraged the guide.

I saw Julie was holding her phone toward the guide. She must be recording him.

"Nine thousand, five hundred between June and October of 1944. One day in 1940, one thousand of our planes flew over in a day."

There was silence as we tried to imagine how the people of south east England must have lived in fear.

My phone vibrated and I looked down at the text. It was Mark. "Are you still in Canterbury?"

I answered. "Yes."

"We have to come up to interview Betty Sanderson. That's where she lives now."

"Are you here?" I asked him.

"Just coming in to the city. Are you available? We could use you in the interview. The psychiatrist I consulted said I should bring a woman with me and we don't have an available female officer."

I scrambled my itinerary around in my head. "I can be available about eight-thirty tonight. That's when my group is going to a play. I could leave them at the play for a few hours."

"Okay," Mark texted. "Travis and I will get a meal, prepare for the interview and set up the time with Mrs. Sanderson. We'll pick you up at The Falstaff."

I agree to that. I was sorry to miss the play. It was Noel Coward's *Private Lives* with Patricia Hodge and Nigel Havers and I'd been looking forward to it. But I also was keenly interested in Betty Sanderson.

CHAPTER FOURTEEN

I deposited everyone at the front entrance of the Marlowe Theatre. I'd gather them after the play and take them to The Old Weaver's Restaurant close to the Great Stour River. They were anticipating the evening with pleasure. Even Richard looked interested.

"They did this play during the war years, didn't they?" Amber asked.

"They did," I said. "Noel Coward wrote it in 1930, but they were still performing it in the late thirties and the forties."

"He starred in the first production," Richard interjected quickly. "He played Elyot."

"That's right," I agreed.

"That's a long life for a play," Julie said.

"It's a good play," Richard pronounced as if he were the arbitrator of excellence in the world of theater.

It *was* a good play and I would like to see it, but Mark needed me tonight. In addition, if I was honest with myself, I was curious about Betty Sanderson and a little afraid of meeting her as well. If she'd been such a monster to Reece when he was eight years old, what was she like now?

I rushed back to Rother Manor, darted up the stairs to my room and did a quick refresh of my mascara, lipstick and blush. I grabbed a different scarf and a light sweater in case it got cool. I was ready when Mark arrived. I slid into the back seat of his unmarked, government Audi. Travis was driving; Mark occupied the front passenger seat. I fished a granola bar from my handbag and munched on it. Dinner was going to be several hours from now.

Travis parked the car at the Tower Car Park. There was no street parking on St. Peters Grove where Betty Sanderson lived. The houses were flush to the street, probably built in the nineteenth century. It was an attractive neighborhood with a green and woodland across the street and a primary school close by.

"What do you want me to do?" I asked Mark as we walked toward Number 41.

"I just want you to be there," Mark said. "The psychologist said Betty Sanderson would be more comfortable with you there and more likely to answer questions."

"What's your approach, sir?" Travis waited for instructions. Travis sounded formal. He might be nervous as well.

Mark looked at him. "I'm a bit out of my depth here. I think I'll just have to wing it."

"Do you want me to take notes?" Clearly, he wanted to know the rules he was expected would govern the interview.

"Of course," Mark said. "And ask any question you think appropriate."

I didn't think Travis would spontaneously ask anything.

The woman who answered the door was about thirty-five, short, with beautiful almost translucent skin. Her blond hair was curly and bounced around her head.

"Do come in," she said. "I'm Elizabeth Sanderson, Betty."

Mark introduced himself and Travis, then me as, "This is Claire Barclay, our consultant." That had a nice ring to it. Much better than 'my girlfriend' or even "fiancé'.

Betty shook hands with us and brought us into her lounge.

The house was beautiful. It was probably mid-nineteenth century but had been modernized. The floors were light oak, the walls a pale yellow, the woodwork painted white. The room was what estate agents called 'light and airy'. There was no fire on this hot July day but it would be a cozy room in the winter. While it wasn't an open floor plan, it felt spacious. The dining room door to the kitchen was open and I glimpsed a garden in the back.

"Do you work outside the home now?" I asked.,

Betty turned to me and smiled. "Yes, I work as a receptionist at the local doctor's surgery, Doctors MacIntosh and Bent."

"Oh, good hours," I said. My immediate thought was that it was a place where she could lay her hands on drugs. "You have children then."

"Yes. I have two: Susan who is ten and Jason who is eight. Do you have children?"

I shook my head.

"It's nice to get it over with when you're younger," she suggested. "I don't think I have the energy for babies at this point in my life."

I glanced at Mark. He didn't want this interview to be about home life and babies.

"We're investigating the murder of Reece Martin as I told you on the phone." He took control.

"That's just so shocking," she said. "Who would want to murder Reece? I know he had his problems, but he was a nice boy."

"What was he like as a child as an eight-year-old when you looked after him?" Mark asked.

"He was typical," Betty said. "He collected football cards. He had favorites and traded them at school." She looked away and half-smiled, then met Mark's eyes. "He used to lay them out for me and tell me all the statistics around those football players. He was an easy child to look after."

"Just to be sure we're talking about the same child," Mark said, "we have a picture here we would like you to identify."

Travis picked a picture from an envelope, a big eight by ten-inch picture which I assumed was Reece as a child. He handed it to Betty. She took it, looked, then handed it back.

"That's him for sure. It makes me cry. Such a lovely little boy." She reached for a tissue and wiped her eyes.

"Somebody thought so," Mark said. "He was sexually abused at that time."

Betty went perfectly still. Her mouth dropped open, and she stared at Mark. "Somebody did that to Reece?"

"Was it you?"

Her face almost drained of color. You can't fake that sudden draining of blood from the face. I worried she was going to faint, but the color came back in a slowly deepening flush.

"Absolutely not! I wouldn't have dreamed of it. It's shocking and ...and...obscene!"

"You spent a great deal of time with him in the relevant period. We need to take your fingerprints to be sure you did not visit Reece in his shed."

"What shed? What are you talking about?" Her cheeks were flaming red now. "No, you can not take my fingerprints. I'm not a suspect here. I want to help nab whoever killed Reece. That person deserves to go to jail, but that person is not me. I'm not taking any responsibility for something that happened to him when I wasn't there. I want you to leave."

She stood, so we stood. I remembered Mark telling me that when asked to leave somewhere he had to leave, unless he had a warrant. We didn't have a warrant, so Travis and I followed Mark to the door.

I stopped and turned to her. "It's the shock," I said. "If you think of anything that would help, call and ask for Mark Evans at the local constabulary."

She took a quick step backwards and slammed the door.

"You got her fingerprints on that photo," I said as we walked along the street towards the car.

"I did," Travis said, "but we can't use them at a trial. If they match anything at the shed, we can demand she give us legal fingerprints."

"She'll figure out that you took them," I said. "She's not short of sense."

Mark glanced at me. "I got that. I didn't do all that well." He looked away and was quiet for a moment. "I rushed her. I should have led her to consider suspects before I accused her." He shrugged. "Damn." He turned back to me. "What do you think about her guilt?"

I got in the car with the two of them, this time in the front passenger seat while Mark drove. Travis climbed in the back. I glanced at my mobile to make sure I had time to talk to them before my pick-up run to the theater.

"I think she was shocked, but I don't know if she was shocked because you knew about the abuse and suspected she had committed it, or she had never heard of it before and was shocked because it happened to Reece. It's hard to tell."

"She works in a doctor's office," Mark said. Betty Sanderson was still a suspect. He pulled away from the curb and headed towards Rother Manor and my van.

"Did you set up that meeting with the teacher, Travis?" Mark asked.

"Lexington," Travis said. "Yes I did, for tomorrow. At his home."

"That's good."

I turned to see Travis reading his notes. "He's married to Daphne Sinclair. He said they've been married about eight years."

"Daphne Sinclair?" Mark said. His voice sounded higher than usual.

"Do you know her?" Travis asked

"I used to." He was quiet for a moment. "She's my ex-wife—if this is the same Daphne Sinclair. Do you have a middle name?"

Travis looked at the tablet. "Dorothy."

"Must be her."

There was silence while Travis and I absorbed the information. Daphne Sinclair. Mark's wife. Divorced now. Mark had told me a bit about her, but the divorce was eleven years in the past. He didn't see her. I expect he hadn't known she lived in Kent.

Mark directed his question to Travis. "Do you think I have a conflict of interest here?"

"Maybe."

"I'd better check it out."

Mark would have to phone Superintendent Addison and ask her what he should do about it. If they had enough staff, they would take Mark off a case.

I left him with his problem. Addison would make the decision for him. I tried to stuff the idea of Mark meeting and investigating his ex-wife into a compartment of my mind to be taken out later and mulled over. Would he remember that he'd loved her once? Would he be attracted to her? I could hear my mother's voice in my head. '*Sufficient unto the day is the evil thereof.*' The old adage made sense. I would not angst about Daphne Sinclair right now. I returned to the Marlowe Theatre to pick up my group.

They had thoroughly enjoyed Noel Coward's play, the Toronto trio because it was set just before the War years and had a flavor of those times, and the others because the actors were excellent and the production well-done, fast-paced and with hilarious one-liners.

"Right nice," Howard said. "Didn't think I'd enjoy it, but I did."

Poppy laughed. "You always think a play is going to be a bore, and you always enjoy going to the theater."

"You might be right about that," Howard said agreeably.

"What about you, Richard?" I asked, daring him to contradict the group.

"It was well-directed. Very good lighting."

Faint praise was better than criticism.

We were in time for our dinner reservation at The Old Weavers Restaurant where they had a varied menu that would appeal to the women and a choice of pies: beef steak and Guinness, chicken, ham and leek, beef steak and Stilton which ought to keep the men happy. Both men wanted hearty meals that included meat.

We prolonged the evening with The Weaver's excellent beer and arrived back at Rother Manor about one in the morning. Everyone seemed mellow and happy.

In the morning, Mark phoned to tell me he was still on the case.

"There's no one to take my place, so Addison told me to stay. Daphne only met Lexington nine years ago, so she wouldn't have any knowledge of an offense committed twenty years ago."

"True," I agreed. "You'll stay on then?"

"For six more days. That's all the time I'm allotted."

"That's unreasonable." Six days? In spite of Deirdre's faith in him, that was not enough time.

"Addison runs on schedule and she ignores anything that doesn't fit that schedule, like the time it takes to collect evidence and do interviews. So whether it's reasonable or not, I have six days."

I'd love to be on the interview with Lexington and Daphne Sinclair. But in the morning we were off to Whitstable for a day of wandering in the shops and exploring the seaside town. I hoped Mark would tell me all he found out in the interview and what it was like to see his ex again.

The seashore with its beautiful pebble beach was tranquil, but the town was crowded, as many people appreciated the bathing here. I'd arranged a parking reservation close to the shore so my group wouldn't have far to walk. While it was a warm July day, the breeze off the sea cooled us enough so we weren't unbearably hot.

I gave everyone a map with some of the sites of mysteries novels marked. *The Whitstable Pearl Mysteries* by Julie Wassmer takes place at a seafood restaurant that the protagonist owns and operates. The author is also a screen writer so they could look for the TV series of the books as well as search them out in bookstores. They could have fun picking which seafood restaurant was the most likely to be the setting for this series.

Two Caravans by Marina Lewycka is set amongst the strawberry pickers in Kent, not in Whitstable. *The Birdwatcher* by William Shaw is set on the coast of Kent and is more a thriller than a cozy mystery. Howard liked thrillers, so he might like that one.

"Somerset Maugham set the last part *Of Human Bondage* in Whitstable although he called the town something else," Susan said.

I answered their questions and helped organize their time as they planned to wander through Whitstable and told them to call my mobile if they needed anything. I extracted the wheelchair and was ready to pilot Susan wherever she wanted to go. She was interested in the shops, but she was especially interested in the people: the young men in surfer shorts congregating on the beach, older women in pastel pant suits eating ices. She commented on the different dialects we heard. I enjoyed her. We met the others for lunch at Samphire. North American tourists didn't seem familiar with the vegetable samphire and were interested in the name. It's called sea asparagus in western Canada and sea beans in the U.S. and grows wild near the ocean, but they didn't seem familiar with the vegetable by any of those names. I went over what they planned for the afternoon on their exploration of the town. It was very busy in Whitstable as many tourist had the same idea we did, but it was lively and cool enough to enjoy meandering. By the time we headed home about five, they'd had a full day.

They were free this evening to find a restaurant and familiar enough with Canterbury by now to make good choices.

Mark texted me and we met at Chapman's Fish Restaurant. He escorted me upstairs where we had more privacy. I had a quick look around on the way up the stairs to see if Julie had found this restaurant, but didn't see her.

Mark ordered some white wine, my favourite Sauvignon Blanc, and handed me a menu. I took a sip of the wine and put the menu down. "What happened in your interview with Daphne?" I couldn't wait to find out how that meeting went.

He took off his new reading glasses. I do love those glasses.

"It was strange. I haven't seen her in years."

"No contact at all?"

"When I heard her mother died, I sent a wreath to the funeral, a phone call and a sympathy card. Other than that, I don't think I've had any contact in a long time."

"How did the meeting go?"

He turned to the server, exchanged the usual "Hiyas", then back to me, waited while I gave my order then gave his own.

I sipped a little more of that crisp Sauvignon Blanc. Daphne Sinclair wasn't important to him any more. I wasn't going to be silly about this.

"To start, they live in a neat two up two down terrace house on a quiet street—with parking. They each have a small car. I saw bicycles in the back hall of their house."

"Any kids?"

"No. Charles has two sons but they're grown up and don't live with him."

I wanted to ask: What does she look like now? How did you feel when you saw her? Instead I asked, "What did he have to say about Reece?"

"Daphne was in on the interview and was her usual demanding self. I didn't want her opinion, but I found it awkward to ask her to leave. Maybe I shouldn't be taking this case, but the local nick doesn't have anyone else." He took a sip of his beer. "She hadn't met Charles when Reece attended the school, so she doesn't factor into this."

"Did she tell you all that?"

"Of course she did. She must have known I knew it, but she had to make sure she had her say."

"Irritating, is she?"

"Very."

I found his attitude satisfying. I was happy to find he had no lingering attraction to her. "What did Charles Lexington have to say?"

"He said he remembered Reece. Nice boy. Quiet, good athlete and had friends. He'd been interested in botany and horticulture. His father was paying the bills and was pressuring him to go into accounting. Quite unsuitable for Reece, according to Charles."

"How did Charles deal with the father?"

"He said he was good at withstanding pressure from paying parents, that such pressure was common."

"Did you ask him about the old police complaint, the one that was unsubstantiated?"

"I did. He said it was a misunderstanding that had been satisfactorily dealt with. I had to accept that. I couldn't compel him to reveal details. He was very dignified and firm."

I thought about that for a moment. "It sounds as though you don't suspect him of being the one who assaulted Reece?

"No. That's my initial impression. He seems like a really nice guy, although that doesn't mean twenty years ago he wasn't a monster."

"Did you get his fingerprints?"

"Yes. He gave them. Daphne protested, but he just smiled at her. I think he's good for her. He didn't seem her type, but he calms her."

I accepted a plate of aromatic, steaming mussels with the accompanying melted butter and started eating. After about six delicious mussels I asked Mark, "What does Daphne do?"

He was rapidly decimating fried oysters and didn't answer for a moment. When he had emptied his plate, he said, "She manages an outdoor outfitters store in Ashford. She'd be good at that. She was always off hiking somewhere." He paused, "In a way, it was good to see her."

"It was?"

"Yes. Good to see her content or at least as content as she'll ever be. And Charles seemed to be fond of her."

"So you don't have to feel any responsibility for her."

He smiled at me. "I guess that's it. I felt relief."

I smiled as well. He definitely had a strong sense of responsibility. It's what fueled his career. It was what occasionally annoyed me. It's hard to get used to the idea that when someone loves you they also feel responsible for you. They want to protect you and care for you, but that has to be within limits. I was working out those limits with Mark.

"How long since you had any contact with her?"

"Maybe six or seven years and then just a brief phone call when her mother died. It's weird. She's such a stranger." He shivered. "I am eternally grateful you are not her."

As declaration of enduring love, it lacked substance, but at least I compared favourably.

CHAPTER FIFTEEN

Even at seven in the morning, the sun was bright. I sat on the window seat of my bedroom for a few minutes, watching the light play on the rooftop of the Marlowe Theatre and beyond it on the spires of Canterbury Cathedral. The cathedral was a site of beauty, history and even mystery as was the city, but I hoped the group had seen all they wanted of it yesterday as we didn't have any more time to explore it today. I was taking my guests to Chartwell, the home of Winston and Clementine Churchill.

We loaded all our luggage into the van as we were returning to Rye at the end of the day. I paid the bill and we headed for Chartwell at about ten. It was roughly an hour's drive to the west and a little north. I'd placed material in their goodie bags this morning: chocolate as usual, some biscuits and brochures that described different tours of Chartwell. There was the War Years Tour that Julie would probably enjoy. I put that one in Richard and Howard's bags as well. I had registered Amber and Poppy in the Artist tour and booked Heather, Trinity and Susan in the Clementine Churchill Tour. Clementine was a remarkable woman and responsible for much of Winston's success. I was going to join that tour to make sure Susan would get rest when she needed it. No one clambered for a change, which I would make if they requested it, but I had judged their interests accurately. That was a relief. I would be embarrassed if everyone wanted to go on the Warriors tour and left two guides with no tourists.

We met the three guides just inside the main door. The art tour group left us and an older woman whom I had hired from the Open University gathered up the war group. I wanted someone who understood Churchill's role in the Second World War and the National Trust didn't offer that option. This woman, a Miss MacPhee, was a retired history teacher. She was tiny, about five foot tall, thin and beamed at Julie, Richard and Howard.

"Good morning. I assume you have all heard of Winston Churchill."

"I was a kid when Churchill died," Howard said, "but I remember him. He had a powerful voice".

Miss MacPhee smiled widely. "He's considered the finest orator in the country, even in the world." she said.

"A great talker," Howard agreed.

"I am so happy to conduct this tour," she said. "Winston won the war for us, you know, and must not be forgotten."

I expect those of us on *Clementine* Churchill's tour might think she had a great deal to do with Winston's oratory and political decisions. I joined the Clementine group. A quick look around told me everyone had joined the correct group.

We toured the beautiful rooms of Chartwell. Susan did very well, managing the few stairs and using the stool I brought when she needed it. We saw Churchill's bedroom, his study and library. It was a beautiful house. We learned how Clementine made sure Winston didn't run through his money in spite of his impulsive financial decisions, and how she kept him from making rash political decisions. She wasn't always successful, but she often was. We joined the others at the café about one and gathered some pot pies to take to the outside tables.

While most were settling at the tables and some were visiting the cloakroom, I found a secluded stonewall to perch on and called Mark

"How did the interview with Malcolm and Vanessa go?"

"A bit better than last time," Mark said. "Malcolm admitted he'd been to see Reece the day he died at about four in the afternoon."

"He did?"

"So he says now. I need to find someone who saw him leave then talk to our friend Drew. He said he saw Reece at six."

"Didn't Beth come later?"

"No, earlier. At two. She was on her lunch break. Travis is going to do a timeline for us and we'll be able to checks facts a little better when we have that." He was quiet for a moment, then asked, "How are your guests doing?"

I expect Mark wanted to take his mind off the muddle of facts and evidence he was looking at.

"The visit to Chartwell is going pretty well. We have three different tours and, undoubtedly, they'll want to discuss Winston Churchill from three different points of view."

"Sounds like they're gelling as a group."

"Perhaps. Richard seems less annoying today."

Mark laughed. "Maybe you're getting used to him."

"Maybe," I agreed.

"See you tonight for dinner. "At the Hoof. Is that all right?"

"It is."

The gardens at Chartwell were spectacular. Susan, Trinity and I explored Clementine's rose garden. The roses were a bit past full glory but still beautiful. The others wandered down toward the two lakes. Susan sat on a bench and watched while Trinity and I searched along the nearby paths for roses we hadn't seen before. I studied a particularly multi-petaled rose. Trinity went back to sit beside Susan on the bench.

"This is incredible, you know," she said to Susan. "I never thought I'd be here."

"What do you mean you never thought you'd be here? Surely, with the optimism of a young woman you must feel almost anything is possible."

"Absolutely not," she said. "I grew up in the foster system near Ottawa, you know, and it wasn't kind."

There was silence while Susan absorbed that. 'Wasn't kind' probably meant it was horrible.

"That must have been difficult."

"Yeah. It was. My parents died in a car accident when I was pretty young. I was moved around and I missed a lot of school. A lot of foster parents really don't care if you go to school or not and sometimes it's a lot easier not to go. I got into a really good foster home in high school. Eileen, the foster mother there, made me go every day and once I *was* at school I could really learn. I learned enough to get into art school. But I didn't see myself traveling to England, or traveling anywhere."

"What happened to make things different?" Susan asked.

"I met Julie and then Amber. They see themselves as citizens of the world. Well…" She laughed. "They see themselves as changing the world."

"And you?"

"I can change the world a bit, maybe. The world needs changing. So why shouldn't *I* do it?"

"Why not, indeed," Susan said.

In the van on the way back to Rye, the conversation centered around the personalities of Winston and Clementine. There was quite a difference of opinion on who was more important.

"Winston Churchill," Richard pronounced, "was the greatest orator since Shakespeare and could persuade the politicians and the people of England to do what he wanted."

"He very often didn't have a good idea of what he should do," Susan said, "but Clem did. We should all be grateful she was so clever."

The argument didn't stop there of course, but it was a civil argument more like a debate, so I just let it roll.

Laura was in the foyer arranging flowers on a side table when I trailed my guests into Rother Manor. I heard her say a few words to Howard and Poppy then ask Susan how she had enjoyed her day. Laura's hands seemed steady, but she looked pale. She had those purple smudges under her eyes still and she stooped a little over the flowers as if anchoring herself to the blossoms.

"Are you alright?" I stopped and faced her.

She turned and met by eyes. "I can go for a little while without thinking of Reece. But then, suddenly, he's all I can think about. It's hard."

I reached for her hands and rubbed them, trying to convey some comfort. "Grief is so unexpected," I said, thinking about how I survived the days after my mother died. "You think you're fine, and then you're not."

"It's like that." She straightened and took on the mantle of the manager of the guest house. "How is your tour going?"

"All right, I think. Have you had any complaints about me or the tour?"

"No. No one has said anything. Has anyone complained about their meals or accommodation?"

"Not yet," I said, "but I'm expecting something from Richard."

She looks startled, then laughed. "He's one of those, isn't he?"

I glanced around quickly and lowered my voice. "He seems to be mellowing, but I can't be sure it will last."

I left Laura smiling and went on to my room. Howard and Poppy stopped me before I could open my door.

"Do you have any recommendations for a restaurant for tonight? We're not sure where to go."

I'd given everyone a list of restaurants when we'd first arrived in Rye, but either they hadn't noticed the list, or they'd lost it, or preferred not to choose.

"What kind of food do you like? I think you like meat and potatoes, Howard. Right?"

"Pretty much," Howard said.

"You'd like something little lighter?" I asked Poppy.

"That's right."

They waited at my door while I found the list of restaurants and a map of Rye. I showed them where the Union Restaurant was on East Street then pointed out the many restaurants on High Street. They should be able to find one they liked in that group.

After they left, I sent a quick text to Deirdre. "How is my wonderful dog?" I asked her.

"Still wonderful," she answered. "Eats well, sleeps well, plays with the other dogs and the kids. No worries."

"Great."

"How's your murder investigation going?"

"It's not mine."

"How is Mark's murder investigation going?"

"It's a bit muddled," I said. "Nothing's very clear."

"That's a shame. Hope you get a break soon."

She still called it *my* investigation but I disconnected without arguing with her.

I was just leaving the guest house for my meeting with Mark when Richard caught me.

"I definitely need more towels," he said. "And better towels. The ones I have are not thick enough. There should be at least three towels per person in each room."

"I'll see to it right away."

"Do that." He turned and walked away. I wondered at his need to always be in charge of something. He could have asked for towels with graciousness, but he was offensive even when asking for something simple. He made his life hard for himself. Heather was going to make it a good deal more difficult when he got home. I wonder if he even suspected she was leaving him.

I knocked on Laura's kitchen door.

"Yes?" she called.

"Richard again." I opened the door and moved just inside the kitchen; Laura was sitting at the table.

"He wants three, big, thick towels."

She rolled her eyes. "I'm on it."

"Thanks."

I walked to the Hoof Restaurant. Mark was there before me and had ordered me a small beer. He had a binder with papers in it beside him on the table. It looked as if this was going to be a business meeting. Good. I wanted to know what he'd found out today. I was grateful Travis had a wife and family to go home to because I got more time with Mark.

"How did your interview with Malcolm Martin go today?" I asked him as I was sitting down.

"Let's order first, *cariad*."

I contain my curiosity while I made the choice of a haddock burger with a side of coleslaw and Mark ordered a sirloin steak with potatoes and carrots. I took a sip of the beer then a couple of more sips and let the tension ease from my shoulders.

After the waiter disappeared, I asked Mark again. "What did you find out today?"

He took a long drink of his dark beer and sighed with satisfaction.

"I found out Malcolm Martin and his wife Vanessa Clark live in a very nice plot of land in a gentleman's house with barns, fences, horses in the paddock and dogs—three of them—in the house. There's money there."

"He's is a dentist," I said. "He would be making good money."

"And she's a veterinarian," Mark said. "Cats."

"What do you mean cats?"

"She just looks after cats, but I think she also inherited money. She wasn't with us very long. Came in, said hello, asked if we wanted coffee and then left."

He smiled at me. "I was glad she left because it's a little awkward to ask a man about his former love and family in front of his new wife."

Mark had just been through that awkward time where he was faced with his old love in front of her new one. Perhaps he saw some parallels and sympathized with Martin.

"You said Martin saw Reece on the day he died."

"In the afternoon. He said he felt a little guilty for not supporting Reece when he was in so much trouble. Then Reece approached him for tuition money for his horticultural course. He felt he should pay for that. Reece was trying to be normal, live a decent life. But he still didn't want Reece anywhere near his kids."

"So that was why he went to visit him?"

"So he says."

"Do you believe him?"

"Well, he gave me a good reason." Mark looked away for a moment, then took another sip of his beer. "There was the check he wrote for the tuition money. It substantiates his reason for visiting Reece that day. He said Reece had to have the money by the following morning so he felt it imperative to drop it off and not put it in the mail."

"That makes sense."

We stopped talking as a waiter delivered our meals. It always amazes me when my fish burger and Mark's steak arrive hot at the same time. I know restaurants do this all the time, but it still surprises me. I suppose it's because I don't cook much at all and certainly wouldn't manage to get two different meals hot at the same time.

When Mark had finished his steak and got the last bit of gravy off the plate, he opened the binder that was beside him. "I asked Travis to make a timeline of who Reece saw on that last day."

That would suit Travis. He liked meticulous detail.

"He did a good job. Have a look." Mark turned the binder toward me.

Travis had constructed a graph with the time along the bottom and little figures inserted above the time they said they visited.

"Laura came over at noon."

"She says she left some muffins for him but didn't stay."

I looked up. "Any collaboration on that?"

He shook his head. "She doesn't have CTV at the back, just at the front and side."

"Then Bethany Williams, the girlfriend." I put my finger on the figure representing her. "She arrived at two and left at two-fifteen."

"They had a quick lunch together. She used the side path, so she is on the CTV. The time is right."

I moved my finger along the graph. "This must be Malcolm. He said he arrive about four?"

"Four-fifteen, according to the CTV."

"And left at?"

"Five. He said he had tea and biscuits with Reece. His wife says he was home at six. She noted the time because she was waiting for him to come home so she could get the sitter. They were going out."

"No nanny?" I said. They sounded rich enough to be able to afford one.

"They have an *au pair* girl but she's gone home to France for a holiday."

I looked at the last figure. Travis had given him a dunce cap. "Must be the friend."

"Drew Jones. Travis shouldn't prejudice our thinking with that dunce cap."

"It's not a professional assessment." I didn't see why a little bit of opinion shouldn't enliven the chart.

"No, but it influences our thinking. Put a dunce cap on him and people will discount him. Many people can be slow but still cunning."

Mark would be careful not to dismiss a suspect too early. "He arrived at eight and left at ten-thirty. Did they have anything to eat or drink?"

"Drew said Reece gave him a couple of beers, but only drank tea himself."

"Hmm." Reminded, I drank the last of my beer. "That seems strange. Do you think it's the truth?"

"Maybe. If Reece was not using, he might have been avoiding any drugs including alcohol."

Drew interested me. "Drew might be terminally stupid, as Travis thinks, but he may be able to follow directions well. If someone said, put this pill in your mate's tea, or offer him these doctored biscuits, he might be well able to do that."

Mark nodded. "If he was on drugs himself, he might need to keep his suppliers happy."

"Anyone might have given him directions, not just a supplier. All they needed to do was convince Drew to do it. And Drew was the last visitor we know about."

"True enough." He closed the file and reached for the bill. "Come on. I'll walk you home."

My group had congregated in the lounge and were sipping tea and eating biscuits. It was the English experience. I expected a few flasks had juiced up some of that tea.

"I'll just give Laura a quick update," Mark said.

"She'll likely be in the kitchen." I gestured toward the back of the house and he knocked on the door.

"Have some tea," Susan offered. She was in charge of the large teapot. I passed her my cup and joined them.

"Milk or lemon?" Susan inquired.

I laughed. I'm sure she didn't have tea that way in her home country, but she was enjoying English traditions.

Mark return from speaking with Laura and paused to wave a goodbye.

"Come and sit yourself down," Howard said. "Don't be a stranger. You can have a cup of tea."

I was convinced Howard had imbibed much more than tea.

"Do join us," Poppy seconded the invitation. "We were just talking about the death of Laura's son. Such a tragedy."

"Do you have the perp in custody?" Richard demanded.

"Not yet," Mark said. He refused the tea but did join us. Mark had experience with my past guests. He knew they were intellectually interested in murder and would no doubt offer to solve the case for him. He also knew mystery novel fans were gratified when they met a real Detective Inspector, and that added richness to my tour, so he was patient.

"We were thinking you should look at old loves." Julie leaned forward.

"Someone who didn't like being dumped by him," Amber suggested.

"A woman scorned and all that," Trinity interjected, "or a man scorned." She added the afterthought.

"Do you have a lot of murders?" Julie asked.

"In England, you mean?"

"Yes."

"Our homicide rate is low, about 1.1 per thousand, but we haven't accurate records on *why* people kill."

"In Canada, our homicide rate is 1.76 per thousand," Julie said. I shouldn't be at all surprised that the readers of mysteries knew the crime statistics.

"Ours is 5 per thousand which ought to give us statistics on motivation," Susan said.

"Oh, motivation," Richard interjected. "That's the bases of Shakespeare's plays and, of course, Christie's too. Motivations are the same the world over: greed, love, hate."

"The seven deadly sins," Trinity insisted. "Pride, envy, greed, lust, anger, gluttony and sloth."

We all turned to her.

She shrugged. "Some of those nun's rants stuck with me."

We considered the sins.

"Not sloth," Amber said. "You'd be too lazy to carry out a plan."

"Gluttony is unlikely. I can't see anyone killing to get more food." Heather said.

"Unless they didn't have any," Trinity said.

"Then it wouldn't be gluttony." Amber said.

"Oh, true." Trinity sat back.

"That leaves five to be going on with. Lots of scope there." Mark stood. "A pleasure to meet you. Enjoy your stay."

I stood as well and escorted him to the door, then down the stairs and under the trees for a good night kiss.

He murmured endearments in Welsh, I understood *Rwy'n dy garu d* as 'I love you'. It sounds more poetic in Welsh than it does in English. I caught *enaid*. That means 'beloved'.

"Mmm." I felt like a cat, adored and content.

"I like your guests," Mark said, playing with strands of my hair. "For the most part, they are nice folks."

I honed in on what constituted 'nice'. "No murderers."

"Just so," he said.

CHAPTER SIXTEEN

We began the tenth day of the tour with a breakfast of eggs, fried tomatoes, sausages, beans, scones and coffee. That ought to keep us satisfied for a while. We were going to Hastings, a seaside resort with a castle, museums, art galleries, shops and ancient history that goes back over a thousand years

I'd been up earlier to clean the van and replace items in their goodie bags. I'd filled their bags but, instead of chocolate, I'd given them some rock candy which was a typical English seaside treat, a map of Hastings with the bookstores, museums and art galleries marked on it, a pass to the West Hill Cliff Railway, information brochures and some vouchers for several ice cream and confectionary shops. The temperature was forecasted to rise in the afternoon and my guests would need to be hydrated and as cool as possible.

"Can we swim?" Trinity asked me.

"You can but the water is quite cold."

"But thousands do swim?"

I agreed they did, although I wasn't one of them. Too cold for me.

"No sharks, though." Amber reassured Trinity.

Hastings is a holiday resort town and near enough to London that it is a popular day trip destination. There would be thousands of people there. Luckily, the roads were wide and the car parks plentiful. I'd booked a tour of St. Clements Caves, an original smuggler's cove of the eighteenth century.

It was used more recently during the Second World War as an air-raid shelter when the German bombs were devastating the town. There had been no anti-aircraft guns installed here until October, 1940 and, even then, it was a hard town to defend because the enemy planes could approach from the sea or over the flat land all around.

We left Rye at nine-twenty and were at the ocean in Hastings by nine-forty-five. We were ahead of most of the day trippers so the streets were quiet and the view breathtaking.

"The English Channel, right?" Amber said with satisfaction in her voice.

"The very one," I agreed.

She grinned. "I can't believe I'm really here."

"France is twenty miles away." Julie stared over the blue water, calm today, as if she could conjure the beaches of Normandy. They were fascinated by the nearness of France. Canada bordered the United States but, other than that one country, oceans separated it from the rest of the world. Perhaps this channel seemed a small separation to them. Brought up in England I was used to thinking of it as a formidable barrier.

I drove them through the town giving them a potted history of Hastings, particularly the Battle of Hastings in 1066 between the armies of King Harold and William the Conqueror. I kept it brief. My main purpose in the tour of Hastings was to orientate them so they would not waste time and energy in getting lost. Misplacing a tourist was one of my nightmares.

"Hastings has a Norman castle, a medieval old town and many Victorian buildings. There is lots to look at."

I parked at the Pelham Car Park, unloaded the wheelchair and escorted everyone to the West Hill Cliff Railway. This is a funicular railway that would take us up to the castle ruins and St. Clements caves. The lack of apostrophe bothered me but I've given up protesting that omission.

"St. Clements Caves were used during the war to hide from the many enemy bombers that pummeled Hastings," I told them.

"They were used by smugglers before that." Julie read from one of the brochures I'd put in her goodie bag.

"It's worth a visit," I said. "You have a voucher for it in your bag."

Although some of the trip in the funicular is in a tunnel, the view when we rose into the clear air was magnificent. I heard the ping and click of cameras and mobiles while they captured the scene,

Susan and I would not go into the caves, as the ground was uneven and it would be a rough ride in the wheelchair. I gathered the other guests around me before they went in and made sure they all knew where Teddy's Beach Diner was and how to get there in case they didn't meet me for the return ride.

"We'll meet at one p.m. at the base of the funicular for the ride to the restaurant," I said. "Please try to be on time as I have a reservation and it can get quite crowded. If you are going to make your own way to Teddy's, please text me that information." I didn't want to wait a half-hour for someone who was already at the other end of town.

"Where are *you* going?" Richard asked. He might think I had sloughed him off onto an inferior attraction while Susan and I were enjoying something luxurious.

"Susan and I will walk along the shore and look at the boats. You are welcome to join us." I said that as graciously as I could, hoping he would reject the offer.

He did. "I'll go into the caves, although I expect they will be tawdry."

"Fun, though, Richard," Julie leaned over to whisper. "Maybe even dramatic. You might get some ideas for production here."

"That's true." Richard brightened and started for the entrance. I saw Heather give Julie a smile of thanks. We all treated Richard as if he were perpetually twelve years old and badly brought up.

I trundled Susan in the wheelchair along the Hastings Seafront. Behind us hundreds of people crowded the beach, intent on getting as much sun and sea bathing as they could. Beside us, the carnival spewed raucous sounds: competing tunes from amusement rides, the screams of those on the roller coaster and the chug of the machinery that drove all the equipment. Smells drifted over us as well: popcorn, chocolate, fried onions and fish.

Once we left the carnival behind, we appreciated the sight of the many fishing boats that remained on the sand when the tide receded.

"This is Europe's largest beach-launched fishing fleet," I told Susan.

"Impressive." We paused for a moment to stare at the boats.

"There is a Lifeboat station here." She gestured to the large building on the edge of the sea walk. There were no boats in front of it—all rescue craft were inside the building—and the sand between the center and the sea was open, devoid of fishing boats or any debris so the rescuers had a clear path to the water.

"That's one of the many Royal National Lifeboat Institution stations."

"I've heard about the RNLI."

"It's a charity staffed mostly by volunteers." It was a popular charity.

"Like a volunteer search and rescue organization."

"Just so" I agreed.

We moved on, taking our time, to the Museum of Contemporary British Art. We didn't stay there long as the art didn't appeal to Susan, although she found the textile exhibit interesting.

"I can see why Trinity is fascinated by fabric." She admired a beautiful wall mural made of a collage of hundreds of pieces of fabric in tones of blue, turquoise and green with some splashes of black and bright yellow.

"It gives the impression of an underwater garden, like an abstract painting." She contemplated it for some minutes.

Back at the van, I helped Susan into her seat, stored the wheelchair and waited for the others. They all arrived. No one had wandered away. They loaded into the van and I drove them to St. Leonard's which is nestled under the cliff on the west side of Hastings. The beach wasn't as crowded as Hastings Beach and Teddy's Beach Diner was the experience of a proper English fish and chip shop with a variety of pub food. We sat outside where we could enjoy the warm sun and fresh air.

"Nice," Heather said as she looked around at the bathers in the sea and the many umbrellas and deck chairs dotting the sand.

I waited for Richard to contradict her. I realized the three young women were also watching him. He didn't disappoint.

"I'll get sand in my food out here. We should sit inside."

"You might get attacked by sand," Julie said. She leaned back and peered onto the shop. "There's one stool left at the bar. Why don't you go inside?"

"I'll do that." Richard stood and disappeared into the diner.

There was a brief silence, then Heather buried her face in her menu and started to laugh. Everyone joined in, but no one made any comment.

I sorted them out for their afternoon exploration of Hastings. The trio asked Susan to accompany them. Richard joined us at the coffee stage and I handed him information so he could choose his afternoon's activities. I felt a little sorry for him. No one wanted to spend time with him. He was, as my mother would say, his own worst enemy.

I deposited them in the center of town, made sure everyone knew where we were going to meet and at what time, extracted the wheelchair and passed it over to Trinity. I parked the van in a commercial spot I'd booked ahead of time close to the seashore. When everyone had dispersed, I found an empty bench that overlooked the sea and sat.

First, I texted Deirdre. She recognized my number and was swift and succinct.

"I'm working. Gulliver is fine."

I disconnected.

I tried Mark next. He didn't answer the text but called me.

"Are you back in town for dinner tonight?"

"No. We're staying in Hastings. I'll be back about ten."

"I'll come to your guest house." He paused for a moment. "Maybe stay over."

I felt a sudden rush of pleasure. That suited me. I much preferred him in my bed than a block away. He must not suspect Laura any more.

I stayed on the bench in the sunshine for a few minutes longer then went into the shops to replenish my supply of chocolate and buy some souvenirs of Hastings to add to the goodie bags tonight. I managed to find a new Sussex mystery writer in Waterstones, Richard Smiraldi. The book was *Seven Murders in Sussex*. I'd read it before I recommended it. Seven murders was excessive.

Everyone except Poppy and Howard arrived at six. I texted Poppy.

"So sorry," she answered. "We are near La Belle Restaurant. Why don't we meet you there?"

I agreed to do that and drove the rest of the group along the seaside.

I escorted them to the crowded restaurant. Servers snaked through the diners who were sitting, standing and generally impeding the delivery of orders. The beer was flowing and the casually-dressed beach crowd was loud. I took my group up the stairs to a reserved table in a quieter part of the restaurant where I'd arranged the set menu to limit the choices and the discussion around the food. Once everyone had their menus in front of them, I slipped down to the sidewalk to wait for Howard and Poppy.

"So sorry." Poppy rushed up to me. "We found The True Crime Museum. It's on Trinity Street really close to here. Does Trinity know about it?"

"Let's ask her," I said and herded them up the stairs to join the others.

"Did you get to The True Crime Museum?" Poppy burst out with the question as she sat down. "Trinity, you must go. It's on your street."

"We did," Trinity said. "Lots of things are named after me." She laughed.

Poppy agreed. "Even a university in Ireland."

"True?" Trinity asked.

"True," Poppy affirmed.

The food was elaborate and delicious. The wine flowed and everyone seemed to be happy with their experiences of the day.

Mark was sitting in his car when I drove into the Rother Manor car park. I escorted my guests inside. Laura was waiting and offered tea and coffee. No one accepted her invitation. They had the makings for tea and coffee in their rooms and probably were looking forward to some privacy after being together all day.

"Thanks anyway, Laura." I appreciated her effort.

"It's fine," Laura said,. "As long as they're happy."

"I think so," I said. "Mark is outside. I'd like to bring him in."

"To see me?" She looked tired, perhaps thinking he wanted to interview her again.

"No, to stay with me."

I knew she would find it hard to refuse—I brought her business—but it was polite to ask.

"It's fine. You're a couple, right? Why didn't he stay with you before?"

"I'm not sure," I lied. I didn't want to say 'because he was investigating you'.

"It's fine with me. There'll be a charge."

"That's expected. No problem."

Before I could go outside to invite Mark in, the Toronto trio tripped down the stairs.

"We're looking for a pub," Amber said. She turned to Laura. "We'd like one with music. What do you recommend?"

Laura thought for a moment then said, "The Globe Inn Marsh, Ypres Inn and the Ship Inn. All should have music."

"And all are within walking distance, but call if you need a ride home," I added.

"We'll be good," Julie said.

"Define 'good'," I heard Amber say.

I didn't hear her answer. I followed them out but stopped at the top of the steps. They glanced back and waved as they entered the street and then they were gone. I gestured to Mark and he joined me on the steps.

"I want to stay over, are you okay with that, *cariad*?"

"More than okay. I told Laura you might."

"I can, She's off my suspect list."

I wanted to hear about that.

CHAPTER SEVENTEEN

The guest house was quiet as Mark and I climbed the stairs. Mark slung his knapsack onto the bed while l cleared a space on the table for his briefcase. I recognized he was still focused on the case. When he was a detective sergeant he told me, he'd always felt scattered, investigating many cases at the same time and responding to requests and orders from several inspectors. Now that he was an inspector, he had the luxury of honing in on one case—at least until the superintendent's time allotment ran out which was two days from now. That was pressure. I knew he hadn't noticed the soft colors of the linens in the room, or the intimate light cast by the lamp. My engagement ring gleamed and sparkled. I suppressed a sigh. I could wait. Besides I had questions.

Mark flicked on the light above the table, pulled his tablet and some papers from his briefcase and sat down. He handed me his mobile and charger and I put his and mine side-by-side on the end table. That looked intimate. I wondered if anyone had ever written a poem about the significance of matching mobiles.

"Sit with me, *enaid*." He gestured to the chair beside him.

I sat. "First, love, I assume you are staying here now because Laura is no longer a suspect. Tell me about that."

He smiled. "I'm staying because I desperately want to, but yes, she's no longer a suspect. She accounted for her time with witnesses. Angela was with her when she was in the house and she had witnesses for her errands outside the house. It is remotely possible she poisoned her son but not likely."

"Thank you."

"*Croeso.*"

I should go online and learn more Welsh words. I knew *enaid* meant dear or love, but I needed more vocabulary than endearments which is what I heard from Mark when he was feeling affectionate or swear words which I heard when he was surprised or annoyed.

Mark looked up. "I need to talk to you about two things: the toxicology report and the time line. Will you put your sharp brain on this, or are you too tired?"

I checked my energy level. "I can manage a half-hour or so."

"Good." He scrolled down on his tablet, clicked a few buttons and read from the report. "Cause of death. Nembutal overdose."

"Flynn didn't think it was common on the street." I remembered that from his conversation in Laura's kitchen.

"Not a street drug. Not commonly used. It's a barbiturate, phenobarbital. It used to be prescribed for anxiety but hasn't been used on people for about twenty years."

"Not used on people any more," I repeated. "So, what is it used on?"

"Animals."

I thought for a moment. "So either someone had some at the back of their cupboards or someone took it from an animal surgery."

"Or it's becoming the next street drug and something we are going to see again."

"Can you check with HOLMES to see if there is any data on it?" The new data information bank was cumbersome when it was first set up, but it was useful now. The name was apt as Sherlock Holmes was noted for collecting details.

"I'll check."

While Mark did that, I plugged in the kettle and prepared tea for us. Laura had left some macaroons and chocolate biscuits which I set out.

"Ta," Mark said absently as he pulled his cup closer, still reading from the screen.

I sipped my tea, a light lemony white tea. Delicious. I pulled my attention back to the HOLMES report.

"No reports of this drug."

"None."

"Nembutal," I mulled aloud. "From an old cupboard or from a veterinarian's surgery."

We looked at each other. "Vanessa," we said together.

"I'll have to interview her again."

We were quiet, then, "No motive," I said.

"True. Not one I've found, in any case."

"What about Charles Lexington?"

"He has an alibi. It seems he was invigilating exams all day and had a faculty meeting in the evening and no fingerprints of his turned up in the shed."

"Daphne will be pleased."

"She was."

"Did she phone you to thank you?"

"She phoned me to berate me for considering him a suspect in the first place."

I smiled at his exasperated tone and thought from what he'd told me Daphne would never be completely happy.

Mark leaned back in his chair and stretched his arms wide, shook his shoulders to relax his muscles then glanced at his tablet. "Help me work out a time line."

"Who did what when?"

"Yes. Reece was working in the communal gardens in the morning. Jas found a witness, a jogger who saw him. Laura visited him at noon. She said she took him some muffins left over from breakfast.

"Just a minute." I extracted some paper and a pen from my pile of supplies and sat back down. "How long did she stay?"

"Twenty minutes." Mark read from his tablet. I knew he had it written down, but I wanted a visual. I wrote on my paper, "Laura. Noon. 20 min."

"Reece was alive after Laura left because Beth arrived at the shed at two on her lunch break."

"Did Reece talk to her?"

"Yes, he told her his mum had brought three muffins and he'd eaten two, He made her tea, and they shared the third muffin."

"Nothing in the muffin then?"

"No, couldn't be, as Beth had no after effects. She said he was filling out the application for the horticultural course. His mum was going to borrow the money to pay for it. Beth said he felt badly about taking the money, but his mum had convinced him it was best. Beth agreed and said she was happy he was doing something positive for himself."

"How long did she stay?"

"Fifteen minutes. Her lunch break was only a half-hour."

That piece of information made me grateful my job allowed for long lunches, often with excellent food and wine.

"Who was next?"

"Malcolm. He arrived at four."

"Did anyone see him?"

"The surveillance camera. He was the one we couldn't identify on first viewing. He arrived carrying a briefcase. He said he stayed about a half-hour. He gave Reece the check for the tuition. The application form was on the table and he made the check out for the tuition."

I could imagine it: Reece sitting at the table with the completed application form. His father leaning over to take the correct name of the institution from the form to put on the check.

"After all this time, why did he offer to help him now?"

"He was honest about that, even though it made him look like a selfish jerk. He said Vanessas insisted. It seems she felt he was morally obligated to help Reece even though he didn't feel that way himself. 'It kept peace in the house' was how he put it which was more honest than his first explanation."

"That he felt guilty?"

"*Ei*."

Aye. Yes. Welsh again. "He won't win any awards for Father of the Year, that one."

Mark raised his eyebrows. "He said the conversation was civil and he left Reece in good spirits."

"Did anyone see Reece after that?"

"Drew. His friend Drew. He came by about eight and stayed for over two hours, according to the surveillance camera."

I added Drew to my list. "What did Drew have to say?"

"I need to interview him again because he said very little."

"He stayed for quite some time. What did they talk about? What did they do? Did Drew sell him some drugs? Did they do drugs together and Reece got a contaminated batch?"

"Good questions. I don't know. I'll see what I can find out tomorrow."

He shut down his tablet and put it on its own charger for the night. He placed the papers into his briefcase and shut it, then turned to me and shed the officer of the law for the lover. "Come to bed, *cariad*."

I smiled. "Good idea."

"We'll talk about marriage soon, won't we?"

"Soon," I agreed. "Just not tonight." I was going to have to consider it. I was willing to be perpetually engaged, but Mark wasn't.

Later as I was drifting off to a contented sleep, I had a sudden thought, "Mark." I pushed his shoulder.

"Wot's up?" he said sleepily.

"In that toxicology report, was there any food in Reece's stomach?"

Mark swung his feet over the side of the bed, shook his head and walked over to the table. I saw the tablet glow. He was silent for a few minutes then came back to bed. He pulled the duvet over us and lay down in the warm nest we'd created. "Just peach pie."

I was silent for a moment then said, "But, Mark, where did he get the peach pie?"

My question hung in the air, getting no response. Mark hadn't heard me as he'd fallen asleep. The question coasted on the edge of consciousness all night. I posed it to Mark again in the morning

"I'm meeting Travis for breakfast and I'll get him on that." He gave me a quick kiss and was gone.

Today was Day 12 of the tour. So far I'd managed to give my guests a full agenda and they seemed happy, except, of course, Richard, but I wasn't hoping for the impossible.

We bypassed Ashford and headed north and slightly west to The Kent and Sussex Tea and Coffee Company factory. I'd arranged a short tour of the plant with a guide to explain the different types of tea. They had many different kinds of coffee as well, but I wanted to concentrate of tea as a quintessentially English phenomenon. I know tea is drunk in many other countries but tourists associate it with England, and we do drink a lot of it.

My group lingered in the store after the tour and bought both tea and coffee and the usual souvenir fridge magnets and tea towels. I bought several packages of tea for myself and Deirdre.

"She let us taste the tea," Trinity enthused as we loaded back into the van. "I bought this," She shoved her package at me.

I read the label. 'St. Clements Tea'. No apostrophe.

"It tastes like flowers," she said. I'd have to try that one but I might have to come back to the factory to get it. Not all their product went out to restaurants, cafés and groceries.

I activated the mic as I drove them through the green and yellow farmland of Kent. "There is hardly a British mystery novel that doesn't include tea," I began.

"For sure," Heather agreed. "Rhys Bowen has Georgiana looking for tea in many books, particularly the first ones where she is so poor."

"I wonder how many plots used poison in the tea? They must have used a stronger flavored tea to cover the taste." Julie was likely thinking of the plot of her latent novel.

I mentioned a few novels and the women kept up a lively discussion. I drove them to The Village Tea Rooms in Headcorn, about twenty minutes away from the tea factory for the High Tea lunch I'd reserved. It was everything high tea should be: three kinds of crustless sandwiches, scones, clotted cream and raspberry jam, a tiered collection of sweets and a vast selection of tea.

I allowed an hour-and-a-half after lunch for them to explore the town of Headcorn. I'd placed maps in their goodie bags that indicated, bookshops, museums and the aerodrome where there was a display of old aircraft. I expected the men and Julie to want to go there. Julie seemed the most committed to their novel and to the history of World War II.

Mark texted me as we were leaving the tea room. "Meeting with Drew Jones four p.m. I'll pick you up."

I answered him. "That should work."

I was keen to be part of this interview. Maybe Drew brought that peach pie. Somebody did unless Reece bought it himself. Or did he bake it? I had no idea if he could make pies.

"What are we doing this afternoon and evening?" Richard demanded as we unloaded at Rother Manor.

It was a beautiful, warm afternoon. I'd stopped in the guest house car park and, when the engine died so did the air conditioner. The contrast between my airconditioned van and the heat radiating off the stones in the car park was uncomfortable.

"Follow me into the lounge," I said as I got up from my seat. "It will be more comfortable there." We caught up to the others.

I extracted tickets from my knapsack. "Here are your tickets for the boat ride this afternoon. It leaves at three so you have a half-hour to change clothes or freshen up and join me in the lounge."

"Are we all going?" Richard asked.

"Susan and I are not accompanying you. You will have a competent, company guide with you," The boat tour was on a Zodiac which smacked the waves when it was moving fast. That would be physically hard on Susan. In any case, the tour company wouldn't take anyone with osteoporosis for fear such rough impacts would break fragile bones. I didn't owe Richard that explanation.

"What are you going to do?" He turned to Susan.

He was less interested in Susan's activity and more interested in assuring himself her activity wasn't more favored than the boat trip.

"I'm going to a pottery," she said.

"Hey, take pictures," Trinity said. "Especially of the glazing. If they let you".

I had talked to Susan about this over email before she arrived and had arranged a private workshop for her. She was going to make a pot. Perhaps they would allow her to take pictures of the process.

"Maybe I should do that. Go with Susan." Richard showed no concern over how I was going to manage such a change of plans.

"You'll miss going to Dover and Eastbourne," Heather said, reading from her ticket, "but that's fine with me."

That convinced Richard. "No. No. I'll go on the boat trip." Heather had skill in managing Richard. He was going to get into a right mess without her.

I delivered them to the boat tour company and a bespoke trip up the coast at a moderate rate of speed. Howard and Poppy were older and might not enjoy a fast ride. I handed over the hamper I'd asked Laura to prepare so my group, who were the only ones on this excursion, would have snacks, a couple of bottles of wine and some sweets.

Susan and I waved them off, then I took Susan to the Rye Pottery where she was welcomed.

I gave her a taxi voucher. "Just call them when you are ready to return to the guest house. I have a meeting this afternoon."

"Now what are you up to?" She cocked her head and looked expectant.

"I'm joining Mark in his interview."

"Ah. Tell me what you can this evening. I'm most interested." Her words were conventional, but her eyes danced with curiosity.

I grinned at her. I wouldn't be able to tell her anything because the interview would be confidential, but I truly appreciated her lively interest. I hoped I'd be that involved in life when I was her age.

I had time to change my capris for a summer dress and grab a light shawl. I was waiting on the steps when Mark drove into the car park.

"Hi, Travis," I said as I climbed into the back seat.

"Ma'am." Travis acknowledged me.

That's what he would call a superior female officer. I didn't merit it. I saw the edge of Mark's mouth twitch. Was he comparing me to his superintendent, the sour-faced Marjorie Addison? She ran the constabulary better than the previous Superintendent Owen, but she was not a friendly woman.

"Where are we meeting Drew?"

"At the Martello, sea side." Mark drove the short ten-minute trip to Rye Harbour and the Martello tower. He parked the car on the adjacent road and we hiked the short distance to the tower. Unlike other historic sites, this one had nothing to attract tourists. It was neglected with ivy growing over the mossy stones and brambles around the base. The locals called it the 'Enchantress'. I couldn't see why it deserved the name.

I *could* see why they built the tower here. It was on a knoll with a view to the south of acres of fields. When this was built in the early 1800s, it would have overlooked the sea at the mouth of the Rother River.

Mark strode past the tower toward some bushes at the edge of a field. I spotted a figure sitting on a rock near a wall. A bicycle lay on the ground nearby. He stood when we got closer, and I recognized him from our earlier meeting when he'd tried to run away from Mark and Travis and from the funeral. He had dark hair, dark eyebrows, and stubble on his chin. He slouched as if trying to shrink his six-foot height.

"Afternoon, Drew," Mark said. "Thanks for making time for this meeting."

"S'alright. Reece was a good mate."

Mark sat on the wall beside Drew. Travis stood a few feet away. He held his notebook and pen.

I sat on the other side of Mark but also a few feet away.

Drew looked at us, glanced around at the bushes then back to Mark. "Can you be quick?"

"You don't want any of the gang to see you."

I expected Drew chose Rye Harbour because gang members were unlikely to come here. If they did, we would be able to see them from quite a distance.

Drew was silent, then said, "I'm here, aren't I? Get on with it."

"Right," Mark said. "You visited Mark about six o'clock on the evening he died. What was he doing?"

Drew looked away as if conjuring a memory. "He was sitting at his little table. He'd been filling out his application to that college so he could learn more about plants. It was finished, printed out nice and just lying there on the table. His old man had left him a check to pay for it. Made out to the College, so Reece couldn't buy anything with it."

"Like drugs, you mean."

"Yeah."

Mark suspected Drew was Reece's supplier, so it made sense Drew would notice where Reece got his income.

"He was still using then?"

Drew shifted a look sideways at Mark and looked away again. He must have found some reassurance because he kept talking. "Not much. A little, mostly on the weekends. It's hard to just quit, you know."

"I know," Mark agreed.

I'd heard it was *extremely* hard to simply quit.

"Cold turkey can kill ya, you know. Me and Mark went to NA together but it was the same old stories and the same stuff that didn't work for us. We were going to go to rehab together. New rehab program. We were both going to try it. Said his old man was going to help but he always thought that—and the bastard never did. Maybe Reece would make it this time."

Drew stared out over the salt flats. We were quiet, waiting. I heard the rolling chatter of a blue tit but I didn't see it. Drew shrugged and continued. "He was starting to talk more. He liked his job. Liked digging and planting. Another thing his old man *didn't* like. Reece was supposed to be a solicitor or a numbers man like a banker, not a guy who worked with his hands. My guv wants me to be someone important who makes a lot of money too, but he doesn't go on about it. Reece's dad did."

"So that was pressure on Reece."

"He was used to it."

I felt a wave of sadness for these two lost young men who tried Narcotics Anonymous, a group that helped addicts deal with their feelings but doesn't give rehab drugs or therapy. It seemed the health care system had abandoned them.

"Had he had supper?"

Drew turned his head back toward Mark. "He had. That sucked 'cause it was early enough and I hoped he'd have some food for me, but he said he'd only had muffins all day and got hungry early. He'd eaten already."

"So you didn't get anything to eat there?"

"I didn't say that." Drew's voice was sharp. "He had a pie he was going to eat later and he gave me half of it."

"What kind of pie?"

"What? What does it matter what kind of pie? It was peach and it was good."

"You ate it later."

"Yes, I ate it later. Reece was generous like that but said he wanted to eat his pie with tea before he went to bed so I took my half and left."

"Did you eat it at home?"

"No I didn't. I'm not like Reece, not generous I mean. If I took it home my old man would take it. I ate it at the park."

Travis wrote something in his notebook.

Drew looked from Mark to Travis and back. "What's this about the pie? What was the matter with the pie?" His voice rose.

"It was poisoned."

Drew stared at Mark. "No."

"We think so."

"Streuth! I ate that half. I didn't die."

"That might just be luck," Mark said.

"For me. Not for Reece." I didn't find Drew at all stupid. He'd seen the importance of the pie very quickly.

"Where'd he get the pie?" I had to know.

Drew looked at me for the first time since his initial glance.

"Do I answer her? Is she a cop?"

"You can answer me. Where did he get the pie?"

Drew shook his head. "I never asked. His mum, I thought. Her and that Angela can bake."

"Did he say that Laura or Angela brought him the pie?"

"No. He didn't say. I didn't ask."

"Was it store-bought or home-made." I wanted to know that.

Drew sat back and looked away. Finally, he said, "I think it was store-bought. I didn't think about that before, but yeah, it was store-bought. Good, though. The peaches weren't mushed together, still in big pieces and juicy. It was a good pie."

I looked at Drew. He was staring in front of him and a tear ran down his cheek. He sniffed and looked away. "Shit," he said. "He was a good mate."

"Drew," Mark said. "Stop dealing. We're thinking about laying murder charges on dealers." The police in general weren't, but Mark was.

Drew rolled his eyes back, then shook his shoulders. He looked around wildly. "I got to get out of here. If anyone sees me, I could get offed." He grabbed his bike and threw his leg over the bar. He paused and looked at Mark.

"You could get it too, cop. They don't like dibbies." And he was gone.

I looked at Mark, realizing how dangerous his job was. By talking to Drew he'd draw the attention of whatever gang Drew was mixed up in. I imagined a target on Mark's jacket, a bright yellow bull's eye. I shuddered. I knew his job put him in danger and I understood that, but Drew's fear made that possibility too real. Loving Mark meant I might lose him

Drew left quickly, mounted his bike and pedaled away home. He hadn't wanted to be seen with Mark or Travis.

"How likely are you to be hit by his gang?" I was still worrying about danger to Mark.

"No more likely than usual." Mark shrugged. "I don't see anyone around, no drones, no cars parked on the street. Drew's a little paranoid."

"Or careful," Travis said.

I spared a thought for Drew. "Poor guy."

CHAPTER EIGHTEEN

"A killer can cry and show sadness and still have done the deed," Mark reminded me as we climbed into his Audi.

I knew that but I felt a wave of pity for Drew. He had cared for Reece and it showed.

"He's still a small cog in the local drug dealings." Travis pegged Drew as insignificant. "I suppose he could have been told to poison Reece, but no one would trust him to actually manage it."

I didn't agree with Travis's rationale, but there was another reason to suspect Drew. "He could eat half a pie without dying," I said. "If he had poisoned it, he'd know where the poison was in the pie."

"You mean if he put the poison in the pie he would know which piece was lethal," Mark said.

"Logical," Travis said. "Theoretically, that's possible, but it would be like Drew to get that wrong." Travis had no faith in Drew even to commit a crime.

"It doesn't feel right." Drew was an unlikely murderer, but I didn't know how persuasive a gang might be.

"If someone else put the poison in the pie," Mark said. "Then our friend Drew Jones just escaped a nasty game of Russian Roulette."

"As did anyone who Reece could have entertained and offered a share of his pie." I shuddered. Laura could have had a piece. Beth could have shared that pie.

"I'd like to know more about the source of that drug and the pie. I'm running out of time on this case." Mark pulled into the car park at the guest house. I opened the back door and hopped out.

"What are you going to do for supper?" he asked me.

I stooped and talked to him through his open window.

"Tonight is the last night for my group. Everyone catches a plane tomorrow so they have a choice: fancy or a pub."

Richard and Heather and Howard and Poppy chose to return to the Mermaid Inn.

"We'll walk back," Heather informed me. "It's not far and it's a beautiful evening."

It was a warm, bright evening. July was usually dry and sunny in this part of the British Isles, but rain could come in any month.

"Just text me if you change your mind," *Or if Richard insisted on VIP treatment.* I didn't say that, but I thought it.

I drove them to the Mermaid and hurried in to leave my credit card to pay for their food and one bottle of wine. They would look after additional alcohol purchases themselves.

The rest of us decided to go to The Ship Inn which was about two blocks away on the Strand.

"It's Saturday night. They'll have music," Trinity said.

"I'll enjoy that." Susan was willing to partake in what might be a noisy dinner. I hoped she'd appreciate it. Many of my older guests found a loud environment exhausting.

We were lucky. The band was an acoustic one without amplifiers or at least with amplifiers that didn't blast our ear drums. We seated ourselves in an alcove in the pub and studied the menus. They served typical pub food here: fish and chips with mushy peas, burgers and steak, but they had some interesting starters: mussels, potted Devon crab and pig cheek croquettes.

I ordered a round of beer for everyone with a glass of white wine for Susan. We ate with enthusiasm and the group was livelier and more spontaneous than it was when Richard's critical

presence hovered over us. The incomprehensible waitress wasn't
working tonight.

We were finished our meal and on our second round of beer—
paid for by Susan—when I saw Beth.

I waved at her. She walked over to me. "Are you alone?" I asked.
"Come join us."

She looked over her shoulder. "I'm with a group from work. I'll
just tell them I'll be here for a few minutes."

"Reece's girl friend," I explained to the others while she was out
of earshot.

They nodded and were friendly when she returned.

"I'm Trinity."

"Amber"

"Julie."

"Susan."

They rattled off their names in rapid order.

"I'm Beth."

"Girlfriend of the deceased. So sorry for you," Trinity said with
the insouciance that two beers provides.

"Thanks."

"Who do you think killed him?" Julie asked.

I thought Beth might get up and leave, but she leaned forward
as if eager to talk about it. Strangers were often easier to talk to
than relatives or friends.

"He was still using, you know, just not as much. It's still illegal
so he had to buy from dealers. "

"Drew?" I asked.

"Probably. Reece wasn't using much, so his addiction wasn't
as expensive as it used to be. His mum said she might give him
enough money to keep him in maintenance drugs."

"Did she?" Laura hadn't told me that.

"She was thinking of giving him the amount of money he
needed to maintain his sanity. He was a lot more stable, though,

when he used only once a week. He had an appointment with a psychiatrist. He just needed help."

"I have friends in that situation," Julie said. "Maybe I should be more understanding."

"No one wants to be an addict." Beth sounded fierce. "It's a terrible disease."

"The problem is compounded," Susan said, "by an outdated morality notion that the addict has control of what his body needs to function. He doesn't. It's like telling a diabetic he shouldn't need insulin."

Amber leaned forward. "And because he can't get it legally, he gets it illegally and then he's a criminal. I have a cousin like that. He was unreliable for years. You had to sit on your wallet if he was around, but they started a program in his area of Toronto where he can get his drug free from the clinic. He goes there every morning now and gets his drug. Then he goes to work."

"That would have been perfect for Reece. He wanted to be normal."

"Maybe they'll get that program here."

"Maybe," Beth said as she stood. "But it's too late for Reece." Julie stood and hugged her. She passed her to Amber and we all took our turn to hug her.

She smiled at us, her eyes shining with tears. "Thanks. It was good to share."

Obviously, it had helped her. I couldn't imagine being so trusting as to unload onto strangers. I felt old. I wondered if the experience of loving Reece was worth the pain of losing him. Perhaps everyone had to risk that.

Julie bought the next round. I switched to water. I had to drive. We stayed another two hours listening to the music and talking. I rolled them all into the van and drove them home about midnight.

We weren't quiet but I managed to deposit everyone to their correct room and join Mark in mine.

He was sitting at the small, round table with his tablet and papers beside him. He removed his reading glasses as I entered. I love those glasses.

I sashayed over and plopped onto his lap.

"Oof."

"Are you complaining?"

"No." He gathered me into his arms. Bliss.

In the morning, I was up early to clean out the van and to fill the final goodie bags. This one did not include their usual small bottle of water as the airlines would only make them leave it behind.

I knocked on Susan's door and handed her the bag I'd assembled for her. I'd put in a small picture of her with the Toronto trio and another of her pottery vase. She had given it to me as she didn't want to carry it on the plane. She didn't know this, but I was going to arrange to have it shipped to her.

"I had a wonderful time, Claire. Thank you for everything you did to make it so special."

"It was a pleasure," I said. It had been.

"I doubt I'll get back another year. I am getting old, but I will enjoy this trip many times in retrospect."

I met Poppy and Howard at the door of their room. They were just going to breakfast.

"Thanks," Poppy said as I handed her their bags. "We had such a good time Howard thinks he will do it again. I had to drag him here, you know," she confided.

Howard agreed. "That's true. The food's a lot better than I expected. Some of the boys at the yacht club said the meals would be all boiled beef and cabbage."

I laughed. "Those days are long gone."

"Sure are. I don't want to miss the breakfast today. That's why we're up so early."

I waved them off and knocked on Richard and Heather's door.

Richard answered the door. "Ah, Claire. Just the person I want to see. I have some feedback for you."

'Feedback' was a euphemism for criticism. I handed him his bag. I'd been temped to put a lump of coal in there, but I rose above my inclinations and had given him a small book of Shakespeare idioms.

I listened to his litany of complaints, trying to keep my temper.

First," he said, "the manor is not as advertised. It is NOT a manor." Second, the manager of the Marlowe Theatre was not sufficiently knowledgeable for a man of my accomplishments. You could have done better. Third,.."

I lost the battle with my temper.

"Richard," I said and looked straight at him. "You have not been happy on my tour in spite of the many concessions and adjustments I made for you."

"You need to supply more information. You aren't intelligent enough to be a tour guide on this type of exclusive tour."

The supercilious, pseudo-intellectual, unkind and downright obnoxious idiot!

"Enough! I said.

He start to speak but I continued. My face was flushed and my voice higher than usual. I had enough control not to yell at him or swear, but I was angry. "I suggest that you never book with me again as neither of us would like it." I waited for his reply. I was sure it was going to be nasty, but he looked stricken as if he'd just realized how ill-mannered he'd been. He sent me a quick look as if he was going to apologize. I was in no mood for an apology.

Heather interrupted. "You'd better go to the breakfast room, Richard, and get that table you like, or those Toronto girls will take it."

Richard agreed quickly. "Yes. Yes. I'd better do that. You hurry."

"I'll be there soon."

We watched him stride down the hall. Then I handed Heather her bag. She patted my arm.

"In spite of Richard, I had a great time. Thanks for everything."

"*You* were a pleasure," I said.

She laughed. "*I'll* book with you again, only next time I'll be single."

"Good luck with it all."

She smiled and I was free of anger. I could see her now as a courageous woman who was coping with an intolerable partner. I admired her for breaking free. She started her marriage with love and hope. When the promise was not fulfilled, she changed to deal with it and then when adjusting became impossible made practical plans to save herself. Good for her.

The Toronto trio were still packing.

"Trinity's not ready," Amber complained.

"I'm almost ready," Trinity whined.

I passed out the bags. "Maybe you two could go to breakfast and I'll give Trinity a hand."

Julie let out a long breath. "Good idea."

I'd hate to have their trip spoiled by impatience at this point.

"What would you like me to do," I asked Trinity when her friends had departed.

Trinity looked around and gave me directions. She was packed and ready in ten minutes.

Mark was at our table when I arrived. I collected coffee which I needed and some eggs, bacon and scones. I checked the time. I could eat, get everyone in the van and delivered to their airline gate with time to spare.

"Can you be back here at one?" Mark asked.

I looked up quickly. "Something happened?"

"Cst Johnson who works on our data analysis program picked up someone reported Nembutal stolen from her clinic. She saw the cross reference to our case."

"Who?"

"Dr. Clarke."

"Vanessa."

"Right. I've arranged to see her at one-thirty at her surgery. Can you come with me?"

I calculated the drive to Heathrow and back. "If the traffic allows."

This was the break Mark needed. If Vanessa was missing Nembutal and had reported the loss, it wasn't much of a stretch to think that Malcolm had taken it.

CHAPTER NINETEEN

I arranged with Laura to stay another day, but I wasn't going to stay without Gulliver.

I drove my guests to the airport and made sure they made it to the security gate. Richard had decided I didn't exist and wouldn't even respond to 'Good morning'. The rest of the group treated him like a sullen adolescent and ignored him. I was happy to see the last of him. I parted from the others with warmth and affection.

"Send me pictures of your art work," I told the Toronto trio. "I'll put it up on my website with buying information."

"Will do," Julie said.

"Tell me when you have a show," Susan said, "and I'll fly up to take it in."

"Now, Auntie, that would be a treat. We'll take you on the town," Trinity said hugging her.

Heather promised to give me her new address and Poppy and Howard told me they'd be back. Richard stood aloof. We didn't miss him. After I saw them off, I drove to Deirdre's house. No one was home as Deirdre, Michael and Josh were at Josh's football tournament and Kala was at a friend's, but I had a key. Gulliver was ecstatic and bounced around me, trying to lick my face and climb onto my lap. Then he raced around the foyer in circles. Pike and Duff were excited by Gulliver's antics and joined in the race. Anticipating the melee, I was sitting on the floor. Those big Labs could knock me over. I eventually calmed them, collected

Gulliver's gear and loaded him into his crate in the van. I left Deirdre a thank you note, some Kent and Sussex tea and a huge box of specialty chocolates—on top of the refrigerator so the dogs wouldn't get into it.

I was back at Laura's guest house by one just in time to meet Mark. He fussed over Gulliver and introduce him to Travis.

"He's coming with us?" Travis did not approve.

"Just pretend he's an Alsatian," Mark said.

My sweet Cavalier King Charles spaniel was no substitute for the fierce warrior of the canine unit.

"Dr. Clarke just does cats," Travis said.

I reconsidered taking Gulliver. He was unreliable with cats.

"I'll leave him. Just a minute."

I took Gulliver back into the guest house, settled him on my bed and told Angela he was there.

"Can I take him for a walk?" she asked.

"Sure," I smiled at her. She appreciated Gulliver on sight. "Thanks."

Vanessa Clarke's animal surgery was off Manorfield Road near a park in the northwest part of Maidstone. The surgery was large with enough parking for several cars and a couple of big trucks. There was a lane at the side of the building that must lead to an entrance for large animals like horses and cows. Travis said Vanesa only treated cats. Perhaps she had a partner or two who looked after horses. The front entrance was a double entrance: one door had a sign "Dr. Clark, Cats Only".

"She must share this building with three of four other vets," Mark said.

I looked at the signs in front of the parking spots. "Five," I said, after counting the 'Dr.' signs.

"She owns the building and collects rent from the other docs," Travis said. "I checked."

"Good man," Travis *was* good with details.

There were two women behind the receptionist counter and three waiting seated in the reception room, each with a cat on her lap. One was a particularly beautiful cat.

"Gorgeous," I said to the owner, a thirties something, blonde women as elegant as her cat.

"He's Balinese."

I nodded as if I understood how special that was.

"Which is a long-haired Siamese," the woman beside her sniffed.

"Balinese" the owner said firmly.

"Claire," Mark said, inviting me to follow him into Dr. Clark's inner office.

Vanessa moved away from her desk and extended her hand. She welcomed Mark first, then Travis, then me. I got the impression that her demarcation of who was the most important was habitual and that she wasn't thinking of what she was doing.

I was the last one in and carefully closed the door behind me. She gestured to the chairs in front of her desk. She was as elegant as before only this time she had a lab coat over her light linen shirt and tailored trousers. The room was as neat but inviting. There was a low, padded bench wide enough to have an enormous cat on it. Photos of cats were tacked to a huge cork board on one wall. There were cupboards behind her desk. Some of them with locks on them, although at least one had the key in the lock.

Vanessa looked at me curiously but didn't object to my presence.

"You reported missing Nembutal." Mark got straight to the point.

"Yes. The veterinary surgeons' regulations demand I report it. I didn't expect such a high-level response." She glanced at the clock on the wall, no doubt calculating how much time she could spare.

"You reported Nembutal missing; Reece Martin was killed with Nembutal."

Vanessa stared at him. Her eyes widened. "Please repeat that."

Mark complied.

"There must be Nembutal in surgeries all over Britain," she protested.

"No one else has reported any missing. It's possible there is no connection."

We were silent as Vanessa continued to stare at Mark.

"But not probable," she said slowly. "Oh. That's ugly."

She looked flushed now; her eyes were bright.

"Are you all right?" I asked.

"No. I'm distressed, upset and beside myself. I do not want to face this."

Mark took her over some facts, no doubt in an effort to defuse emotion and make it easier for her. Vanessa wasn't a suspect. She wouldn't have reported the missing Nembutal if she had used it to kill Reece.

"How did you discover it was missing?" he asked.

"After you came to the house, I worried that my cupboards weren't secure. I do keep narcotics here. I checked my meds. Everything was fine except one package of Nembutal. It's phenobarbital, in pill form. I rarely use it as the liquid injectable Nembutal is more effective. I only checked it because I was being thorough."

"What was missing?" Travis asked. He had his notebook on his knee and paused his writing. Dr. Clark glanced at him, then ignored him and faced Mark.

She got up, went to a cupboard, unlocked it and returned with a package of pills, a blister pack of twelve with four empty compartments.

"There were eight capsules in the package. There should have been twelve."

"Would that be enough to kill someone?"

"Most definitely. And kill them fairly quickly."

"How quickly." Travis paused, his pen above the notebook.

"Maybe twenty minutes."

Mark bagged the evidence, labelled it and handed it to Travis.

"This will have your fingerprints on it but we may find others."

"Probably not. I handled it quite a it. Turned it around, smoothed it out. I couldn't believe it. Sorry."

Mark nodded, acknowledging she hadn't been thinking forensically.

"What's its effect on people?"

Vanessa sat straighter. "Usually, it causes vomiting in people, then sleepiness and, if they have enough, respiratory arrest."

"Why would a person use it?" Mark asked.

"To commit suicide," she said. "People buy it on line. They aren't supposed to, but they do. Vets are asked to supply it sometimes—relatives, friends ask us. It's a problem but we never do supply it to people. We'd risk our licence."

"Did Reece ever come to your surgery?" I'm glad Mark asked that question. Did Reece kill himself?

"No. Never. Malcom didn't want him here."

Malcolm had said *Vanessa* didn't want Reece visiting. Reece hadn't visited so he hadn't had any opportunity to steal it. Another argument against suicide.

There was silence. Finally Mark asked, "Who do you think stole it."

"Someone who had access to my clinic keys and the keys to the narcotic cupboard." Her voice was even but she was twisting her rings, showing some agitation.

"Your staff?"

"Possibly. They might have a friend or relative who wants to die and couldn't get medical permission."

"Who else?"

"The cleaning staff? They might have filched the keys when I was busy."

Mark was implacable. "Who else?"

She stared at him, anguish in her eyes. "Malcolm," she whispered.

There it was. The reason she was distressed, upset and beside herself. She was afraid her husband had killed his son.

She put her head on her desk and her shoulders shuddered. Mark glanced at me. I stood and moved in beside her, rubbing my hand on her shoulder and down her back.

She stopped shaking, took a few deep breaths and raised her head. "Thank you." She looked straight at me.

"Are you all right?"

She didn't answer me but spoke to Mark. "He came home that night and seemed happy. He'd stopped at the bakery and bought us a peach pie. I love peach pie. It was so thoughtful."

I repressed a shudder of my own and tried to keep my face blank. Reece had eaten a peach pie. Probably laced with Nembutal. Vanessa had no idea she'd just handed Mark a crucial piece of evidence. He'd trace that bakery and Malcom's purchase.

She found a tissue in her desk drawer, wiped her eyes and blew her nose. "I'm all right," she said.

I sat back in my chair. I admired her courage. With what she suspected, she could have kept quiet about this, never reported the missing Nembutal and pretended she hadn't discovered the loss. But she'd chosen to face facts. Even if she was wrong and Malcolm was innocent, which was looking more and more doubtful, she'd allowed suspicion to enter her mind. He wouldn't forget that, and neither would she.

"I will have to talk to him. Tell him about the missing medication. He will have to explain himself or he will have to leave."

We said nothing. If Malcolm did take the Nembutal, he was in much worse trouble than a confrontation with his wife or a failed marriage.

Mark called in a forensic team to dust for fingerprints and any DNA they might find. He didn't hold out much hope, but he followed the correct procedure. He left Travis interviewing the staff and guarding the office and took me back to Laura's. He dropped me there and went on to the nick. He was going to send Jas Sandu out to look for the bakery. Mark would want to get evidence from the bakery before confronting Malcolm.

Gulliver was not in my room. I found him on a mat in the kitchen, happy to have company.

"Don't tell the Health Department," Laura said.

Dogs were allowed in restaurants but not in commercial kitchens. It wasn't logical, but it was the rule.

"Wouldn't think of it," I said, I sat on a chair and snapped my fingers. Gulliver trotted over and hopped onto my lap. I cuddled him. He gave me reliable, consistent affection. No game-playing, no deviousness, no false professions of sentiment. He was easy to love.

Laura was kneading bread dough, her strong hands creating rhythmic thumps on the marble counter while Angela chopped fruit, preparing tomorrow's breakfast.

"He's quite the sociable character." Angela paused in her work to admire Gulliver. "He wants to stop and chat with anyone and everyone."

"Thanks for taking him out."

"No problem. You need some time with your bloke."

It wasn't exactly couple time, but I didn't tell her that.

"Tea?" Laura offered and nodded toward the kettle on the Aga.

"Lovely. Thank you."

I gave Gulliver another pat, dumped him to the floor and found a mug.

Laura worked quickly, shaping dough into buns and placing them in a pan. She covered them with a linen tea towel and placed them on a shelf above the Aga to rise. She fetched herself a cup of tea and sat at the table with me.

Angela put her bowl of cut fruit in the fridge. "I'm off," she said. "I'll be here at eight tomorrow morning. You get some sleep tonight, luv." She patted Laura's shoulder as she passed.

We sipped our tea while the house settled around us. We heard the outer door close then listened to the silence. This must be the only time of the day Laura had to herself...after the guests left for the day and before they returned in the afternoon and evening.

"You aren't sleeping?" I asked.

"No. Not surprising really. I'm a bit of a mess of guilt and grief."

I remembered my own experience. "We don't have any defenses against grief. It overwhelms us unexpectedly. All we can do is feel intensely and wait until it passes."

"It's like waves come out of nowhere."

It was like that and it seemed to go on for a long time.

"Why guilt?"

"Oh, it's a mother thing. What should I have done? Why didn't I know Reece had been abused? Why didn't I suspect it? Why didn't I get him help?"

"I'm sorry." She would probably always be tortured by those thoughts.

"And then Malcolm came by earlier." She turned her mug around in her hands.

"He did?"

"Yes. He said he wanted to pick up the check he'd made out to the College. The check is valid even though Reece can't present it and it's for quite a lot of money. He wanted to make sure it was destroyed."

"Did he find it?"

"I wouldn't let him go into the shed. I couldn't stand the idea of him searching through Reece's things. He wasn't looking for a picture of Reece or a memento. He just wanted his check. Selfish bastard. I told him I was sure the police had taken it and he should ask at the police station."

I could understand him trying the chase down that check. Perhaps he was afraid the police would send it on to the College. Or Laura would if the police returned it to her. But I understood her anger. He hadn't come to offer her support or comfort, or to grieve about the loss of his son. Sending Malcom off with a flea in his ear would have felt satisfying.

"Did he leave?"

"He left, but not before he tried to convince me that Reece had deliberately killed himself."

I thought about the timing. Malcolm was here while we were talking to Vanessa. I looked at her. "You didn't think Reece did that. And neither do the police."

"I told him Reece had been poisoned."

"He said Reece had used a drug people who want to kill themselves can buy on line. Nembutal is an Exit drug, a common drug used in suicide, he said. I should stop wasting the time of the police and face facts."

She twisted her mug around in her hands again and stared at it.

I thought about that for a moment. "Laura," I said. "Did you tell him what the drug was called?"

She looked up. She shook her head. "I didn't remember what it was until he said the name. Detective Sergeant Flynn told us, didn't he?"

"How did Malcolm know?"

CHAPTER TWENTY

"Call Mark," I said.

"It's probably nothing." But she pulled her mobile from her pocket and hit Mark's number. "No doubt the police told Malcolm."

"Possibly," I said. "But Mark can sort it. Best if we don't assume anything."

She walked up and down the kitchen while she reported to Mark what she had told me. The sunlight through the high kitchen window lit her blond hair, leaving her face in shadow. I knew she was strong, but she looked delicate.

"I need to do something to keep me busy." She disconnected and put her mobile in the pocket of her jeans.

"I have some time. Can I help?" She seemed calmer today, although I expect she was still emotionally fragile and would be for some time.

She glanced around the kitchen then out the window as if she was mentally sifting through all the chores a house this size demanded. She turned to me. "I need to sort out the garden shed. Not all at once. I'll do a few hours every day over the next few weeks, but I haven't been able to get started. I think it would be easier if I had company."

"Gulliver and I would be delighted to help."

Laura brought boxes out to the shed and we began to go through the drawers and the shelves. Gulliver was a positive distraction.

We had to stop many times and remove unidentified food from his mouth or rescue a piece of clothing he thought would make a perfect chew toy, but fussing over him lightened the mood.

"I should have bought Reece a dog," she said. "Gulliver would make anyone happy."

"He's a love," I said. "Have you thought about getting one for yourself?"

"I've always thought it would bother the guests, but maybe I could share one with Angela."

"That might work. Then you could leave him with Angela when a guest objects. I find Gulliver can go with me most of the time."

In a couple of hours we had four boxes ready to be taken to Laura's storage unit. I helped her carry them to her car. "It will take me about an hour. I'll be back in time to look after the guests. Thanks so much for helping. You and Gulliver." She hugged me then drove way.

She looked, not happy, but less sad.

I lifted the key from the peg board by the kitchen door and took Gulliver into the communal gardens. Reece had done a good job. All the spring flowers had been cut back to make room for the roses, larkspur and daisies. There was a beautiful sweep of purple lavender and sage against the far wall. It was dreadful he couldn't have continued to make the landscape beautiful. Laura was going to think of him every time she walked here.

Gulliver sniffed along the pathways. I didn't know the garden well enough to let him off leash, but he enjoyed the new sights and smells. I locked the gate when I returned and glanced at the shed as I passed it. I saw movement. I stopped.

"Do you need more help?" I said as I opened the door and walked in. "Weren't we finished for the day?"

It wasn't Laura. Malcom Martin was standing in front of the kitchen cupboards. He had taken a board out from the back of the cupboard revealing a small recess.

"Does Laura know you're here," I asked.

It really was none of my business, but she'd told me she didn't want him rooting around in Reece's possessions. If she knew he planned to come back, she would have mentioned it, even of it was just a comment that she wanted everything out of the shed before Malcolm showed up. Gulliver sniffed the floor and pulled me over closer to Malcolm. Malcolm leaned down and petted him.

"Her car's not here so I just came ahead."

I could feel the anger start to rise in a hot flush to my face. I was incensed enough to be frank. "A bit much, aren't you? Leave the kid alone for years and then show up to go over the pickings?" He wasn't *my* guest. I didn't have to be polite to him.

"Who are you? Something to do with the police, aren't you? I remember you. You came to the house."

"I did, but I'm not a member of the police."

"So you don't have any right to be here."

"More right than you have. What are you looking for?"

I could see Malcolm struggling to control his temper. He took a deep breath and tightened his lips. He gestured towards the chairs and sat down. I sat opposite him and Gulliver bounced up onto my lap. I stroked Gulliver's head while Malcolm talked.

"Reece used to keep a diary when he was a kid. That Miss Weatherby at the funeral reminded me. He kept it when he was a teenager too. He probably still kept one. I don't know why I forgot that; I suppose I thought he was too old for it, but I need to find it. It should be here somewhere."

"The police have it."

He stared at me. "I asked the investigating officer and he said they hadn't found it."

That was devious. I suppose Mark didn't want Malcolm to know he had it. I might have caused a problem here by admitting they collected it. "They didn't find it; Laura did."

Malcolm looked sick. "Did she read it?"

"I suppose quite a few people have read it by now." I didn't answer his question.

He slumped in his chair as if I'd hit him. "This is not good."

I said nothing. Whatever he feared was in the diary was of vital importance to him.

He straightened and stared at me. "I have it all, you know. A beautiful wife. A wealthy wife. Two little girls who adore me. A good profession."

"And Reece threatened that." I was getting an inkling of where this was going.

"He was going to a psychiatrist to tell everything. After all these years, he'd decided to bare his soul to a psychiatrist. He wanted me to come with him. Admit to what I'd done. Help him get through it with the psychiatrist." He sounded sarcastic and bitter.

I tried to remain still and not show what a revelation this was for me. It had been Malcolm who had abused Reece. No wonder he'd left Laura. He'd been afraid she'd find out; afraid Reece would tell her and she would report him. That would mean jail. Even when Reece didn't tell Laura, the abuse ruined the marriage. Malcolm wouldn't have been able to have an honest relationship with her so he detached and withdrew. He wouldn't be able to have an honest relationship with anyone, hiding a past like that. Thoughts about his abuse and the reactions to it flashed through my mind. But I couldn't think about them now. Malcolm was almost yelling.

"Those psychiatrists have to report any criminal offence, you know. They're compelled to by their professional association. Dentists, teachers, nurses, we all have to report it to the police. My son was going to turn me over to the police." He sounded more insulted than contrite.

"And you couldn't have that."

He shook his head. "I couldn't. Vanessa would leave me and take the girls. I'd never see them again. I'd lose my practice licence. I wouldn't have a way of making a living. It's been a strain living with the threat of Reece going to the authorities. I was always afraid he'd tell Laura because she would go to the police, inevitably." He sounded as though he thought it was unfair.

My stomach rolled. "So you abused your son."

"He wasn't my son. He was Laura's."

"He thought he was. You adopted him. That made him your son."

"Not really." He shrugged. "I guess legally. I was good to him when I was with Laura."

I stared at him. "Good to him? How can you think so? You abused him, abandoned him then murdered him when he asked for help. What does that make you?"

He was silent for a moment. He was a handsome man with a film star, blond classic face. It hid his appalling morals. "It makes me a practical man. Laura and Reece were in my past. I didn't need them any more."

"Reece carried the past with him. Your child abuse ruined his life."

He looked around the room as if to make sure we were alone. "There is no proof. No one is going to find out. I'll say Reece was lying."

"Vanessa knows," I said flatly. His criminal self-absorption was nauseating. "She knows you took the Nembutal from her office. She told the police."

"She doesn't." Color drained from his face.

"She does. I was there when she told the detective."

He pushed away from the table, leaned back in the chair and stared over my shoulder as if looking into his future. There was silence for a few moments. I added pressure.

"The police know you bought the peach pie. They're tracing your purchase."

That was out of my mouth before I thought that Mark might not want me to tell him what evidence they had.

"Vanessa knows I took the Nembutal?" He went back to what he thought was important.

"She does."

"She won't forgive me."

"For killing your child?"

"There's no proof. No one can prove anything. But she'll suspect me. She'll always suspect me."

We were both silent for a moment. Then Malcolm took a deep breath and seemed to come to a decision.

"I'll leave here. Go up north. Start again."

"You'll leave the girls behind?"

"Vanessa won't let me see them. Not if she thinks I took the Nembutal. She and her family will see to that. I'll have to leave. Fuckin' Reece."

He was blaming Reece? A young man trying to deal with an ugly situation, murdered by someone who should have loved him. This was Reece's fault? I felt a deep and passionate anger rise up and free my tongue even more.

"You won't be able to work anywhere else. Even if the police can't prove you killed Reece, Vanessa, her family and Laura will see that everyone is your new town knows what you did. Any patient you manage to get, any woman gullible enough to be charmed by you will get a visit from someone who will inform on you."

He stared at me. He was intelligent. He could see the truth of what I said. His belief in his abilities was high, but he had a formidable set of in-laws who would persecute him.

"So Reece ruined me after all." He sounded like a child. It was someone else's fault.

"You ruined yourself." I was disgusted, and it showed.

He shrugged, pushed away from the table and stood.

"The police have Reece's journal?"

I nodded.

"And he wrote down what I did to him?"

"He did"

"Why didn't they come for me then?"

I didn't want him to know Reece hadn't named him.

"They wanted to gather more evidence. That's what they are doing now. I expect they'll come for you tonight."

I was lying. I had no idea if Mark had enough evidence for an arrest, but Malcolm didn't have any right to the truth as far as I was concerned. I was happy to add pressure to his life.

He headed toward the door. "This conversation never happened."

I didn't answer. Of course, I was going to tell Mark, but Malcolm was telling me he would deny it.

I didn't think Malcolm would go home to Vanessa. I doubt she'd let him in, but maybe she would? Maybe she would ask for that 'explanation' she mentioned? If he was going to bolt, he'd need to get papers, credit cards, clothes, so he'd be unlikely to leave straight away. If he didn't go home, he'd probably find a hotel and make arrangements from there. If he was running away to the north, it would take him days to leave. My brain buzzed with the possibilities. Then I thought about myself. Was I in danger from him? Possibly. Would he regret telling me? Of course, he would and he might decide he needed to silence me. I shivered. The sooner I told Mark, the safer I'd be. I fished out my mobile.

CHAPTER TWENTY-ONE

I wondered what Malcolm would do. He could face Vanessa and try to convince her he was innocent. I remembered Vanessa's face, her realization that Malcom had killed his son. She didn't need evidence; she knew. Perhaps she had indications earlier, small discrepancies, a few lies. She was a bright woman. She would put it together. She was also a strong woman and I expect, at the very least, Malcolm would be out of the house, his comfortable life style shattered, his prestigious position in the local social world of Maidstone and London stripped from him, his daughters would be kept from him. Vanessa and her parents would see to that.

I reported the whole conversation to Mark.

"Did he threaten you?"

"No. He said he'd deny everything."

"I'll pick him up on the sexual assault charge."

"That should keep him while you get the evidence for the murder."

"I'm on it," he said and disconnected.

Mark should add a pedophile charge, because that is what Malcolm was, a pedophile, a social pariah, the most despicable of men. I expect there are people in the world —psychiatrists, counselors—who try to help predators with their cravings so they don't abuse children, They were the helping professionals with amazing compassion and understanding. I didn't have either. It surprised me. This implacable disgust. This lack of any effort to understand Malcolm. If that made me a flawed human being with a limit to compassion, so be it.

I wondered what he'd told Reece to keep him from divulging all to Laura when he was first assaulted. That the police would come and get his dad if he told anyone? That the police would come and get Reece? He'd been only eight. He'd trusted his dad. He'd loved him. Wanted to please him. He would have been so confused. Then Malcolm abandoned him for years without any help dealing with his feelings. He left him on his own with the emotional turmoil he'd caused. When Reece finally got the courage to look for help, Malcolm killed him to protect himself.

Even now, he was looking for a way to slither out of the consequences of his actions. I expect he was planning on booking a flight, getting his money transferred to a different account or a different bank and fleeing.

Mark texted. "A constable will pick you up and bring you to the nick in Ashford."

I checked with Laura. "Is it all right to leave Gulliver in my room while I go out?"

"Going to dinner, are you? Sure. He can spend it with me."

I didn't correct her assumption. "Thanks."

I waited on the steps for the police car and jumped in when it pulled up.

"What's happening?" I asked.

"I'm sure I don't know, madam." The constable was not someone I'd ever seen before. I wouldn't get anything out of him.

"What's your name?"

"Constable Riley, madam."

"So, Constable Riley, are you a native of Kent?"

"Yes, I am. Grew up in Folkstone."

"Busy place. Ashford must seem sleepy after Folkstone."

"Different, anyway."

He navigated the streets of Ashford with their confusing

names: Tufton Street made a right angle turn and changed its name to Vicarage Lane, while what should have been the extension of Tufton Street became Church Road. You had to memorize your path through this town; names didn't help.

The station was a solid, brick Georgian style building, dwarfed by a tall, ugly modern building which I assumed was part of the police complex. I found my way to the reception area where Mark had arranged a pass for me. Another constable, this one, young, female and black, escorted me to an office.

"Claire," Mark rose but didn't approach me. "Thank you for coming." He gestured to a chair and I sat.

"Johnstone," he said to the constable. "Would you like to sit in on the interview with Martin and take notes?"

"Yes, sir." She smiled.

"Keep your eye out at reception. Flynn should be in soon with our chummy." He glanced at his watch. "In about ten minutes. Interview room five."

"I'll be there."

"Recording and notes," Mark instructed.

"Do I join the debriefing afterwards?"

"Certainly."

She grinned. "Thank you, sir."

She shut the door behind her.

"A new detective constable? You made her day."

Mark smiled. "I suppose. Yes, she's new. She has a degree in computer science." Mark was almost reverent in his admiration for anyone who understood the nether counties of the computer world.

"What's happening?"

"Travis is picking up Martin at his dental office and bringing him in for questioning. I can't use anything he told you because there were no witnesses to the incident. You didn't record it?"

"Sorry." I wouldn't have been able to do that surreptitiously. Malcolm was too astute to miss it. In any case, I hadn't thought of it.

"Tell me what you remember. Word for word if you can and I'll record it now."

It took about fifteen minutes for me to recount the shocking revelations Malcolm had made. I felt sick when I again imagined what Reece had faced.

Mark shut off the recording and stared at me. "This is going to be difficult." He spun around in his chair and stared out the window for a moment, then spun back. "He thinks Reece named him in the journal?"

"Yes, I let him think that."

"I can't *say* Reece named him. That would be an outright lie and jeopardize any trial. I'll see what I can do."

"I *really* don't want him to walk free,." I said. I was vindictive. I wanted Malcolm to suffer. I was not sure I liked that revelation about myself. I hadn't known I was capable of such a deep hatred. But I passionately wanted to punish Malcolm.

"Believe me, neither do I."

Travis texted Mark to say he was waiting for Malcolm to finish with his patient then would bring him in. Mark ordered tea for me and put me in a room that had a huge window which allowed me to see into the interviewing room.

"One-way," he said. "You can see and hear him but he can't see or hear you."

The chair was comfortable. The tea was surprisingly good. Travis joined me at the end of a half-hour. He shut the door and dropped onto the remaining chair.

"Polite bastard," he said. "All grace and condescension. He had already called his solicitor when I arrived. He knew we would be coming for him. That's his gabber there." He pointed to a sixties-something man in a gray suit.

I imagined how Malcolm would handle this interview. "He thinks Mark is going to charge him with murder. He'll deny he said anything to me. Maybe imply I was working on Laura's behalf to frame him." I worried the nail on my thumb and stared at Malcolm.

"He will underestimate DI Evans." Travis sounded confident.

I agreed. "Mark will play up the ignorant Welsh boy image."

"Maybe." Travis looked worried for a moment. "It's going to be tricky, like trying to get a wild pony into a barn."

"Have you ever done that?" I was curious.

"Aye. I grew up on a farm in Kent, not far from here. I did all sorts of daff things when I was a teen." University and years had put a cloak maturity on Travis but I had a sudden glimpse of an impulsive younger self. Perhaps his memories made him tolerant of Jas Sandhu, someone who still seemed like a teenager.

Constable Johnstone came into the interview room next and took a desk in the corner of the room. Then Mark arrived with a folder full of papers and Reece's journal. It was letter-sized with a thick, hard cover which had some stains on it in rings, as if Reece had carelessly placed a wet coffee mug on it.

Mark announced the date, the time and the names of the people in the room. The solicitor was a Mr. Fetterly. Mark opened the file but placed the journal on top of the papers.

Malcolm stared at the journal.

"We are considering two charges here," Mark said calmly. "The first is the murder of Reece Malcolm Martin."

Malcolm started to protest. Mark held up his hand. "Let me finish, boyo. You'll get your chance to sputter. And your man here will be sure to help you out." Mark was letting his Welshness rise.

The solicitor half-smiled but continued to write in his notebook.

"The second is pedophilia, the sexual assault of a minor, Reece Malcolm Martin."

The solicitor's pen stopped and he stared at Malcolm.

Malcolm's fingers drummed on the table.

"He wasn't expecting that," Travis said.

"He was at some level because he'd been searching for the journal. He just didn't know if the police had read it."

"Is that Mark's journal?" Malcolm needed his worse fears confirmed.

"It is," Mark said. "And it's fascinating reading. Your son was in the habit of keeping a journal."

"Has done since he was a kid." Malcolm's voice was stilted, his face a bland mask.

"At least since he was eight," Mark agreed.

"He's sweating," Travis said.

I could see the beads of sweat glistening on Malcolm's forehead under the overhead light. He believed Mark had evidence.

Mark put his hand on the journal. "There are no statutes of limitations on child abuse or pedophilia. We're going to charge you. You thought he'd keep your secret. He had kept it for twenty years. But he was going to tell a psychiatrist."

"He was lying in that journal. He was going to lie to the psychiatrist."

"He was going to tell the psychiatrist you'd abused him when he was eight?"

"Yes. He didn't care how much damage that was going to do in my life. Maybe he wanted to do damage."

The impassive face of the solicitor twitched.

"Got him!" Travis was excited. "An admission that the abuse Reece wrote about in his journal referred to his father. That was as pretty a piece of manipulation as I've ever seen. Mark gave him a chance to incriminate himself and he did. Martin offered it up, so it will stand as evidence."

"He will say Reece was lying."

"The court will decide if they believe him, but since he admitted he thought Reece had named him, the court will wonder why he made that assumption. At least we have a case now."

"That's the first charge," Mark said. "The second charge is murder of Reece Malcolm Martin."

"You can't prove that."

"Mr. Martin," his solicitor said. "Let the inspector give us information."

Malcolm sat back in his chair. "Go ahead, then."

Travis snorted. "He's trying to take charge of the conversation. Hear him. He's giving Mark permission to speak."

"The first charge is sexual assault of Reece Malcom Martin when he was eight. The second charge is the murder of Reece Malcom Martin twenty years later."

Mark leaned forward and his voice became firmer and more abrupt. "You stole Nembutal from your wife's surgery. Quiet!" he shouted when Malcolm started to interrupt.

"You bought a peach pie, two peach pies. One you brought home to your wife and daughters. There was nothing wrong with that one. The other you gave to Reece with enough powdered Nembutal in it to kill him."

There was silence.

"Here's what's going to happen today" Mark said. "I am sending an officer with you to your home to pick up your passport."

Malcolm started to protest. Mark held up his hand and silenced him.

"He will also take your home computer and your mobile. He will then drop you at your office where you left your car. Do not leave the country. Stay in touch with your solicitor and await the delivery of the charges."

Malcolm turned his solicitor. "Can he do this?"

"He can. He can do worse." The solicitor's face was again smooth.

Malcom stared at the journal on the desk. "Where did you find it?"

"Laura gave it to us."

He looked down. "She knows." Soon, everyone would know.

Mark didn't answer him. He spoke to the solicitor. "Get him out of here."

CHAPTER TWENTY-TWO

After Malcolm and Mr. Fetterly left, I joined Mark and his officers in a conference room where there was a long table, a computer with a huge screen on a desk at the front and a cork board. Mark sat at the end of the table and spread his papers out in front of him. Constable Johnston sat beside him, Travis sat beside her, and I took a seat beside Mark.

"First, we need to collect some evidence." Mark stabbed a few numbers into his mobile and spoke into it. "Jas, I want you to bring Martin's computer to Constable Johnston and his passport to me."

He disconnected and put his mobile on the table and turned to his officers. "What do we have?"

"LOB," Travis said.

I translated that to 'a load of bollocks', or useless information. He was obviously more comfortable with Mark after working with him for a week.

"I don't know how you had the nerve to charge him on either count. Our evidence is so thin." He was worried.

"He convicted himself on the assault charge." Mark's tone was mild. I think he had a great deal of satisfaction from getting that admission from Malcolm.

"Bloody miracle."

Mark directed a smile to me. "We had help from Claire."

Both Travis and Constable Johnstone turned to look at me.

"Moving on," Mark said. Both heads swiveled back to Mark.

"Karen, take that computer apart when you get it. See if you can find emails between Malcolm and Reece. Look to see if he promised to bring a pie."

"A pie, sir?"

"Yes. A pie. Travis, put someone on watching Malcolm. Claire thinks he will leave the house."

"Why" Travis asked me.

Mark nodded to me, requesting an answer.

"Because Vanessa won't have him there. He knows she is through with him. He needs to get out before she comes home from work which is six o'clock. He might have a friend's place he can go to, but I suspect he'll find a hotel." I hesitated a moment struck by a thought. "Unless they have a summer house or an apartment in London."

"They might," Mark said. "If we can't find him we'll ask Dr. Clarke."

Travis went out into the hall. We could hear him giving directions, the tone but not the words.

Jas appeared with Malcom's computer and passport. It was always a pleasure to look at Jas. Today he wore a black T-shirt, black capris that ended at his calves and yellow trainers. "Here you are, guv." He handed Mark the passport and another piece of paper. "That's the name of the bakery. I got it from Dr. Clarke. And the other paper is a disposition from the bakery owner, a ferocious old bird called Mrs. Nesbit, attesting to the fact she sold Martin two peach pies. She finally gave me the time and date taken from the till information. 'And tasty pies they be, sonny. None better. So don't you be putting it about that there was somet'in wrong wid me pies.'" His mimicry was amazing.

Mark smiled. "Excellent, Jas."

"Miracles any time," he said and sat beside Karen.

"Before you get too comfortable, Jas, I want you to go back and keep surveillance on Martin."

"Have I got time for tea?" Jas asked as he stood.

"Take it with you."

Jas gave us all a quick smile and left. I was beginning to understand why he was valued here.

Mark continued giving orders. "Karen, enter the verbatim report of the interview into the file under 'On-going Investigations-Malcolm Martin', print out a copy and leave it on my desk along with any pertinent emails you find."

She picked up her notebook and prepared to leave.

"If you can get into his email, monitor it to see if he books a flight or a train ticket. His phone records might not reveal that. He could pick up a replacement mobile and might use his email."

"What about checking his credit cards?" I asked. "Can you do that?"

"Not without his permission or a court order." Mark's voice was curt. It must be frustrating to be constricted by that law.

"Banks are tight," Karen said.

"Off you go then," Mark said. She took her papers and the computer and left.

Travis returned and passed her in the doorway.

Mark spoke to him before he could sit down. "Travis, join Sandhu on surveillance. Let me know where Martin goes as soon as possible."

"Will do." He turned around and left us in the conference room. Mark placed his papers in the folder and closed it.

"Do you have enough to charge him?" I wasn't clear on that.

"Not on the murder charge. We need more. We can charge him now with sexual assault because he admitted Reece would have named him in the journal. Without that admission, I couldn't have charged him on anything. His solicitor will now request a copy, read it and realize we had nothing. *Now*, we have a case. I'll call Addison. I need another few days."

"Will she grant them?"

"Assuredly. We are close to ending this.""

"What do you think Malcolm will do?"

"He'll take what he needs from the house as quickly as he can which may include items Vanessa wouldn't like him to have like cash and jewellery. Then he'll find a hotel, get on the new mobile which I expect he's already bought and contact a locum to take his patients and manage his practice while he arranges to sell it. Charges and prosecution take time. He has no priors, so the courts will grant him bail, probably low bail, because the assault is an old offence and they won't see him as a danger to anyone."

"You think he'll sell the practice here and move? He said he might move north but that Vanessa would hound him."

"He'll head for a bolt hole of some kind. I don't know what all his choices are, but we will be looking for evidence to substantiate a murder charge while the other charge goes forward. He knows that."

"I bet he spends hours on the phone with his solicitor." I hoped his life was going to get complicated and difficult.

I accompanied Mark back to the office he was using and waited while he added some notes to the central case file. It was after six when we left the building and Mark hadn't heard from Travis.

I was impressed with the way Mark and the officers talked about Malcolm without heat or anger. He was the object of their investigation, a player in the game of justice, and they didn't seem to waste any emotion on him.

I, on the other hand, had a hard time keeping my anger at bay. Every time I thought of the smarmy goat taking advantage of his son, I could feel my stomach knot. I needed to find some of that detachment. Mark had other things on his mind. "Do you know a place around here where we can have dinner while we're waiting? We might as well eat."

I mentally reviewed our choices. "The Skye Restaurant. It's close by; they have an excellent menu and you can get a good burger and beer if you want."

"I haven't tried there yet. Let's go."

We left his car at the nick and walked the block to the restaurant.

True to form, Mark had the burger. I had their wild mushroom risotto. We both had beer. Aside from the white linen on the table, which Mark could have done without, he liked the place.

We had finished our meal, left the restaurant and were just getting into Mark's car when Travis phoned.

"Finally!" Mark said and put his mobile on speaker.

"What happened?" Mark asked.

I suppose the delay in getting a message from Travis meant something had happened.

"Our chummy has landed in clover. He's registered at Eastwell Manor."

Mark whistled. I was impressed as well. Richard would love that place. It truly was a manor house—large and elegant—and used now as a hotel for the wealthy, but too pricey even for my tourists. "Our Malcom does well for himself."

"He needed a place to stay, why not the best? He probably headed for the first oasis he thought of," Travis said. "He didn't get out of his house before his wife came home, though. She caught him loading his car. Jas and I were close to the entrance hidden by a bush and we heard every word."

"Good man. Can you remember what they said?"

"I can do better than that. I can play you a recording."

Mark grinned. "Brilliant."

I don't know what kind of mobile Travis had or how close he was but the sound came through clearly. Of course, both Vanessa and Malcom were yelling.

"Go and never come back!" That was Vanessa. She yelled even louder. "If you ever try to come near the girls or contact them I swear I'll kill you."

"Be reasonable, Vanessa. I have a right to see the girls."

"You have no rights. You're a killer. You killed your son."

"No one can prove that."

"I don't need legal proof. I know you did it. Keep away from my daughters."

"They're my daughters too.

"Not any more."

"Vanessa!"

She interrupted. "You have no daughters now and no friends. The friends we have are my friends. Don't try to contact any of them. I am going to make sure everyone knows about you. I will write a letter. Better still, my solicitor will write a letter to your dentists' board and insist you are removed from the list of active practitioners. I will hire a detective and make sure no other woman is ignorant of what a beast you are. I'll do that because what I *really* want to do is kill you. If I could get away with it, I'd murder you and with nothing so peaceful as Nembutal. How could you be so despicable? Don't answer. There is nothing that would justify murdering your own child. I hope they convict you. I wish we still had hanging. Now get out of here."

We heard a car door slam then the roar of the motor as it passed then diminishing sound.

"Well, she was definite," Mark said.

"She was amazing," Travis said. "I got close and could see them both. Magnificent woman. She's tall, almost regal, and was so angry she was like one of those avenging furies the Vikings believed in."

"Malcolm is going to be smarting from that."

"Vanessa's not going to allow him to set up a cozy new family somewhere else." I said. "His choices are getting limited."

"Where are you now, Travis?" Mark asked.

"I'm just outside the front door of the hotel. We followed Malcolm and I waited until he registered before calling you. I explained to the manager we were watching Martin and promised to be discreet. I sent Jas for some dinner. I'll leave him in the lobby with the security guard and send a relief at midnight. The hotel is fine with that. They think we're protecting him. I said we didn't want him to realize it."

"Good man. I'll take Claire back to the guest house then go back to the nick and prepare the assault charge. We can serve it on him in the morning. Go home and get some sleep."

"Right you are." He sounded happy.

Mark got a call from Superintendent Addison. He did not put it on speaker.

"Did you get your extension?" I asked when he disengaged.

"I did." His voice was full of satisfaction.

Mark drove me back to Rother Manor. It was a half-hour drive each way from Ashford but he said it gave him time to clear his head.

"Finally, the evidence is slotting in behind the logic."

He sounded happy. He could see an end to this. He might start singing. I smiled at the notion. Richard was a direct contrast to Mark. Mark had at his core a sense of honor and integrity. His world reached far out from his own concerns. He cared about me, his family, his friends, and everyone he was responsible for. His ability to love was huge. I was lucky he was in my life. I felt a rising surge of love for him. Imagine if I'd never met him! It was clear to me how deprived my life would have been. I reached out and lay my hand on his arm.

He looked over at me. "We haven't had much time to enjoy each other lately."

"We mix in our businesses and it gets busy." Between his investigation and my tourists, we didn't get much time to just relax.

He parked in a far corner of the Rother Manor car park and turned to me.

"Can we talk about marriage again?"

This wasn't a surprise. I knew our marriage was on his mind. He'd told me so. He was a straightforward man. I didn't have to guess or try to infer what he wanted.

I considered marriages: Vanessa's, Laura's, Deirdre's, Mark's parents and my mother's with Paul. Mark and I might drift apart, hate each other in a few years—or find we were more in love. There were no guarantees. I knew I loved him, but following my feelings could get me into a mess. I had to have a good reason to marry him. I gathered my scattered thoughts and concentrated. He was a good man; he was trustworthy; and he loved me. That should be enough. Besides, I might not *have* Mark in my future if I didn't take a chance and that brief look at what the future would look like without him was frightening. That made it simple.

I took a deep breath and said, "The wedding date? Sept 16ᵗʰ, this year. Small, just family, lunch at Jack's pub after."

"Done," Mark said with satisfaction. "I'll arrange it. You send out the invitations. I'll give you a list of those I think should be invited."

"A short list."

"Agreed."

He kissed me then. I felt a strong sense that marriage was the right decision. I'd probably second guess it later, think about all the reasons it wouldn't work, but at the moment, it felt right.

"Let's work out a marriage to suit us," Mark said as he turned on the ignition. Even while we were discussing important, personal subjects, he had one part of his mind on his work. He had to get back to the station.

"What do you mean 'to suit us'?" I opened my door but didn't get out immediately.

"A marriage that isn't like anyone else's. One that we negotiate. Something unique."

I thought about it. "With Adam I tried to be the 'good girlfriend' and I never felt comfortable."

"With Daphne I tried to be the 'good husband' and it didn't fit. I didn't have a nine-to-five job. I'm probably never going to have a nine-to-five job."

"Me neither," I said.

He grinned. "There you are, then. We'll work it out."

I smiled, shut the door and watched as his car turned onto the street. Maybe he had enough optimism for both of us.

I reunited with Gulliver, thanked Laura profusely and took Gulliver for a walk.

This time I didn't go into the gardens. We took the path to the Cricket Club, then walked along the edge of the pitch to the river. There, I let Gulliver off leash and watched him run and splash in the water. I'd have to wash him when I got back to the guest house, but he deserved some play time. It was a warm night. The sun while low in the sky had not set. Someone was fishing from the other side of the river. A few boats were pulled up on the bank. I heard a blackbird call its melodious song. It was peaceful. I had just promised to marry Mark in September. I checked on my feelings about it —something that's not easy for me to do—and was surprised to find I was happy.

CHAPTER TWENTY-THREE

Mark arrived in my room a little after mid-night. I was sitting up in bed reading the novel I'd picked up in Hastings. There really were too many bodies in this novel. Mark put his wallet and his phone on the table and plugged in the charger. He gave a huge yawn.

"I documented all the evidence, filled out all the forms and forwarded the charges to the crown prosecutor's office."

"Do you have enough evidence?"

"I think so. I hope so. First, I have his admission that he abused Reece witnessed by Constable Johnstone, his solicitor and me, as well as you and Travis behind the mirror, but I won't need you two."

"That's very good evidence." I smiled at him. He looked tired but satisfied. There were so many times when justice was not served. This time it looked as though Reece was going to get justice, perhaps not for his murder, but at least for his assault.

"Then, there's irrefutable evidence that Johnston uncovered on his computer: twenty-year-old videos of Reece being assaulted."

My stomach rolled. "Oh God. That poor little boy."

Mark shoved his hair back and rolled his shoulders as if uncomfortable. "Abused by someone he loved and trusted. The worst kind of abuse."

I swallowed. It had occurred twenty years ago. There was no point in getting upset now. I bit my lip and took a few slow breaths.

"Malcolm's hands are in the video," Mark said. "Hands are distinctive. We can match his hands with those in the video."

"And there's the fact that it was on his computer. What did he do, call it up every so often and gloat over it?"

"Perhaps."

"Don't tell Laura he had that video. Don't let her see it. It will torture her."

"I won't if I can keep it away from her, but it will come out in evidence so she may hear about it if she attends the trial."

We were both quiet for a moment. Then I focused on the present. "What about the murder charge?"

"We need more evidence, but we have the motivation. He didn't want Reece to tell the psychiatrist about the abuse. I'll put Johnston on combing through his computer for proof he researched the drug he used."

"Are you seizing his office computer as well?"

"I have that lined up for tomorrow. It will be a busy day."

But in the morning Mark got a hysterical call. I could hear shrieks.

Mark interrupted. "Am I speaking with Ms Stanford, the manager of Eastwell?"

The high-pitched squawks moderated slightly and I could understand what she was saying.

"Mr. Martin. He's dead. He's lying in bed and he's dead. You were watching him. Was he murdered? Are my guests in danger here?"

"Did you call an ambulance."

"No. He's dead."

"Just a moment, madam."

Mark held out his hand for my phone. I punched in 999 and handed it to him.

"This is Detective Inspector Evans. We need an ambulance to Eastwell Manor. A man is apparently dead but I haven't seen him and I need a positive diagnosis."

He waited a moment.

"About fifty, six-foot-three. Medium build. Ingested possibly some hours ago and likely Nembutal. Yes. Speed is important. We may have to defend our response time in court."

As an incentive to hurry, that would be a winner.

He disconnected, handed me back my phone and spoke to the waiting manager.

"Please go to the front entrance of the hotel and escort the ambulance to Mr. Martin's room. I will be there as soon as possible."

I heard a squawk.

"I realize that," Mark said. "But your pronouncement of death isn't enough. I am sorry that it will disturb your guests. We'll be as quick as we can be."

She squawked again.

"Who discovered him?" Mark ignored her questions. He glanced at me and put the call on speaker.

"The room service waiter, Nigel." I heard her answer. "He was delivering Mr. Martin's pre-ordered breakfast."

"Give the man a chance to calm down and keep him in your office until I get there which will be forty minutes. Don't let anyone in Martin's room. I'll send an officer to guard it, but no, I don't believe it was murder."

He disconnected, disengaged the speaker and hit a speed button. "Travis, can you send a constable to guard Martin's room at Eastwell. The hotel manager thinks he's dead but I've sent an ambulance to make sure." He listened. "No. I expect we'll find he killed himself. Well, yes, it could be murder if Vanessa got to him, but I don't think so. She had protected her children and was planning other ways to destroy him. Don't do a search until I get there, but keep anyone from going in."

"Suicide?" I queried. I was at the door as I had been going to take Gulliver for a quick walk before breakfast.

"Probably," Mark said as he put his wallet and mobile in his pockets. "Unless Vanessa or Laura got to him. They seem to be the only ones with motive."

"There might be others."

"There might." He kissed me and held the door open for me. "But, I expect we'll find it's suicide. If he's dead."

"He might not be?"

"He might not be. Nembutal is phenobarbital. It has a wide range of lethal dosage and it can be idiosyncratic to the victim. If he is alive, there isn't much they can do but keep him on fluids and let the body get rid of it."

"He might survive?"

"A slim chance, I'd say. If he isn't dead already. The manager seemed definite."

Malcolm dead? I couldn't dredge up an ounce of regret.

Mark picked up a hard-boiled egg and some toast which he folded into a napkin to eat on the way back to Ashford. He filled his travel mug with coffee and left. It might be some time before he could eat again.

I spared a brief thought for Miss Weatherby. She wouldn't have any idea that she had precipitated Malcolm's search of Reece's shed with her casual comment about his journal. And she wouldn't have any idea that a newsworthy story was taking place without her. I felt a little sorry for her. She's been a catalyst for tragedy and she was oblivious to it. The sensational journalistic coup would likely always elude her. She would speed over the countryside on her bicycle, chasing stories just out of her reach.

I snapped on Gulliver's leash. We walked past the shed and into the communal garden. It was pleasantly warm this early in the day. The heat would come later. Gulliver advanced to sniff at an apricot poodle while I exchanged the usual compliments of besotted dog owners. My mouth accomplished this inane small talk several times during our walk but my mind was occupied with what Mark was discovering. Had Malcolm killed himself? He knew he was going to be charged with assault of a minor and would have to face the social ostracization that would engender. Vanessa threatened him with professional ruin and Mark held out the spectre of a trial for murder. That could have sent him into despair, a realization that his future was hopeless. Or did one of his wives murder him? Laura didn't know it was Malcolm who had abused Reece those many years ago, but she resented his indifference. She might have been furious enough to kill him. Between the two of them, Vanessa was more likely to do the deed. She was capable and almost overwhelmed with anger. But she already was in control of Malcolm and had sent him away.

I took Gulliver back to my room and fed him. Then, I went to the breakfast room and ordered a hot breakfast from Angela. It wasn't long in coming. Angela was full of news.

"Laura got a call from your Mark," she said as she delivered the poached eggs on toast with avocado and salsa. She topped up my coffee and set a small carafe on the table. "Seems Malcom tried to off himself."

"Tried to? He's not dead?"

"Apparently it's touch and go. The medics got to him before he drifted away completely. He's not out of the woods yet."

Mark was right to call the ambulance but the result wasn't just. If I was running the world, Reece would have survived the Nembutal poisoning and Malcolm would have died. I wondered if he'd left a note.

"Makes you think he was the one who did away with our Reece." She sniffed and straightened her shoulders. "If he did, I'm sorry he's still with us."

I watched her walk stiffly back to the kitchen. I expect she would bang pots, slam doors, sit down at the table and have a cry.

Mark texted. "Come to the nick in Ashford. Martin did try suicide. The medics revived him. But he left a note."

"Was it a confession?"

"Good enough."

I hoped so. That would help Mark conclude the case.

I had to finish up here and go home. First, I packed, loaded my suitcase and briefcase into my van then searched for Laura both to pay for my stay and see if the news of Malcolm's attempt to die had upset her.

I found her in the kitchen. There was no sign of Angela.

She petted Gulliver. "I'm going to miss you, luvie. I will think about getting a dog."

"How are you dealing with the latest news?"

"I don't know why he would have tried to kill himself," Laura said. "Maybe he and Vanessa had a falling out. It wouldn't be over Reece. He didn't love him. I wouldn't have thought he'd care enough about anyone to take such a step. He seemed to me to care only about himself."

Obviously, Mark hadn't told her the whole story. *I* wasn't going to tell her. That was Mark's job. Besides, I didn't know how to break news that Malcolm had treated Reece so horrifically. She was right about Malcolm. His efforts to leave the world had everything to do with him and his image of himself. He might have been escaping from public condemnation and punishment. It was hard to know what made him choose such a drastic solution to what was facing him but I expect Malcom was trying to look after Malcolm.

When I got to the Ashford police station, the investigative team was assembled in the conference room. They appeared relieved, almost jubilant.

"Thanks for coming, Claire." Mark turned to the officers I hadn't met. "This is Claire Barclay. She was with Laura Wright immediately after she found her son's body and she had a revealing meeting with Martin." He paused. "And she is my fiancé. The wedding's in September."

He beamed at me. I flushed. Did he have to announce it at work like that? There was a murmur of congratulatory noises. Travis smiled. Jas, dressed in dark purple T-shirt today, gave me a thumbs up.

"And this is Gulliver."

Gulliver was hard to ignore as he was pawing Mark's trousers, trying to get attention. Mark reached down and petted him, then turned to me, all business now. "The team would like to hear about your confrontation with Martin in the shed."

I assumed they were conducting an end-of-case debriefing. Everyone had papers and tablets in front of them.

Mark passed me a cup of tea. I took a sip and tried to give an accurate rendition of that encounter. They listened quietly. Karen made notes.

"Thank you," Mark said when I finished. "That shows us Martin's thought process. It makes his choice of suicide more understandable."

"That and what I heard Vanessa say to him," Travis offered. "She was going to hound him."

"That might have been motivating," Mark agreed, "but we won't mention that to her."

"You said he left a note?" I asked Mark.

"Yes. He said he was sorry. He'd always regretted abusing Reece, but he hadn't known what to do about it. He tried to help him when he could, but he knew others would judge him harshly, so he had to kill him."

Travis spoke. "I'm glad he admitted it. That saves tons of work. I suppose he wanted to escape all the social condemnation. But what is most important is he confessed to the murder." He turned to Mark. "What did the hospital say?"

"They said he's going to recover."

"Good." Travis said. "He'll go to trial."

There was a satisfied murmur around the table.

"What else did the note say?" I asked.

"He sent his regrets to Vanessa, his love to his daughters and his apologies to Laura."

I thought for a moment. "Those girls are going to miss him;

Vanessa is going to be relieved and Laura? I don't know how Laura will feel."

I looked around the room "But a tidy ending of the case for the team."

Karen agreed. "Better than trying to put a case together and chasing him all over Britain. It will take some work to get all the evidence together, but we have it all now. He'll be in jail a long time. And he's no loss to those girls. Who knows what he might have done?"

There were nods all around. There was no tolerance for Malcolm's actions, no shades of gray, no culture where such actions were acceptable. There was no forgiveness here.

CHAPTER TWENTY-FOUR

I was packed to travel home but decided to take Gulliver for a long walk and try to share some of his buoyant energy and his ability to be happy in almost any circumstances. Peasmarsh Walk is a four-mile easy stroll through woods and fields. I let Gulliver off leash for part of the walk and only attached the leash when we travelled through farm yards. The air was warm but there was a breeze when we were in the open fields. I brought water for both of us and we had several drink stops. There were few birds sounds at this time of day and few sightings. It was too hot for birds. Gulliver didn't have the excitement of flushing a grouse. It was quiet and tranquil. No guests. No threatening killers. I felt my shoulder muscles relax in the warmth from the sun. This was perfect. My mobile rang.

Mark.

"Have your left for home yet?"

"No. I'm a little northwest of Rye, walking in the countryside."

"Can you meet me at Laura's? I need to tell her we know Malcolm killed Reece. You heard him admit to it, so you can collaborate what I tell her."

There went my peaceful day. This was not going to be an easy conversation.

I waited in my van in the Rother Manor car park until Mark arrived. When we got out of the van to meet Mark, Gulliver barked, excited to have his pack of three together. Mark squatted to pet him and scratch behind his ears. Gulliver loved that.

Laura was expecting us because Mark had called her. She ushered us into the kitchen where we could converse privately. The recently arrived guests were away at the moment, either on jaunts around town or looking for places to dine, but they could return at any time and we didn't want interruptions. She leaned down, patted Gulliver and slipped him a crumb from the pan of warm muffins on the counter. Then she gestured to the table and we sat.

"What's this about?"

"Malcom is likely going to recover, but he will be in police custody. He left a suicide note." Mark handed her a copy of the note. It was short.

Laura read it. "He killed Reece?" She stared at Mark. He glanced at me.

I took a breath and said, "He admitted that to me as well. When he was ranting at the world in the shed. He also admitted to sexually abusing him"

Laura's eye widened in shock. "Malcom abused him? Malcolm?"

I nodded, watching her carefully. She had gone so pale I was afraid she was going to faint.

"It never occurred to me. I never thought of him doing that. Why didn't I know? Oh, poor Reece. *Malcolm!*"

I continued my explanation. "He knew Reece was going to talk to the psychiatrist, Dr. Masterson, and tell her everything. He was sure the psychiatrist would report the offence and the police would investigate. He didn't want Vanessa to know."

"No, he wouldn't. Image was important to him. He had to be important." She said that quietly as if thinking of something else. Then she burst out with, "How could he do that to Reece? And then what? Pretend he hadn't done it? Abandon Reece and let him deal with it himself? Malcolm always put Malcom first. Always." She stared at the note. Then she looked straight at Mark. "So he stopped Reece from talking. It was *Malcolm* who killed him. *Malcolm!*"

"Yes." Mark waited.

"He said so." I reached out and touched her arm.

She turned and looked at me. "That's obscene."

"Vile," I said.

"Yes, wicked."

Tears trickled down her cheeks. I don't think she knew she was crying. I got up and ripped a paper towel from the roll and handed it to her. Gulliver put a paw on her knee. She patted his head and sniffed.

We were all quiet, respecting her grief and shock.

She turned back to Mark. "You were going to charge him?"

"We were readying a charge of sexual assault to be served on him today. He knew we were going to do that. It would take more time for us to gather evidence to get the murder charge in order. But yes, that was our plan. Now he is under guard at the hospital and will keep him in custody when he recovers."

Mark's voice was firm. He looked implacable as if centuries of laws lined up behind him to convince us that, indeed, Malcolm would be charged.

"Murder? So he murdered him."

I added more information. She would go over this information many times in the days ahead, so she needed as much as I could give her. "Mark told him the crown would charge him with murder, so he must have anticipated the publicity that would cause. Vanessa threw him out. She suspected he'd stolen the drug he used from her surgery and accused him of killing Reece. Malcolm told me Vanessa and her family would hound him. He must have felt there was no place for him to go."

Laura straightened and lifted her head. "I'm glad he didn't die. I want him to suffer. Really suffer. I hope he'll be humiliated and reviled. Suicide would have been too merciful."

Mark and I were silent. This was going to be difficult for her to process.

She handed Mark the note. "Thanks for everything you've done."

"You can keep the note. It's a copy."

She looked at it. "I'll call Angela and Beth. They can read it. And then we'll burn it."

I could imagine the three women making a ritual of thrusting the note into a fire and speeding Malcolm to hell—after prolonged suffering on earth.

"Do you want me to call Angela?"

Wordlessly, she handed me her phone. I found Angela's number and called her.

"She's on her way."

Mark stood and said his goodbyes. I waited until Angela arrived and moved close to give Laura a hug before I also left.

"Thanks, Claire." She stepped back, grabbed a muffin and held it out to me. "For the trip home." Always the host. I hoped her job would sustain her in the months ahead. Grieving was going to be painful.

I drove home, mulling over the mess people made of their lives. Laura and Malcolm had started their life together full of hope. Once Malcom had abused Reece, they wouldn't have been able to keep a happy family. The undercurrents would pull them apart, even when Laura didn't understand why. My father tore our family apart with his drinking and his rages. I made a poor choice when I first tried to find love and then couldn't deal with the violence that came with it. So why did I think Mark and I had a chance? Because he was a solid, reliable honest man and because loving someone meant taking a chance. I hoped I wasn't fooling myself.

I arrived home just after Mark. My flint and brick semi-detached looked peaceful in the late afternoon sun. There were no cars parked in front of my neighbor's house, so Patrick and Rita Stonning must be in London this week. I liked the cheerful colors of my garden: red roses, purple salvia and yellow marguerites. A colorful choice of my taciturn and sedate gardener, Peter Brown. I made requests which he sometimes ignored, but I admit he did a better job than I could have.

I let Gulliver into the back garden which was walled and fenced. Mark had deposited his carryall in our bedroom and stopped in the kitchen.

"I'm going to the nick but, if I'm lucky, I'll avoid Superintendent Addison. Why don't I pick up some take-out?"

"You may end up spending hours dealing with the paperwork from the Martin case and with whatever has piled up on your desk. Why don't you get yourself some take-out and I'll pull out something for me from the freezer?"

"Good enough," he agreed.

"You know you aren't marrying me for my culinary skills." There! I'd brought up our wedding. I had to get used to the idea.

He grinned and reached for me. "True enough."

He kissed me thoroughly. "About that wedding date?"

I was a bit breathless. "September 16th."

"How about this Saturday?"

"Mark. No. That's too soon."

He laughed. "No pressure."

I heard the front door close behind him.

No pressure? What else would you call that suggestion for a wedding on Saturday? But I was smiling.

ABOUT THE AUTHOR

© Duke Morse

Emma Dakin lives in Gibsons on the Sunshine Coast of British Columbia. She has over thirty trade published books of mystery and adventure for teens and middle-grade children and non-fiction for teens and adults. Her memoir *Always Pack a Candle: A Nurse in the Cariboo-Chilcotin* received the Lieutenant Governor's Community History Award, but she keeps returning to her favorite genre, cozy mysteries. Her love of the British countryside and villages and her addiction to reading cozy mysteries keep her writing about characters who live and work in those villages. She enjoys those characters and trusts you will as well.

www.ingramcontent.com/pod-product-compliance
Lightning Source LLC
La Vergne TN
LVHW032355270225
804780LV00042B/1892